Cinderella
IN THERAPY

Cinderella IN THERAPY

A Novel by LeeAnna Neumeyer

Artwork by: Brian Camden
Book design by: Maureen Cutajar, gopublished.com

Print ISBN: 978-0-9911740-3-4
Ebook ISBN: 978-0-9911740-4-1

For my sister, Mary

❧ ACKNOWLEDGEMENTS ❧

Great friends and family inspired me to put this all together. John and Ann Neumeyer, Brian Camden, Jorge Enrique Ponce, Norman Orenstein, Erika Coleman, Amanda Buchanan, Gayla Nethercott, Judy Karfiol, Rachel Balfoort, Melissa Baumbach, Jonathan Howard, Drew Ruselowski, Kim Ooi, Barb Frederick, Gilley, Bridget Briley, Martha Sanchez, Jackie Ono and Hyuk Song (for keeping me healthy and balanced). John, Paul and Robert. Kathy and Mary. Dylan, Miranda, Nathan and Eric. I love you all. And to Robert Neumeyer (Uncle Bobby), you're forever in my heart.

❧ AUTHOR'S NOTE ❧

In this book, I will be breaking one of the cardinal rules of psychiatry, that of doctor-patient confidentiality. The patient I will be
sharing details about is someone universally known, and who
has already been written about in hundreds, possibly thousands,
of published books. You may Google her if wish to find specific
facts, but let it be known that there are facts in my book that cannot be found anywhere else since it is based on my own personal
association with Cinderella. Yes, *the* Cinderella.

You may be saying to yourself, "But that's impossible!"

Believe me, I was once where you are now, and the very
reason why I've decided to write this book. It is my hope by
doing so I will prove once and for all that, truly, nothing is impossible.

—Boris Berger, MD, PhD.

(By the way, Cinderella had granted me permission to write
and publish this book, so no need to condemn me, nor my
profession).

➤ Prologue ≪

inderella had been living "happily ever after" for many years before I met her – more accurately, decades. No, centuries. It's hard to say exactly since she lives in a kingdom where there is no time. Yes, they have clocks to tell the hour for breakfast, lunch and dinner. Even sleep. But there are no calendars. No need for those. The seasons are almost all the same, always sunny and warm, like the first day of spring, or a clear skied, breezy June afternoon, or an Indian summer. Snow falls only when ordered by the King, usually on special occasions such as Christmas day, but it has to fall softly and only enough to blanket the landscape, then it has to be gone by the next morning, returning everything back to a lush green.

How do I know this? I've been there, but that is another story that will some day be written. For now, allow me to stick to this one.

Everyone in the kingdom lives in perfect, identical cottages. There is no mildew, decay or rot – not ever. One would not usually describe a cottage made of mud, brick and straw as pristine,

1

but these are. And all are spaced with acres of property between them, property filled with the healthiest of livestock. Pigs, goats, chickens and cows –and all, of course, clean. Horses graze quietly in the grass. Birds chirp together in harmony. There are no insects, mosquitoes or termites. Rats exist, but are not a threat. They play in the shrubbery with the chipmunks and squirrels. Every animal in the kingdom is friendly and harmless.

And then there is the castle. It's as beautiful as you can imagine, yet more beautiful than you could ever imagine. It's made of the finest of stone that changes in color depending on the time of day. In the morning, it sprays a perfect array of orange, yellow and pink upon it. By mid-day it sparkles shiny silver with what looks like little specks of diamonds. In the afternoon it takes on a soft, ocean blue tint, and by night, it's black but for the rows of lighted windows, complimented by the moonlight that drapes spectacular shadows down its walls and pointed towers.

And that's just the outside. The inside is majestic with its exquisite interior of marble floors and regal furniture, and as it should be since this is the home of the royal family – the King, the Queen and, of course, the Prince. The Prince is quite possibly the only adult male in all of fiction, as well as in real life, who actually loves living with his parents. And why shouldn't he? They adore him and have been captivated by his charm since the day he was born. He has the same effect on everyone in the kingdom. He is simply irresistible.

And this, dear reader, is Cinderella's "happily ever after." That is, until one day, all of it – the castle, the kingdom, and everything in it, even the Prince, became suddenly unbearably, disgustingly and unexplainably oppressive to her. And so, with that, we begin our story.

Once upon a time...

One

It was night in the kingdom. As usual – an enchanted evening. The sky was a dark, velvety blue. Stars twinkled. Actually, they did more than that. They *sparkled*. Suddenly, a single star fell gracefully from the sky right next to the castle. When it hit the earth, it burst into a firework of colorful dust.

Inside the castle, all was quiet, and was lit only by the bright moonlight that gave it a soft, romantic ambiance. Upstairs, in the master bedroom, upon a large bed with satin pillows and silk sheets, slept the one and only, Cinderella. Next to her, in a blissful slumber, wearing a sleep eye mask made of the finest silk was Prince Charming.

A clock on the mantle ticked a soft, rhythmic beat. Tick...tick...tick. When it struck midnight, a soft chime resonated from it, signifying the hour. Suddenly, in one frantic movement, Cinderella sprang up from her sleep in terror, gasping for air. Her wide, bulging eyes darted around the bedroom. The stillness of it contrasted the frenzied, twisted look on her face. She glanced over at the prince. He was still sleeping soundly. This strangely bothered Cinderella. She thought was there nothing that disturbed this guy? Then her eyes slowly narrowed and a rage began building from deep within her.

Like a crazed banshee, she began kicking the Prince violently, as her arms swung punches to his head. This woke him immediately. He tried to rise, but was unable to since Cinderella had locked her legs around his and continued to aggressively pummel him with her fists. The Prince covered his face to avoid her assaults, and let out a painful yelp after she punched him hard in the stomach.

The Prince's nose began to bruise and swell after Cinderella gave him a good hard whack to it. Her diamond wedding ring cut his lip, causing blood to form in his mouth and trickle down his chin; his face clawed by her fingernails. He did his best to block her punches, but she had the advantage since he'd never experienced such a confrontation before. Plus, she was strong. When vengeance was the reward, Cinderella, fighting like a wild cat, was determined to win it.

She shouted at him all the things that brought on her wrath. "I am sick of *you*...and your *castle*...and your *kingdom*...and your stupid *family*...and your –"

Just then, the clock on the mantle struck midnight, the soft chime signifying the hour and, in one frantic movement, Cinderella jolted up in bed, gasping for air, with beads of sweat on her forehead. Her bulging eyes darted around the room. What she had experienced was all just a terrible nightmare. Her heaving breaths awoke the Prince. He sat up, pushing his sleep mask to the top of his head.

"Cinderella, my darling – are you all right?"

The Prince's sincere and loving question had the opposite

4

effect on Cinderella. It would have been better if he didn't wake up at all.

"Go back to sleep," she muttered without looking at him, and lowered her head, exhausted.

"But, my love –"

Cinderella shot him a bothered look, daring him to say another word. Getting the hint, the Prince slowly slid back down beneath the sheets, but continued to look at her.

Feeling his eyes upon her, she barked, "Sleep!" as if an order.

"Yes, my love," said the Prince obediently as he pulled the sleep mask over his eyes and fell back into a peaceful slumber almost immediately.

Cinderella pushed away the sweaty hair that stuck to her face and rubbed her tired eyes. Knowing she wouldn't be able to get back to sleep, she crawled out of bed and dragged herself into the bathroom. She turned on the light and entered, closing the door behind her. She approached the mirror and looked at herself. Staring back was a very haggard looking woman. Her eyes were bloodshot, her complexion grey. That nightmare wasn't the first. She'd been having them for months, but told no one. This most recent one disturbed her the most. Although it was just a dream, the thought of harming her husband still lingered. However, instead of feeling shame or regret, she found a strange sense of pleasure in it.

She used her fingertips to pull down the skin just below her eyes to see how bloodshot they were. As she did this, she noticed a small stain on the counter. How odd, she thought, since everything in the castle was always spotless. Choosing to ignore it, she went back to looking at her weary eyes, but that stain was hard to overlook. She leaned forward to make better inspection of it. It was a stain all right, and one that she felt the compulsion to get rid of immediately.

Cinderella opened the cabinet beneath the sink and saw inside a tray of cleaning supplies – several rags, a couple of sponges and a can of cleaning powder. She grabbed hold of the tray, placed it on the counter and smiled eagerly at the materials, as if eyeing jewelry. It had been years since she had the opportunity to clean anything, and revisiting what she knew best, gave her a sense of belonging that she had missed. She found a pair of scouring gloves under the rags and put them on. The feel of them on her hands was nearly orgasmic as she stroked the sides of her face. The feeling of latex on her skin made her swoon.

With unexpected glee, she grabbed the can of cleaning powder and began dowsing the sink, counter top and toilet. She stopped to inhale the ammoniated scent, which caused her to close her eyes and grin. She then took a sponge, ran it under some cold water and began scrubbing. It felt good not only to be cleaning, but releasing her aggression as well. The stain came out immediately, which pleased her, but she didn't stop there. She went on to scrub the counter and sink, making them sparkle. Then she moved to the toilet.

She knelt before the porcelain bowl and began to scrub vigorously. Wanting to be sure to get it extra clean, she reached for a toothbrush that was near the sink and used that. Cinderella was happy to be so diligent in getting every part of that bowl spotless, and made sure to scrub extra hard.

Meanwhile, in the bedroom, the faint sound of the toothbrush brushing in the toilet bowl could be heard. The Prince stirred once, then twice, before he sat up, pushing the sleep mask up on his head. He looked over and saw that his princess wife was not next to him. Seeing light coming from beneath the door of the bathroom, he got up and approached it. He put his ear to the door at first, listening to the strange sounds of grunting and scrubbing coming from inside, then put his hand on the door handle, turned and opened it. The sight inside gave him a shock.

"My darling! What are you doing?" he asked, horror-struck.

Cinderella was on her knees in front of the toilet with toothbrush in hand. She looked up at her Prince, aghast, then quickly stood. Thinking fast, she smiled with quivering lips and said, "I was just brushing my teeth," and with that she shoved the cleaning powder tainted, toilet water drenched toothbrush, into her mouth.

She did her best not to gag, or contort her face from the taste, although her left eye fluttered and watered as she managed a forced smile. It took all the strength she could muster to move the toothbrush across her teeth, which she did.

Unbeknownst to her, this caused the cleaning powder to create bubbly foam in her mouth, which slid down her chin. The Prince looked on in loving disgust then gently told his wife to come back to bed once she was done, and left the bathroom, closing the door behind him.

As fast as lightening, Cinderella turned to the sink and spit out the hideous drool. She turned on the water and splashed her tongue and teeth vigorously, shaking in revulsion. She kicked her legs, a dance of agony, from the pain of the ammonia that was burning her lips.

After finally feeling relief from the pain, she leaned against the counter, exhausted. When she went to push her sweaty hair from her face again, she realized she was still wearing the scouring gloves. Rolling her eyes at the sight of them, she quickly snapped them off, tossed them into the trash and let out a frustrated sigh.

Gathering the little strength and courage she had left, Cinderella headed out of the bathroom and returned to bed.

Before getting in, she looked at the Prince who was again sleeping soundly with the sleep mask over his eyes. She stared at him with contempt, hating how easily sleep came to him. Part of her felt the urge to slap him, but she knew he meant well. He was not a bad guy, she thought. He'd given her everything she could possibly want and more. But maybe that was the problem. He was good at giving her things, but never what she truly needed, which, at the moment, was sleep.

She slipped back into bed, pulled the covers to her chin and stared up at the ceiling. She tried to focus on the things she did have as opposed to what she didn't, but this brought only temporary relief since deep down she was miserable. She didn't know it yet, but she was in denial. And this was why she did not get much sleep that night.

Two

everal hours later, Cinderella was still lying awake and staring at the ceiling. Seeing that dawn was about to break, she slipped quietly from her bed. She wanted to get up before the Prince because she was in no mood for a round of sweet "good mornings" from him. Perhaps a walk around the castle would help, she thought as she slipped into a beautiful silk gown, one that she would only wear once and never again because that's what princesses did, though she didn't bother to straighten or zip it correctly causing it to hang on her lopsided. She was much too tired from lack of sleep to notice, or even care.

Cinderella shuffled quietly down the hallway with its marble floors and marble ceilings since she didn't want the servants to hear her. She knew if they did, they would swarm around to make sure she didn't lift a finger. When she first moved into the castle it took her a long time to get used to having people wait on since she had spent the majority of her youth waiting hand and foot on her stepmother and two stepsisters. She felt a burden to

9

these kind strangers who serviced the King, Queen and Prince since she knew the long, treacherous hours and labor it took to have such a job. But once she saw that the King, Queen and Prince didn't abuse or belittle their staff, as her stepmother and stepsisters did with her, she was able to adjust more easily and was able to accept it. Still, in the mood she was in, she couldn't deal with anyone fawning over her. Not today.

There was something dark building inside Cinderella as she walked alone in what had come to resemble a marble prison. She felt her mood growing steadily sour, especially when she reached the top of the long staircase that led down to the main floor, and saw the Grandfather clock at the bottom of it. The ticking of it was no longer endearing as she used to think it was. Now, it only reminded her of each second of her misery passing. Plus, it was giving her a headache.

She slowly descended the stairs, eyeing the grandfather clock as if it were the enemy. When she came face to face with it, she opened its glass case, reached in and grabbed the pendulum with both hands. With all her might, she wrestled with it and yanked it out. The silence was most welcoming, and the action of breaking something made her feel better.

To make the better feeling last, she happily wielded the pendulum, pretending to be a Samurai. She did this as she passed the front door of the castle, until she saw a guard walk past. Not wanting to be seen, Cinderella quickly ducked behind a marble column. Peering around it, she wondered to herself why they even needed guards. Nothing dangerous ever happened in the kingdom to warrant this. The pointlessness of these guards only added to her anger, but, as was her nature, she swiftly dismissed the thought, buried those angry feelings and decided to try another part of the castle to "escape" to before the Prince awoke and came looking for her.

As Cinderella made her way down a long hallway, swinging the pendulum at her side, she passed walls that held framed paintings of beautiful landscapes, as well as of the castles' still living occupants. The perfection of how they were placed in neat little rows created a feeling of claustrophobia for Cinderella. The only thing she could think of to ease the feeling was to whack each frame with the pendulum, which would make them crooked. And that's just what she did. She gleefully smacked each portrait hard, releasing some of that pent up frustration.

By the time she got to the end of the hall, she turned and smiled for the first time that morning, enjoying the jagged disorder of the frames, then continued on her way.

Setting things out of order triggered such giddiness in Cinderella that she began to look for other things to dismantle. She went into the main living room and scanned it carefully. There was a lamp on the table that immediately caught her eye. One that would look much better on its side she thought, so, lifting the pendulum, she took aim and – Whack! Knocked it clear across the room.

Smiling at her achievement, she then saw an ashtray on the coffee table. She went over and picked it up. Looking at this odd shaped piece of glass, not knowing what it was, or its purpose because smoking did not exist at all in the kingdom, she wondered if it might be some relic from another century. Not caring, she threw it down hard on the floor – Crash! It shattered into a hundred pieces.

She giggled at the glass chaos she created, but her giggle was no longer the sweet peal that so delighted the Prince and all who knew her. Instead, it came from a shadowy place from deep within and sounded more throaty and wicked.

A sinister glean was now in her eyes as she glanced around

the room for other things to obliterate. As if on a mission of destruction, she began using the pendulum like a baseball bat, toppling over chairs and knocking frames off mantles. She then began tearing flowers from vases and throwing them into the air, laughing out loud as she watched them scatter to the floor.

The next thing that caught her eye were the long draped curtains that were tied perfectly back by thick, knotted gold ropes. She shoved the pendulum in the crack of a nearby couch and walked over to one of them. She untied it, letting the curtain dangle loose, then swung the gold-knotted rope above her head in a frenzy and let it go. Swooosh! She watched it fly and crash into a mirror, causing it to loosen from its hook and slam hard to the floor.

Perversely excited, Cinderella rushed over to the next window, untied the knotted gold rope and did the same thing again, swinging it over her head, letting go and watching it slam into a chandelier, breaking its glass pieces that rained to the floor. She did the same with the next curtain, and the next, moving around the room and watching the gold ropes fly out of her hand hitting more wall frames and fixtures. Each time letting out a gleefully, wicked laugh.

She soon found herself out of breath, but was far from finished. Standing near the last curtain, she grabbed it with both hands, and gave it a good yank hoping to pull it down. But the curtain was made of strong material. She yanked at it again, and again defying the fact that she simply was not strong enough to pull it down, but this did not cause her to stop. It only added fuel to her internal raging fire.

Meanwhile, the sun was up and the servants were now all on duty. Two older female servants were polishing the banister of the staircase that Cinderella had descended less than an hour earlier. They hummed in unison as they rubbed their rags along the railings. When they got to the bottom of the stairs, one noticed the open glass case of the grandfather clock and its missing pendulum. Perplexed and worried, she called the other servant over to take a look. They both stared at it then eyed each other in confusion.

The one who noticed it first quickly got on her knees and tried to repair what she could of the clock while the other stepped into the hallway. She let out a mortified gasp and motioned for the servant on her knees to come and see what she was seeing. The other servant did, and both stood in the hallway looking aghast at all the framed paintings tilted lopsided along the walls.

Quickly they made their way down the hall fixing each one by putting them back into perfect position. Then, hearing a low grunting sound coming from the main living room, they cautiously approached the doorway and peered inside. Their expressions turned from hurried confusion to complete disbelief.

They watched Cinderella climbing up the thick curtain, as one would a rope in gym class, making her way to the ceiling. She had been yanking at the curtain so hard she unwittingly started to climb it, grunting and sweating all the way. Once Cinderella realized she was at the top and was not able to bring down the fabric monster, she let out a crazed snarl then a primal scream. Panting when she finished, she glanced over her shoulder and saw the two servants staring up at her, covering their mouths in horror.

Quickly coming to her senses, Cinderella gingerly slid down the curtain and stepped away from it as soon as her feet hit the floor. She calmly straightened her lopsided gown and fixed her sweaty, matted hair. The two servants watched with worry as she strode past them as if nothing unusual at all had taken place, and sweetly greeted them with "good morning" before she left the room.

The servants, though still confused, bowed out of respect then quickly rushed into action. One went for the lamp that was on the floor across the room while the other got on her knees and began carefully picking up the shattered pieces of glass of the chandelier, for they so loved Cinderella and were in alliance never to mention any of this to anyone.

Three

⇻ The Perfect Argument ⇺

Later that morning, the Prince, looking well rested and handsome (as usual), was eating his breakfast in the grand dining hall. Sitting across from him was Cinderella, rubbing her shoulders in pain from her recent curtain climb. She looked at the Prince who was obliviously content with himself and everything around him. Again, that urge to reach over and slap him occurred to her, but she was able to suppress it. However, with all she had been through already that morning, the suppression turned into a silent, angry boil, until finally she could no longer stand it.

"I can't take it anymore!" Cinderella shouted.

This so startled the Prince that he nearly choked on his food. "My love," he said, swallowing hard, "Take what?"

"All of *this*! Everything. It's all too perfect. The castle is too perfect. The staff is too perfect. *You're* too perfect."

"Yes, I am," said the Prince, proudly.

Cinderella glared at him. It frustrated her that he was ignorant to what she was trying to say.

15

"Can't you see I'm suffocating?" she blurted out.

The Prince was taken aback. This was hard for him to comprehend. His mind raced to figure out how to best make everything right as soon as possible. A thought came to him instantly, and he smiled.

"Then I will get for you the most beautiful dress. No, I will get for you the most beautiful necklace..."

"No!" snapped Cinderella, as she pushed her plate away in frustration. "You're not listening! That's not what I *need*."

"What then? Tell me what it is you need," he asked her.

Cinderella looked at him, annoyed, but felt that more with herself since she couldn't put her finger on what she needed. Then suddenly, it came to her.

"An argument!" she announced, excited by the thought. "Argue with me."

"Argue? What about?"

"Anything," Cinderella said with anticipation. "Or rather, tell me something I do that makes you really angry."

The Prince let out a slight chuckle, amused by his wife's obvious joke. "There is nothing you do, my Princess, that angers me."

"There has to be," said Cinderella, sitting forward in her seat and wanting her husband to be brutally honest. "Come on...I can take it."

The Prince pondered this hard. He even stared up at the ceiling thinking with all his might, but shook his head as he looked back at Cinderella and said, "No. There is nothing," then he happily went back to eating his breakfast.

Determined to have a real argument, Cinderella declared, "All right then, *I'll* start one."

She looked at him, thinking. Suddenly something that truly irked her came to mind. "You agree with me on everything."

The Prince smiled, proud of this fact, and said, "Yes, I do. You are right."

This was the response Cinderella expected, but also the one she didn't want. She looked at her husband, frustrated. Suddenly, something else that bothered her came to her. "Everybody *likes* you," she said with irritation.

"Is that so awful?" asked the Prince.

Knowing that it wasn't, Cinderella started to lose momentum and said, "No, I suppose charming isn't a flaw. You can't help it."

The Prince smiled and continued with his breakfast. Feeling defeated, Cinderella tried to go back to hers, but had no appetite. She was looking for a fight, a good one, too, but didn't know how to start it. Then suddenly, an idea struck her.

"What about your parents? Don't they make you angry sometimes?"

The Prince answered her without hesitation. "No. They have been very loving and supportive of everything I do. How could I possibly be angry at that?"

Cinderella looked at him as if that couldn't be true and asked, "You've never gotten into trouble?"

Again, the Prince answered without even a thought, "No. I was obedient."

Cinderella rolled her eyes and said snidely under her breath, "And perfect. As usual."

The Prince heard this. He smiled with clueless satisfaction, "As are you, too, my darling."

The last thing Cinderella couldn't bear was being called "perfect," and this sent her into a fit of despair. "But I'm *not*! I'm lazy. I do nothing all day."

The Prince let out a slight chuckle, still amused by his wife's relentless yet entertaining conversation. "There is nothing for you *to* do. The servants take care of all your needs."

"And you see nothing wrong in that? I never do anything on my own!"

The Prince looked at her, ready to take care of this problem. "All right, tell me what need it is you wish to fulfill on your own, and I will make sure to have the servants take care of it."

Cinderella shot him a death stare, then, giving up, sat back in defeat. "To be honest, I – I don't know what I need."

"Well, I *do*," said the Prince with a smile.

Cinderella looked up at him, surprised, and watched as he carefully dabbed the corners of his mouth with his napkin and said with confidence, "I will regale you with a story. You've always loved my stories."

Before Cinderella could beg him not to, he began, "Once upon a time, I went on a long journey across the kingdom. I rode my best steed, Chase. I soon came upon a brook and dismounted. As Chase drank from the brook, I watched a bird fly from a long branch on a tree to another, then back again."

He looked at Cinderella, pleased. She looked at him, waiting for the rest of it.

"And?" she asked.

"And what?" he asked back, confused.

"Then what happened?"

"I mounted Chase and came home, of course," he said, smiling, as he lifted his fork and continued eating his breakfast.

Cinderella gave him another long, hard stare and responded flatly, "That *didn't* work."

The Prince stopped and looked at her, again perplexed. "Well then," he said thinking, "I will share with you another story."

"No, please –" Cinderella began in hopes to stop him, but it was too late. The Prince wasn't listening.

"Once upon a time, I went on a long journey across the kingdom. I rode my best steed, Chase. We came upon a meadow of soft grass, and I dismounted. As Chase grazed, I watched a –"

"Oh, for God's sake, *stop!*" shouted Cinderella.

"But I didn't finish," said the Prince, looking shocked since he'd never been interrupted before.

"You really think a stupid story is going to help me? That's not what I need!"

The Prince was stunned by her tone. "What then?" he asked. "Tell me what it is you need."

"A break," she said.

"A break?" asked the Prince, confused.

"Yes. I need a break – some time away from all of this...even *you*," she said knowing this would probably hurt his feelings, but at this point she no longer cared.

The Prince did look hurt, understandably, but grinned and said, "Then you shall have it!"

He quickly removed the napkin from his collar, placed it down on the table and left the room.

Cinderella sat there, astonished. He finally listened? Alone and content, she lifted her fork and began to eat her meal in peace. Several moments passed when suddenly the Prince entered, took his seat again and smiling proudly.

"What are you doing?" asked Cinderella.

"I gave you a break. Just as you've asked."

"Are you kidding me? That was less than two minutes! What is *wrong* with you?"

He grinned confidently. "Nothing – of course."

Cinderella dropped her fork in frustration and rose from her chair. "I'm out of here. I'm going to see my Fairy Godmother."

"Whatever for?" the Prince asked, surprised.

"Because I can't sit here and be around someone so -" She stopped herself before letting off a stream of insults. Instead, she rolled her eyes in annoyance and shook her head. "Oh, just forget it."

With that, Cinderella angrily stomped out of the room. The Prince sat pondering all that had just taken place, but too much thinking disturbed his tranquility, so he refocused and tried to eat more from his plate only to realize he was no longer hungry.

Suddenly, from outside the castle window, he heard a carriage and its horses approach. The Prince stood, went to the window and looked out. Below, he saw his princess being helped into a beautiful, oval shaped carriage by a powdered wigged coachman. The coachman closed the door, climbed in front and took the reins. He snapped them twice causing the horses to pull away from the castle down a pathway lined with lush greenery. The Prince watched this with great puzzlement and concern.

Four

❧ RETIREMENT ❧

Cinderella, was happy to be out and away from the castle, but sat anxiously in the carriage as it moved down the path and onto the main road. Yes, she lived in perfection and was sincerely grateful for all of it, but something was wrong though she couldn't figure out what. She even thought about how best to describe it to the Fairy Godmother, but couldn't come up with the words. It had been a long time since she had last seen the Fairy Godmother, so she was looking forward to simply being in the comfort of her much needed company. Perhaps once she got there she would know how to explain herself.

In a small glen on the outskirts of the kingdom sat one of those pristine cottages. The carriage pulled up in front of it and Cinderella got out. She hurried to the door and knocked. There was no answer. She knocked again. Nothing. In desperation, she pounded on the door and shouted, "Fairy Godmother! Where are you?"

Suddenly, there were loud noises heard from inside the cottage of things being knocked over, then of a glass breaking as

21

footsteps came to the door. A moment passed before the lock un-hitched and the door slowly opened.

The Fairy Godmother peered out, blinded by the sunlight. She was dressed in a ratty old bathrobe and even rattier look-ing slippers. Her hair was in complete disarray. She rubbed her eyes as she tried to focus on Cinderella who was taken aback by this unkempt sight.

"Are you all right, Fairy Godmother?"

"I was trying to get some sleep," the Fairy Godmother an-swered in a grouchy mood.

"But it's almost noon," said Cinderella, as if sleeping any time past the break of dawn was some unspoken crime.

The Fairy Godmother didn't care, and responded with a curt, "What do you want?"

"May I come in?"

The Fairy Godmother hated the idea of anyone entering her home, and most definitely did not want company, but gave in. She tried to open the door wider for Cinderella, but it was too tight – years of no guests and neglect. She stepped out and used her shoulder to give it a good shove. It moved just enough to let Cinderella in, then the Fairy Godmother shuffled back inside as Cinderella followed.

The cottage was dusty and old with cobwebs on the furni-ture. The immediate stench of mold, stale beer and wine stung at Cinderella's nostrils causing her to cover her nose delicately with the back of her hand. The Fairy Godmother kicked sever-al wine bottles under a table in the hopes to hide her obvious vice, though Cinderella noticed. She made no comment as she looked about the room with concern.

"Why are you sleeping in the middle of the day?" Cinderella asked.

The Fairy Godmother replied with a gruff, "It's called retirement. You know, happily ever after?"

"Are you happy?" Cinderella asked, as if in desperate need for the answer.

"Of course!" exclaimed the Fairy Godmother. "I've hung up my wand, no more magic potions or spells. Never been happier."

Cinderella frowned, and said, "Well, I'm not."

The Fairy Godmother quickly shot Cinderella a look of alarm, snapping her out of her sleepy state. "What?!"

"I'm unhappy," Cinderella said followed by a deep sigh.

The Fairy Godmother suddenly became frantic, rushed at Cinderella and clasped her hand over Cinderella's mouth.

"Never, *ever*, say that! Not here!" the Fairy Godmother hissed in a panicked whisper as her eyes darted cautiously toward the windows. With her hand still on Cinderella's mouth firm, she asked, "Has anyone heard you say that?"

Cinderella winced in pain from the tight grip the Fairy Godmother had on her mouth and shook her head no.

"Are you sure?" the Fairy Godmother asked with terror and fear still in her eyes.

Cinderella, getting scared herself, nervously nodded her head yes.

The Fairy Godmother glanced to her right, then to her left and said, "I'm going to move my hand away but you're not to repeat those words. Do you understand?"

Cinderella nodded in earnest as the Fairy Godmother moved her hand slowly away and whispered guardedly, "Everyone is happy here. It's the *law*.

"But –" began Cinderella.

"No! No but's! You represent something bigger than you can ever imagine. If any woman were to hear you utter those words it would send an irreparable shock wave deep into women's psyches all over the universe. And we *don't* want that."

"No, no. Of course not," agreed Cinderella, although she wasn't sure what exactly any of it meant.

"This is very troublesome, Cinderella," said the Fairy Godmother as she paced the room, wringing her hands. "I'm not sure I understand. I mean, you have the Prince and the castle...and that stepfamily is finally out of your hair. What more do you *want*?"

Again Cinderella sighed, "I'm not sure. All I know is I'm un –"

"*Don't!* What did I just tell you?" asked the Fairy God-mother shaking her finger at Cinderella. "Oy, you princesses," she sighed then quickly asked in a gossipy whisper, "Is it the Prince?"

"No. I mean, yes...I mean, no. I mean...oh, I don't know. He's perfect, as usual, which grates on my last nerve. I'm not sure if I was wise to marry him. Maybe I should have waited. Just being around him is driving me crazy...giving me night-mares...and thoughts of dying."

"Oh, dear," said the Fairy Godmother. "You're suicidal."

"No, no. Not me, the Prince. Thought of *him* dying...and at my hand."

"Oh," said the Fairy Godmother, worried. "Oh, dear."

"So, I need to get away from here. I've never been without someone telling me who I am, and what to do. I need time to find out who I really am without everyone interfering," Cin-derella bemoaned, then added in anger, "Especially the Prince!"

"Ok, Ok," said the Fairy Godmother waving her hands at Cinderella. "Let me think here."

No longer the symbol of purity, the Fairy Godmother scratched her rear and said, "Sounds like a mid-century crisis to me, Cinderella. It happens to all of us at one time or another. Just ask Rapunzel...or Rumpelstilskin. Now *that* was a crisis!" She mumbled, "Going after first-borns. What a mess," then she let out a sigh. "I'm not quite sure what to do for you, Cinderella. A miserable princess, who knew?"

Cinderella, discouraged, sat down next to a bowl of rotted fruit on the table. She looked at it, hungry, remembering she didn't eat her breakfast.

"May I?" she asked pointing to the fruit.

The Fairy Godmother looked at the moldy, wrinkly fruit and held up her hand indicating for Cinderella to wait as she went to a shelf and sorted through several dusty jars. She found one filled with blue stardust. She took it down, shook it, and then tried to open it. She struggled with it until finally handing it to Cinderella for help.

Cinderella opened it after a few hard twists, then handed it back. The Fairy Godmother removed the lid and sprinkled the stardust on the fruit. Within seconds they magically turned from rotten to fresh. The Fairy Godmother smiled and motioned for Cinderella to help herself.

Cinderella took an apple from the bowl. She bit into it, enjoying its sweet taste, as the Fairy Godmother plopped down on a dusty couch across from her.

"So, you're stuck in eternal bliss. Why can't you just suck it up and enjoy it like the rest of us?"

Cinderella looked despondent. "I can't. I need something real."

"Real, *schmeal*," retorted the Fairy Godmother. "Can't you just fake it?"

"I'm tired of faking it. I'm unhap -"

"*Don't you dare!*" snapped the Fairy Godmother.

"Sorry," said Cinderella, as she lowered her head.

Just then, horse hoofs were heard outside followed by a man's voice shouting, "Whoa!" The Fairy Godmother, bothered already by Cinderella's presence, was even more bothered by the possibility of someone else's.

"Oh, what now?" she groaned as she pulled herself up from the couch.

The thought that it might be the Prince made Cinderella's anger surface. She spoke through clenched teeth, "I swear, if the Prince followed me here, I'll rip his head off his neck and feed it to a pack of starving warthogs!"

The Fairy Godmother was so startled to hear such a nasty tone come from such a sweet princess, that she nearly lost her balance walking to the door. She shot Cinderella a look of shock and worry as she cautiously opened the door. A tired and out of breath royal Page was standing there holding a scroll. He gave her a short bow and said, "Greetings, M'lady."

The Fairy Godmother rolled her eyes and told him to get to the point of why he was there. The Page explained that he had an invitation to a ball that was being thrown by his Royal Highness, The Prince, and handed her the scroll. The Fairy Godmother glanced over her shoulder knowing this would surely set off Cinderella, and it did. Cinderella came to the door, having overheard.

"Did you say a *ball*?" asked Cinderella, in anger.

"Yes, your Highness. Everyone in the kingdom is invited. But please, if you will excuse me, I must go. I have many invitations to distribute." He bowed then walked to a horse drawn cart that was overflowing with hundreds of scrolls.

Cinderella grabbed the scroll from the Fairy Godmother's hand and turned back inside. She angrily unraveled it and read it aloud.

"His Royal Highness extends this most wonderful invitation to be his guest to a ball in celebration of His Beloved

Cinderella. To partake in a reminder of the happily ever after-ness that she has achieved in joining a most perfect union"

Cinderella held it up in confusion. "What the...? It doesn't make grammatical sense, let alone regular sense!"

The Fairy Godmother seeing Cinderella ready to go into an angry tirade, stepped forward and said gently, "Now, Cinderella..."

Before she could say another word, Cinderella began ripping up the scroll in a frantic rage and let out a scream of crazed frustration.

The Fairy Godmother, taken aback, tried to calm her. "He means well, Cinderella."

"No he *doesn't*," Cinderella sneered. "He thinks everything can be glossed over with just a smile, or a necklace, or...a *ball*! I'm so sick of it!"

She shoved what was left of the shredded scroll into the Fairy Godmother's hands as she reached for her apple and angrily threw it across the room where it hit a wall and smashed to the floor.

"*That* should be his head!" shouted Cinderella.

The Fairy Godmother was horrified. Cinderella noticed and, realizing her anger was out of control, quickly composed herself.

"I – I'm sorry. I'll clean it up," she said with intense regret.

As she moved across the room, the Fairy Godmother grabbed her arm and stopped her. She couldn't have a princess cleaning up anything. It was not allowed in the kingdom. She motioned for Cinderella to step back and pointed to a chair. Cinderella grudgingly took a seat and tried to calm herself, letting out a deep, frustrated sigh. Then tears welled up in her eyes.

"Oh, Fairy Godmother...what's *wrong* with me? What am I to *do*? I can't go back to the castle."

"No, you can't," the Fairy Godmother agreed.

"And I can't stay here," whined Cinderella.

"No, most definitely *not*," said the Fairy Godmother, not wanting anyone encroaching on her precious privacy, as she bent over to pick up the smashed apple.

"Where will I go then?" asked Cinderella, despondent.

When the Fairy Godmother stood, she looked at the sloppy pieces of apple in her hand. Suddenly, an idea came to her.

"The Big Apple! You'll go to the Big Apple!"

"What's the Big Apple?" asked Cinderella, perplexed.

The Fairy Godmother hesitated for a moment, unsure if she should tell Cinderella, and then slowly sat down next to her.

"How do I explain this? What you're going through, Cinderella is called perfection overload. It happens...I've been there."

"You?" asked Cinderella, surprised. "What did you do about it?"

The Fairy Godmother looked away for a moment, again hesitant, then said, "I probably shouldn't be telling you this, but what I did was...I left. But just for a little while. I heard about a doctor named Sigmund Freud who was good at fixing people. You know, going deep into your head kind of stuff. So, I went looking for him."

"Did you find him?"

"No. I thought he'd be at this convention where all the same sort of doctors got together, but he wasn't there. Instead, I found someone else, a really nice gentleman, too. He completely fixed me."

"What was wrong with you?"

"Well, he, this doctor, said...let me see if I can remember...oh, yes, he said I had eccentricities of character, and that I suffered from moral anxiety. Oh, but that I had a healthy super-ego and dipsomania, which only means I like to drink. He also said that my narcissism was strong, and that I had something called illusory superiority, whatever that means. Anyway, he fixed me and that's all that matters."

"Do you think he can help me?" asked Cinderella, eager and desperate.

"He might," said the Fairy Godmother. "Let me check to see if he's still in the same place."

The Fairy Godmother got up and went to a corner of the room where there was a large closet. She opened the door and inside was a giant, hand-cranked Rolodex with cards that were 30 x 24 inches in size, about the size of a wall poster. On each card had thousands of names along with cities in tiny print next to them. The Fairy Godmother grabbed hold of the crank and heaved it forward causing the large cards to flap downward.

Cinderella peered inside the closet. "What is this?" she asked.

"These are the names of some people I know, but most are all the people who make wishes. I had them alphabetized."

"How did they know to send their wishes to you?"

"That damn cricket. And that *song*! Ever since it became popular, everyone and their mother has been wishing on a star. Why do you think I haven't been able to sleep?"

The Fairy Godmother went back to cranking. After several exhausting turns, she stopped, out of breath. She then reached for a magnifying glass from a shelf and began studying the names. Squinting to read, she finally found what she was looking for and scratched down a name on a piece of parchment paper that she had stashed in a wooden box, then walked out of the closet, closing the door behind her.

"OK, here is it. He'll definitely remember me. Just tell him that I sent you, and he'll know what to do," said the Fairy Godmother as she handed Cinderella the piece of paper.

Cinderella looked at the name. "Boris Berger?" she asked wearing a quizzical expression.

"That's right. He's in New York. The Big Apple is just a nickname for the place. Go to him and get yourself straightened out."

"Wait...he's not in the kingdom? I can't leave the kingdom!" exclaimed Cinderella nervously.

"Are you kidding me? You stood here just minutes ago telling me how badly you wanted to get out of here!"

"I know, but...but..."

"But nothing! You have no choice. We can't risk the threat of you blurting out that you're unhappy. Those words coming from you would not only mean the end of everyone here, but will crush the fantasy for women everywhere. You're an icon, honey, you have responsibilities."

"But...how will I get there?" Cinderella asked, worried.

"Good question. I'm not sure," said the Fairy Godmother rubbing her chin.

"Isn't there just a spell or a potion you can put together for me to make me happy again?" Cinderella asked.

"For what you have? No. There's no potion or spell strong enough. You need to go work this out in another way...and with a doctor...and *not* here," said the Fairy Godmother as she walked over to a huge book of spells that sat open on a stand. "Now, let me see how to get rid of...er, I mean, get you on your way."

Cinderella let out a sigh of resignation and said, "I will do as you say, Fairy Godmother. You've helped me before. I trust and thank you."

"Well, don't thank me yet. Like I said, I haven't made a spell in ages. I'm rusty," the Fairy Godmother said as she flipped through the pages of the huge book. She took a long time searching for what she was looking for until she finally stopped on a specific passage. Holding her face close to it, she read it carefully then slammed the book shut.

"All right – seems we just need to do what we did last time when I sent you to the ball," she said as she motioned for Cinderella to get up. "Come on, let's go and find a pumpkin."

Cinderella stood and followed the Fairy Godmother to a back door. Filled with anticipation, she asked, "Do tell me about this Big Apple, Fairy Godmother. Is it a place that is real?"

"More than you could ever imagine," replied the Fairy Godmother as she opened the back door and stepped out.

Five

✦ THE JOY OF DEPRESSION ✦

It was late afternoon in the Big Apple, otherwise known as New York City, which is one large mass of skyscrapers, theatres, stores and honking traffic, along with a sea of people moving in every direction.

The city is also home to many of the finest hotels in the world. One of *the* finest, and grandest, is the historic Waldorf Astoria, which has a gorgeous lobby with marble floors, towering pillars and where everything seems laced in gold.

There are exquisite banquet halls and majestic ballrooms where all sorts of events take place. And where one was taking place on that particular day. At the entrance was a sign that read: *American Psychiatric Association Annual Meeting – The Future of Psychiatry.*

This is where I come in.

Inside the luxurious ballroom, psychiatrists from all over the country mingled in groups, enjoying cocktails and eating hors d'oeuvres. In one group stood three distinguished looking male psychiatrists and myself. I was the youngest of the group, at 43.

I am the quiet, intellectual type, which is also how many describe me, though my quiet demeanor that day was mostly due to an inner disappointment that I couldn't bring myself to share with any of my colleagues. You see, they were all quite successful as I was not. At least not at their level, so the best I could muster was a weak smile when one of them would even bother to glance in my direction.

The most boisterous in the group was Rodney Klein, a pompous, womanizing, ego-driven jerk in a tweed jacket who liked to hold a pipe just for show.

"I'm telling you, Gentlemen, it's stimulating to have one book on the best seller's list, but it's *invigorating* when you have two!" he boasted, holding that stupid pipe.

A fellow doctor, just as pompous replied, "When mine was listed at number one for six weeks in a row – it was *orgasmic!*"

As all the men chuckled and nodded in arrogant agreement, I did my best to manage a sincere smile. Then Rodney looked at me.

"And what about your book, Boris? Finished yet?"

There it was. The dreaded question I hoped would never be asked. I wanted to slink away, but that would have been cowardly. Instead, I decided to face the question head on – and lied.

"Uh, yeah. Just a few more chapters."

"What is your subject?"

Oh, no. Not another question. "Relationships," I muttered. Marriage."

I wasn't sure whether to be insulted, or relieved that Rodney gave no acknowledgment that he heard, or cared, about what I had said when he raised his glass and said, "A toast! To best sellers!"

The other psychiatrists quickly raised their glasses proudly as I reluctantly raised mine, feeling like the outcast I obviously was. When I couldn't stand the façade any longer, I skillfully took a step back from the group, then another...and another, until I was able to set my glass down on a nearby table and slip out a side door.

I had been at the Waldorf all weekend and planned my exit earlier that morning. I already checked out and had my bags in the trunk of my car. Now it was time to go. I walked as fast as I could down the hall, trying not to make it obvious that what I really wanted to do was run. I felt a wave of relief at every step when suddenly I heard my name shouted from behind me. It was Rodney. He'd followed me out. I stopped and closed my eyes, wincing that I'd been discovered, then opened them and turned around wearing the best professional smile I could, though I'm sure to anyone paying closer attention, it looked more like I was trying to disguise a horrible toothache.

Rodney was carrying a large leather satchel over his shoulder as he approached me. "Heading out already?" he asked me.

I was ready to give my answer, but he had one for me.

"I totally understand. A room full of pompous shrinks talking about themselves. Can you think of anything worse?"

I squinted at Rodney looking for even a hint of self-awareness. There was none.

"So," he began with his mouth twisting into a conceited grin, "What'd you think of my lecture?"

"No comment," I responded curtly, and then turned to go but he grabbed my arm.

"Boris, come on...your great grandfather contributed a lot to psychiatry. You should be proud of him."

"I'm not," I said. "And I wish you hadn't done –" I began to say, but was interrupted.

"He was a pioneer, a trailblazer! Without him, we'd all go a little...well, nutty," Rodney chuckled.

I was not amused. "I have to go, my son is waiting –"

Completely blind to the fact that I didn't want to talk to him, he asked, "Right…and the Mrs.? How is Helen?"

That was the other question I had hoped to avoid during this entire event since my wife and I separated several months earlier. I hadn't told anyone. I tried to hide my pain with a smile and, again, lied. I was getting good at lying, but it was not something I was proud of.

"Oh…fine. She's…fine," I muttered. I was getting good at muttering, too.

"Well, let me know when you finish your book. I want a signed copy. Oh, and speaking of –" Rodney said as he dug into his satchel, pulled out a copy of his book and handed it to me.

I looked at the cover. On it, in large letters, was the title: *The Joy of Depression*. Was this a joke?

Rodney leaned in closer to me and whispered, "Depression is so overrated," then slapped me hard on the back.

As this happened, a very pretty young woman walked passed. I thought Rodney's head would twist off the way it turned and followed her.

"I'll be in touch," he said as he winked and moved with determination in the young woman's direction, like a wild tiger ready to pounce.

Oh, how I hated Rodney Klein.

The late afternoon traffic out of New York City was bumper to bumper, and I was right in the middle of it, yet feeling too apathetic to care. As I rubbed my eyes and got comfortable in my car seat, my cell phone went off. I answered it on the speakerphone. From it came a booming voice that was demanding, unsympathetic and to the point. It was Helen, my estranged wife. I sat up immediately and hopeful, even though she sounded annoyed and put out. She'd been unfriendly with me for some time. How I wished she wasn't.

"Boris, it's Helen," she snapped. "Why are you dragging your feet with the divorce papers?"

I didn't want to answer her, but I knew I had to. I also knew she wasn't going to like what I had to say. My voice involuntarily quivered, much to my embarrassment, as I tried to lace it with sweetness and optimism.

"Helen...can't we –" was all I got out before she began shouting with angry authority.

"No, Boris, it's over, so just sign the papers and let's get on with our lives."

Helen had left me just three months earlier. It was entirely her decision. I was a failure in her eyes. I suppose I was one in mine as well. I had a quiet and fairly successful practice, but was also focused on getting my name on the New York Times bestseller's list like my colleagues. I suppose my pursuit became somewhat of an obsession, as much as it was also very time consuming. I felt I had something to prove with my book, and in doing so, neglected my role as husband at times. However, I didn't agree that it was enough of an excuse to run out on me.

Perhaps it was "too late," as she described it, but, in my opinion, nothing was ever "too late" when it came to love and family. Helen obviously disagreed, but now that I think about it, we usually disagreed on everything. Still, I loved her and swore never to give up on her and our marriage, although she clearly was done with it.

I shook my head feeling depressed, and said unintentionally aloud, forgetting I was on speakerphone, "This isn't how I ever thought it would be."

Helen quickly snapped back, "That's because we don't live in a fairy tale, Boris. This is real life."

Those words struck a deep nerve in me, and she knew it. The mention of 'fairy tale' was a cheap shot about a dark secret that had haunted me most of my life. It angered me that she 'went there,' but I refrained from a fight since I knew this was clearly what she wanted.

I also knew there was little I could do to convince Helen about changing her mind about our marriage, and I hated that part most about her, about us. She was so stubborn. So, I resorted to the only thing we shared that was beautiful and perfect to reach her. I asked in a tone daring her to snap at me again, "When are you going to come see Walter?"

"Kyle has a thing about kids. He's not ready," she said about the man she left me for. A man I knew little about. I thought many times of standing up to Helen and demanding she tell me who Kyle was, but deep down I didn't want to know and I've always had trouble standing up to her anyway.

But the one person I never had a problem standing up *for* was our son, Walter. My demeanor changed when I heard what she said and knew how to fight back.

"So, your son just sits around and misses you as he waits for Kyle to be *ready*?"

There was a sudden silence on Helen's end. An odd stillness that caused me to lean forward as if she was actually in the car with me, and gave her a tense expression that she would never see.

"The truth is, *I'm* not ready," Helen said calmly with a twinge of vulnerability in her voice.

Her honesty plucked at my heart, and I suddenly felt regret and sadness for her, for both of us. I went soft and said with heartfelt sincerity, "Helen, no matter what happens, I still believe in –"

"Sign the papers!" she quickly barked one last time, and then hung up.

I finished my sentence anyway. "Us."

Just then, traffic started to move. It was a needed distraction. I gently moved along with it when suddenly my cell phone rang again. Relieved that Helen still had a heart, I answered it, but it wasn't Helen. It was my attorney, Greg, a man who also liked to get right to the point.

"Got some bad news, Boris. Your publisher called. They've decided not to move forward with the book. Writing about how to maintain a happy relationship while you're going through a divorce is too much of a hard sell. Sorry."

That was to the point all right. I was crushed. And traffic stopped, making everything worse. Greg tried to be optimistic.

"Hey – you can always write about something else."

I grimaced. Yes, I could write about something else, but relationships was my expertise – or so I thought. This new doubt was now worsening my already aching heart and mind. Not wanting to even engage in a conversation that I knew would go nowhere, I thanked Greg and hung up.

As traffic began to move again, I looked down at Rodney's book that I had thrown on the passenger seat along with my jacket. The words, "The Phenomenal #1 Best Seller" were emblazoned above the title *The Joy of Depression*. I felt nauseated and could no longer take the frustration, so I rolled down my car window, grabbed the book and tossed it out.

Six

⤜ RUSTY SPELLS ⤛

The Fairy Godmother carried a heavy pumpkin across her lawn and dropped it on an empty patch of grass. She let out an agonizing groan as she held her back in pain. Cinderella stepped up next to her, excited, holding a small box with several mice in it.

"I have the mice for the horses!" she said as if her collecting the small rodents was some great accomplishment.

The Fairy Godmother shot her a frosty look. She then shook her head and asked, "And the rats? You need coachmen."

Just then, Cinderella saw two rats rustling in the shrubbery. She started for them then stopped. "I – I can't," she said as she bristled her shoulders and made a 'grossed out' expression.

Annoyed by Cinderella's lack of backbone, the Fairy Godmother bit her tongue as not to make the wrong comment, went back into the cottage and returned with a small block of cheese. She placed it near a tree, then walked over to the shrubs, bent over and dug her hands in. Within a minute, she had two rats by their tails. She stood with them both dangling

39

from her fists, went over to the pumpkin and the cheese and dropped them.

She then walked over to Cinderella and, with a sour look, took the box holding the mice from her, opened it and let them scurry over to the cheese. Then the Fairy Godmother wiped her hands and looked carefully at Cinderella.

"Are you nervous?" she asked.

"I have to admit, I am, but I'm also strangely excited. I think this will be good for me."

"Let's hope so," said the Fairy Godmother. "Now what about the Prince?"

"Oh, I don't care," Cinderella said, flippant.

The Fairy Godmother shook her head. "OK, I'll figure that out later. Let's just get you out of here."

"How long will I be gone for?" Cinderella asked.

"A fortnight," answered the Fairy Godmother.

"A fortnight?!?" shrieked Cinderella.

"Isn't that how long everyone from our world usually goes away for? It's only two weeks. You should be able to accomplish what you need in that time. Now let me find my wand, and let's get this show on the road," said the Fairy Godmother as she went back into the cottage.

Cinderella stood there excited yet worried. She held her hand to her chest, trying to still her rapidly beating heart. She had never traveled outside the kingdom and never been away from the Prince for more then – well, ever. But as she said, part of her heart beating so fast was the thrill of going on an adventure. Also, she knew if she were to stay it would surely put more stress on her relationship, as well as threaten the Prince, the kingdom, and possibly the entire universe if she were to ever say aloud that she was unhappy, although she didn't understand what the entire universe had to do with it.

She looked again at the piece of parchment paper the Fairy Godmother gave her and sighed. Just then, the Fairy Godmother came out of the cottage holding her wand. It was covered in dust, so she blew on it then wiped it on her sleeve to polish it.

"It's been so long since I've used this, Cinderella," she said looking unsure, as she gave it a few flicks with her wrist.

Cinderella saw that several rats were sniffing at the block of cheese. Excited, she told the Fairy Godmother. Seeing this, the Fairy Godmother was relieved that they now had all she needed to get Cinderella on her way. It was time to break in the old wand, so the Fairy Godmother gently pushed Cinderella back to give herself some room, and held out the wand. She scratched her head, trying to recall what to say.

"Uh, let's see now...OK...*a fortnight for the pretty bumpkin/Come a carriage from this pumpkin!*"

She waved the wand. Suddenly, pink and purple stardust appeared and sparkled around the pumpkin. Within seconds, it splashed into a stunningly beautiful white carriage with gold trimmings. The Fairy Godmother looked at it with prideful surprise.

"It worked! I still got it!" she shouted.

"Yes! Now do the rats," said Cinderella, egging her on.

The Fairy Godmother nodded, appreciating the encouragement as she held up her wand and tried again to recall the spell.

"Uh...OK...*another fortnight with gentle pats/Turn two coachmen from these rats.*"

She waved the wand. This time, green stardust formed around the rats then splashed them into two handsome coachmen in blue riding suits with silver buttons. The coachmen looked at each other, surprised and impressed. Then looked over at Cinderella, more impressed.

One of the coachmen gave her a sly smile with a raised eyebrow, and slowly approached her. He leaned in and asked seductively, "How you doing?"

The Fairy Godmother saw this and protectively stood between him and Cinderella. "You'll be the driver," she said with a threatening glare.

The coachman shrugged and obeyed. As he made his way up in the driver's seat, the Fairy Godmother went over to the mice while still casting protective glances at the lecherous coachman.

On a successful spell roll, the Fairy Godmother held up her wand and said, "*A fortnight once/A fortnight twice/ Make horses from these tiny mice!*"

She waved her wand. Yellow and orange stardust appeared this time and sparkled around the mice. It flashed into a bright light then, within seconds, standing in front of the carriage were four beautiful horses.

"YES!" exclaimed the Fairy Godmother, again proud of herself.

Cinderella started for the carriage, eager now to get on her way, but the Fairy Godmother stopped her noticing the beautiful gown she was wearing. Knowing that where Cinderella was going she would stick out like a sore thumb if she wore it, she positioned Cinderella in front of her and took several steps back, holding up her wand.

"*Not too much like a pathetic dork/Make Cinderella fit New York.*"

She waved her wand. There was a sudden explosion of rainbow colors that swirled around Cinderella. When it cleared, Cinderella had changed from her beautiful gown to a dress out of the late 1800's. It was pale blue/grey with a high neck, an hourglass corset, puffed sleeves and a bell-shaped skirt. Her shoes were high tab made of dark blue suede with huge buckles.

Cinderella looked down at the clothes, smiled at first then grimaced from the snugness of the corset.

"This is what they wear in the Big Apple?" she asked.

"I suppose," said the Fairy Godmother, not really caring, as she gave a shrug and began to lay the ground rules for Cinderella about her trip.

"Two weeks from this night, the carriage will return to the same spot where it lands, so *don't forget* where you land. Look for a sign that says "New York." It will lead you into the city. Again, in two weeks remember to be at the same spot by midnight or you'll turn back into a princess – and that could get ugly."

Cinderella nodded as the Fairy Godmother went over to a small vegetable garden and pulled up three heads of cabbage. She found an old burlap sack nearby, shook the dirt off, and placed the cabbages into it.

"Here – you'll need these to buy food and clothes. Last I heard "cabbage" is what they called their currency. When you arrive, these will turn into just that."

Cinderella took the burlap sack and headed for the carriage. The Fairy Godmother followed and stood by the door.

"One more thing, Cinderella, I am granting you three wishes. They are to help you when you need them most. Use them wisely."

She waved her wand three times in front of Cinderella for the wishes to be with her, and then helped her climb into the carriage. It was a struggle with Cinderella's corset so tight, but she got in.

"Good luck, Cinderella," said the Fairy Godmother as she closed the door.

The other coachman took a seat next to the driver. The driver shook the reigns and the carriage started to move slowly forward. The Fairy Godmother walked to the gate and opened it. As the carriage rolled out and started down a path, it began to lift off the ground. It bounced several times and nearly crashed into trees, causing the Fairy Godmother to wince in fright, but soon it took off into the night.

The Fairy Godmother closed the gate and let out an exhausted sigh as she headed back into the cottage, muttering to herself, "*Now* maybe I can get some sleep."

Seven

4am.

n a small patch of forgotten field, all was quiet and still when suddenly Cinderella's carriage landed hard on the earth. It bounced several times causing the coachmen to nearly fall off before it came to a complete stop.

One of the coachmen, still woozy from the ride, jumped down from his seat, balanced himself and opened the passenger door. A shaken Cinderella carefully stepped out. She winced, still getting used to her corset, and held tight to the burlap sack. She took several steps from the carriage, swaying and trying to walk in her shoes, as she looked around perplexed.

It was a strange looking place with brown grass, weeds and broken chunks of cement scattered about. This sight left Cinderella and the coachman speechless. Suddenly, the sound of a blaring horn was heard beyond some thick shrubbery in the distance. Cinderella and the coachman shot each other startled glances, never having heard such a sound before and headed in its direction to investigate. They pushed the shrubbery aside and cautiously stepped out onto a gravel road, which was on the side of a dark interstate highway. Once again, it was still and quiet.

"Where are we?" asked the Coachman.

Cinderella looked above and saw a green highway sign which read: *Interstate 95 South – Newark.*

"New Ark? Hmm. I thought the Fairy Godmother said New York," Cinderella whispered, confused. "Did I hear her wrong?" she asked the coachman. He shrugged, not knowing.

"She told me to look for a sign. New Ark...New York. Sounds the same. This must be it, and that's the sign. I'm in the Big Apple!"

"Are we supposed to just leave you here?" asked the Coachman.

Cinderella didn't know. The Fairy Godmother apparently gave little direction on what to do once they arrived. The Coachman looked around, worried. Just then, a blue Honda Civic seemingly came out of nowhere and sped by. Both Cinderella and the Coachman crouched down in fear as it passed.

"What was *that*?" asked Cinderella.

"A metal monster," replied the Coachman.

"But it looked like a carriage of some sort. There was a driver," said Cinderella, perplexed, as she stood.

"I'm not getting a good feeling about this, M'lady. In fact, I'm not feeling too well at all," said the Coachman, as he held his hand to his stomach, looking queasy.

"Oh," said Cinderella, concerned for him. She opened up the burlap sack as if searching for a remedy, but all she pulled out a handful of hundred dollar bills. When she held them up to show the Coachman, a look of horror came across her face. The Coachman's face had started to turn back into a rat. He had a snout with whiskers with patches of fur covering his face.

Seeing the terror in Cinderella's expression, he touched his face and realized what was happening. After all, the Fairy Godmother did say she was rusty. Knowing time was of the essence, the Coachman said he must return immediately to the kingdom before it was too late. Cinderella agreed and told him to hurry.

When the Coachman turned toward the shrubbery, a tail protruded from under his coat. Cinderella gasped when she saw it, and watched as he disappeared into the shrubs. His tail a second behind, whipped wildly twice, then was gone.

Cinderella stood alone on the side of the highway, and then noticed in the distance a huge truck was fast approaching. Unafraid of "metal monsters," she stepped out onto the highway and waved at it. The truck's lights flashed, and slowed down, as it got closer to her. It pulled over, making a loud breaking sound in the process. Cinderella held her ears and winced. When the truck stopped, the passenger's door swung open. Cinderella cautiously approached it and looked inside.

In the driver's seat was Yegor, a very lean and happy man of Russian descent. "Hello, beautiful person! Vhere are you headed?" he asked cheerfully.

Cinderella was relieved to be welcomed by such a friendly man, and told him New Ark, since that was what was written on the sign.

"Get in, I vill take you!" said Yegor with a huge grin.

Cinderella held tight to her burlap sack, lifted her skirt, took hold of the door and clumsily lifted herself up into the truck's cab. She wiggled to get her corset straight, and then took several hard tugs at the door to get it closed, but once she did, the truck pulled back onto the highway and headed down the interstate.

Inside the truck, Yegor looked at Cinderella and smiled broadly. Apparently, smiling was something he couldn't stop doing.

"My name is Yegor," he said, "This is second veek for me on my new job. My seventh month here in America. Land of free, home of brave! Vhat is your name?"

"Cinderella," she answered cheerfully, as Yegor's manner and mood was contagious.

Yegor stared at her for a brief moment, looked back at the road. He then stared at her again, the second time more carefully. Seeing her clothes were obviously from another era, recognition quickly set in.

"Yes! I have heard of you! You are very famous! This is exciting for me. Cinderella – in *my* truck!"

"Yes! That's me!" Cinderella exclaimed, relieved to have been recognized. She now knew that she most certainly was in the right place.

They both smiled at each other, naively happy, as Yegor continued down the highway.

Eight

✥ BRICK CITY ✥

Newark is the largest city in New Jersey. At the time of this writing, it is ranked the least friendly city on earth, just ahead of Islamabad, Pakistan. But I personally don't think it's all that bad. Yes, Newark has its violence, and most of its people are considered rude, but it does have its own airport, and like many cities, it looks pretty at night.

The sun was already up in Newark, and the morning was busy with commuter traffic and stores opening for business as Yegor's truck inched its way through the tight traffic. It finally pulled up to a curb and stopped. The passenger door swung open and Cinderella, once again holding tight to the burlap sack, climbed carefully down from the cab, trying hard not to get tangled in her skirt.

She wished Yegor well, and thanked him profusely for the ride. Yegor, in return, told her it was his "sincerest honor" to have given "the most famous voman in the world" a lift.

Which reminds me, if you ever come across a "selfie" on

the Internet of a Russian truck driver with our heroine, you'll know it's real.

Cinderella pushed the cab door shut and waved as Yegor pulled away. She looked around, amazed at the magnitude of this busy metropolis, and started to walk. She wasn't paying much attention to where she was going since she was so taken by the sights and sounds, as well as the strong smells of shrimp Empanadillas, car exhaust and urine. The odors were an assault to her senses, and she had to cover her nose several times due to it, but still, she was fascinated by it all.

Cinderella had never seen so many people of different color and nationalities. Most were of Portuguese and Brazilian descent, as well as African-American and Latino, but all were unique and diverse which, unfortunately, made Cinderella stand out like a sore thumb. Of course, she was oblivious to this and couldn't help but stare as she passed the locals. They in turn either ignored her, or stared back since she was a blonde, white girl wearing a dress that made her look like a character from a Henry James' novel.

When Cinderella arrived at a busy intersection, she stopped not because of the traffic light, but because she was amazed by the tall buildings and the many "metal monsters" that raced passed. As she took in the magnificence of it, she exclaimed aloud, "I love New York!"

Just then, an angry young man wearing a hoodie passed. He overheard her and responded in tough defiance, "Screw New York!"

Cinderella was taken aback and watched as the young man walked away. Thinking this was some sort of popular local slang, and wanting to "fit in," she exclaimed aloud and even more enthusiastically, "Yes! *Screw* New York!"

Smiling, she began crossing the busy intersection, not knowing the rules of the road, when a rusty, old Camaro came to a screeching halt, just inches from hitting her. The guy in the car was enraged.

"Hey!" he screamed as he leaned out of his car window.

Cinderella, startled, stopped and stepped out of the way. The guy flipped her the 'finger' and drove off. Thinking this was a local gesture, like a wave, Cinderella raised her middle finger in the same manner, shouted back, "Hey," and waved it happily back.

As she continued her walk, she waved her middle finger at other passing cars. The drivers, incensed, flipped their finger back. Cinderella giggled, enjoying this new way of greeting people and thought them all so very friendly. It was exhilarating to be liberated from the confines of the castle and the Prince. For the first time in her life she felt free. "Yes, *screw* New York," she said aloud, as she gaily continued on.

Nine

⟩⟩ JERSEY GIRLS ⟨⟨

That same morning, not far from where Cinderella was walking was a four-story building that had seen better days called, The Castle Condos. Inside was a three-bedroom condo with interior that screamed gaudy, nouveau riche. Dean Martin's, "Volare" was playing loudly from a small CD player on a counter in the kitchen where Maria Mortadella, a typical New Jersey housewife, was sitting at her table. She had big hair, lots of jewelry and was "hard" in that bitter, divorced woman sort of way. She sorted through a stack of bills as her long nails made a "tat-tat-tat" sound on the keys of her calculator.

Her eldest daughter, 22 year old, Angelina, shuffled in. She wore pink sweatpants and a cut-off t-shirt that had the slogan, *Jersey Girls Don't Do Dishes* emblazed across it. She was lazy, spoiled and extremely self-centered. Tired of her mother's music, she turned off the CD player, opened the refrigerator, and stood there as she stared inside it. Mrs. Mortadella looked up and saw this.

"Pick something and close the door. You'll get cancer."

"Refrigerators don't cause cancer. They makes holes in the ozone or something," Angelina snapped back with misinformed authority, as she grabbed a diet soda.

Just then, her sister, Nikki entered. She was just as bad as Angelina, if not worse. At 21, she wore tight jeans and a tank top that had the word "Princess" written on it in glittery script. Mrs. Mortadella made a comment that it was about time she woke up. Nikki ignored her mother's comment, as she almost always did, and took a seat at the kitchen table. She propped her bare foot on the table and began checking out her painted toenails. Mrs. Mortadella stopped tapping the calculator and looked at her daughter's foot.

"Ya live in a barn?"

Nikki grudgingly swung her foot off, but continued to examine her toenails by placing her foot on the corner of the chair. She glanced at all the papers surrounding her mother and asked what she was doing.

"Your deadbeat father stopped sending money. We have to cut back until the lawyer straightens it out. I'm getting rid of the maid service. Youse girls are gonna have to start cleaning up after yourselves."

Angelina stretched out her "Jersey Girls Don't Do Dishes" t-shirt in front of her mother and said, "Uh – hello!"

Nikki chimed in, "I'm not cleaning up nothing."

Mrs. Mortadella, not accepting her daughter's attitudes said, "It's time you make some sacrifices. Get jobs."

Both girls rolled their eyes, as if that was ever going to happen, as Mrs. Mortadella pushed the calculator away and stood. She suggested that unless her daughters began helping out with the household expenses, the family would have to move since they could no longer afford to live in the condo.

"And go where? Down the shore and live in an apartment?" asked Nikki, horrified.

Angelina chimed in, "I'm not moving there. No way!"

"Well, something has to change. We're, like, the last Italians left in this city. There ain't much for us here, especially without money, so start figuring something out," Mrs. Mortadella said as she grabbed her gaudy gold purse that was attached to a gaudy braided chain, and headed for the door. "I got things to do. I'll see youse two later," she said as she walked out the door.

Ten

➤ THE PUSHOVER ◀

inderella continued to walk along the sidewalk carrying her burlap sack, enjoying this strange, new world she'd entered when a young teenager approached, sucking on a Slurpee. He attempted to toss it in a nearby trashcan, but missed and it splattered right at Cinderella's feet. The teenager kept walking; unfazed.

Cinderella stopped, stunned and appalled. By force of habit, she bent down, picked up the Slurpee cup and put it in the trash. She quickly noticed other pieces of trash lying about. Bothered by all the litter, she moved down the street collecting it. As she did this, she happened upon The Castle Condos.

Drawn by the word "Castle," she stopped. Just then, Mrs. Mortadella walked out, and breezed past Cinderella without noticing her. But Cinderella saw her and started following her, calling out, "Excuse me! Hello?"

Mrs. Mortadella stopped. She turned and saw Cinderella standing there dressed in her turn of the century attire and holding the trash. She gave her a disgusted look. Cinderella saw the look, followed her gaze and, thinking it was the trash in her hands she was looking at said, "People here seem to keep dropping their things all over the place. It's so untidy."

Thinking Cinderella was a disturbed street person, Mrs. Mortadella began to walk away. Cinderella called out for her to stop. Mrs. Mortadella did. "What do you want?" she asked with great impatience.

"I'm new in town and looking for lodgings," Cinderella answered sweetly.

Lodgings? Who says that? Mrs. Mortadella thought, then said, "Check with the manager," as she started to walk away again.

Cinderella followed her. "Manager? What is that?"

Mrs. Mortadella stopped, now creeped out that this strange woman was following her. "The super. The one in charge," she answered, annoyed.

"Who is in charge?" asked Cinderella.

Mrs. Mortadella rolled her eyes in frustration, ignored her and began walking away.

"Wait!" called out Cinderella.

Mrs. Mortadella waved her hand and said, "Take it up with someone else, freak."

"But...but...perhaps I can *pay* you to help me?" shouted Cinderella.

Mrs. Mortadella stopped immediately at the mention of payment. She turned around and approached Cinderella with suspicion and asked, "You got money?"

"Yes," replied Cinderella, happy to have her attention.

Mrs. Mortadella checked out what Cinderella was wearing. "Hey, this isn't one of those prank people on the street sort of things for YouTube, is it?"

"You...tube?" asked Cinderella, confused.

"Yeah. YouTube," repeated Mrs. Mortadella.

Cinderella tilted her head, still confused. Mrs. Mortadella eyed Cinderella carefully, from her strange looking boots to her weird high collar.

"Who are you supposed to be? Wife of Jack the Rippa?"

"No. I'm Cinderella."

Mrs. Mortadella shifted her weight to one side and, thinking this *was* a joke said, "You're kidding."

"Oh, no. That is my name," Cinderella replied with great earnest.

"Let's see the money," said Mrs. Mortadella, ready to end this charade.

"Oh, yes," said Cinderella as she opened the burlap sack and held it out to Mrs. Mortadella.

Mrs. Mortadella leaned in carefully, expecting something disgusting to be lurking inside, but when she saw the sack was loaded with hundred dollar bills, thousands of them, in fact, her eyes nearly popped out of her head. Her mood swiftly changed to mock sweetness.

"Well, I guess people name their kids just about anything these days. Come on, I'll show you where you can, er...lodge."

She motioned for Cinderella to follow her back toward her building. Cinderella hiked up her long skirt and followed, smiling at the wonderful luck that had just befallen her. When they entered the building, Mrs. Mortadello walked Cinderella through the lobby and up the stairs to the door of her condo. She opened it and they entered.

Cinderella followed Mrs. Mortadella into the living room where Nikki was on the couch lazily flipping through a magazine, and Angelina was painting her nails.

"Girls, I want you to meet someone. This is Cinderella," Mrs. Mortadella announced.

Cinderella smiled, waiting for them to acknowledge her with the kindness and respect that she was used to, but Nikki and Angelina looked at her and busted out with laughter.

"She's not Cinderella," said Nikki.

"No, more like that chick from Titanic," said Angelina.

"Totally!" Nikki agreed, then they both "high-fived" each other and went back to what they were doing, completely disinterested.

As Cinderella's smile began to turn into a frown, Mrs. Mortadella pointed to each daughter and said her name. Cinderella said a meek hello, but they still ignored her. Mrs. Mortadella, getting annoyed, blurted out, "She's going to be living with us."

Nikki and Angelina suddenly flew up from the couch in angry protest.

"She's not staying in *my* room," Nikki shouted in defiance.

Angelina snapped, "She's not staying in *mine!*"

Mrs. Mortadella knew this would be their response, so she gave a wink and motioned for both of them to follow her down the hall. They did, leaving Cinderella alone in the living room.

"It's only temporary," whispered Mrs. Mortadella as she stood by a hallway closet. "She isn't bright, but has a lot of money. I think I can get her to pay half the rent."

"But where are we gonna put her?" asked Nikki.

This was something Mrs. Mortadella had yet to figure out. The two girls stood there staring angrily at their mother. Getting an idea, Mrs. Mortadella opened the closet door and peered in. It was a cramped walk-in, but with enough space for a small bed.

"We can put her in here," said Mrs. Mortadella. "We'll get her a futon," she added as an afterthought.

Nikki and Angelina shrugged, uncaring. Now that their space would not be invaded, they walked back into the living room where Cinderella was waiting patiently. She smiled at them as they walked past her, but they didn't smile back.

Mrs. Mortadella began to tell Cinderella about her new "room" and what the house rules would be when Nikki rudely interrupted.

"You have to buy your own food."

Angelina followed that with, "And you can only use the bathroom after *we're* done."

Cinderella nodded in agreement. Seeing what a pushover she was, Nikki threw in the fact that she would also have to do the housecleaning. Angelina added that meant *all* the housecleaning. Cinderella smiled, appreciating that she had a place to stay, and agreed without hesitation. Mrs. Mortadella and the girls looked at each. This was way too easy.

Angelina took it one step further by telling Cinderella that all this hospitality would cost her a thousand dollars in rent – a week. Mrs. Mortadella and Nikki shot Angelina a hard look. That was pushing it, they thought, but Cinderella quickly agreed, much to their surprise.

Cinderella then opened the sack and pulled out a handful of hundred dollar bills. She counted them out as they watched with their mouths open in disbelief. Cinderella handed the money to Mrs. Mortadella and thanked her for being so generous.

Mrs. Mortadella quickly folded the cash, then went into the kitchen and grabbed a spare key from a sugar bowl. She returned and handed it to Cinderella, telling her she could move in immediately. Cinderella cheerfully clapped her hands together and promised to make them dinner.

"Dinner?" all three asked in unison.

"Yes. I'll make venison with potatoes, and a creamy broccoli soup to start."

The two girls stared at their mother in confusion. Mrs. Mortadella, gob smacked, said, "Uh...well...we don't have any...er, venison in the house." She then she gave her daughters a confused shrug.

"Oh, then I must go shopping! I promise to make supper as soon as I return!"

Cinderella thanked them several times again, then flipped them her middle finger, still thinking that was a friendly local custom and walked out the front door.

"What the hell was that?" asked Mrs. Mortadella, confused and insulted.

But Nikki and Angelina didn't care. They quickly snatched the money from their stunned mother's hand and shouted that they were going shopping.

Eleven

The streets of Newark were bustling and Cinderella was excited to be a part of it as she walked cheerfully once again along its sidewalks. Sometimes she would stop to look at something we humans take for granted, such as a bus, or the saggy jeans that hung low on the street kids. She was also captivated by those hand held, metal objects people were talking into, or listening to with tiny earplugs.

While waiting to cross a street, which she now learned how to do properly, she would lean in and try to get a good look at what those metal objects were, and what she later came to understand was an iPhone. Until that, she thought people just walked around talking to themselves.

Cinderella wandered a little south, passing St. Michael's Hospital, and then headed closer toward my alma mater, Rutgers University, where I received my Bachelor, Masters and Doctoral degrees in Health Sciences, specializing in Psychiatric Rehabilitation. She stared up at the large buildings that made up the campus and was intrigued by the influx of students moving in all different directions. Cinderella smiled at anyone who made eye contact with her, although few returned the smile. They all seemed too preoccupied to even try, she thought, and she was right. Most just stared in confusion at her odd appearance since she was still wearing that outfit from the 1800's.

After meandering around the campus for a while, she headed a little further south to Halsey Street, known to some as "restaurant row," and was relieved to finally come upon shops and cafés. It was the smell of freshly baked bread that grabbed her attention – a comforting scent that emanated from a small café nearby, so she immediately went inside and headed straight for the glass counter that was filled with delectable pastries. Her eyes gleamed at the delicious selection. It was a difficult decision which one to choose. She secretly wanted them all.

As she was trying to decide, nearby were two young women sitting at a table having coffee with their backs to Cinderella. One was talking about her recent breakup with her boyfriend as the other consoled her. Their conversation caught Cinderella's attention when she overheard one of the women say with a half determined sigh, "But we can't give up. Our prince is out there somewhere." To which the other woman responded, "Maybe. Unless Cinderella hogged all that perfection for herself."

Cinderella stood there in shock. Who were these women and why were they calling her a "hog?" she wondered. And if they knew how it really was being married to the Prince, surely they wouldn't be talking in such a manner. Cinderella forgot all about the pastries and panicked just a little when she saw the women grab their purses and walked out of the café.

Wanting to hear more of their conversation, Cinderella followed them out. She was careful to walk a safe distance away, but close enough to overhear them talk about the "asshole" the one woman described her boyfriend as, and something about buying some sort of vibrating instrument in his place that Cinderella did not understand.

The women walked at a clipped pace that Cinderella struggled to keep up with due to her the turn of the century shoes she was wearing. Eventually, she followed them up several concrete steps that lead into a massive brick building that was the Newark Public Library. Once Cinderella entered through its arched doorway and passed a marble-clad vestibule into a wide and spacious central court, she forgot all about the two women and stared in awe and delight at her new surroundings. A massive marble staircase caught her eye and she looked upward to where it led, which was to reading rooms and collection areas.

Was this the home of a king and queen, she wondered, as she gazed upward, and if it was, then why were all these people visiting? Were they friends of the royals, or did the king and queen simply allow the towns people to freely enter and occupy their residence?

In the lobby there were display cases. Some filled with new books, others with artifacts or letters of interest. People were leaning over them, studying what was inside. Cinderella peered over several shoulders to see what they were looking at, but nothing in the cases interested her. Instead, what grabbed her attention was the sight of a little girl wearing a princess dress and holding a wand with a sparkling star at the tip of it. She raced happily across the lobby shouting, "Cinderella! Cinderella! I love Cinderella!"

Cinderella was thrilled to be recognized, and held out her arms to embrace the little girl, but she whizzed past her and disappeared down a hall. Cinderella, surprised and perplexed, followed her. As she did, something made her stop dead in her tracks and caused her jaw to drop to her chin.

It was a big cartoon cutout of Cinderella and Prince Charming staring into each other's eyes. Next to it were copies of the fairy tale book with a display sign that read: *Follow Cinderella to Happiness! Read the Classic Tale All Over Again!*

"Follow me to happiness?" Cinderella said to herself, confused and appalled.

Feeling violated and puzzled, she looked around and saw a bored looking male librarian at a nearby information desk. She quickly approached him. The male librarian saw her and was taken aback by how she was dressed.

"Are we going to a costume party?" he asked with a friendly smile.

"No, but I'd love to," answered Cinderella, waiting for his invitation.

They stared at each other in awkward silence until finally he asked, "May I help you?"

Cinderella asked about the display. He answered in a cynical tone, "She's every girl's fantasy, especially the little ones. They start them early with all that happily ever after stuff."

"But it's not *real!*" Cinderella said with great dismay.

The male librarian put on an agreeing, sarcastic sneer and said, "Tell me 'bout it."

Taking his words literally, Cinderella began to tell the young man her story. "Well, when I was a small child –"

Suddenly, the male librarian's cell phone rang in his pocket. He put his finger up to Cinderella, as if to say, "one second," but once he answered it, he turned and walked away, ignoring her completely. Bothered that the male librarian was also a slave to one of those small metal devices, Cinderella looked once again at the hideous display of her "story," then went in search for the little girl who was dressed as a princess.

She made her way down a hall and came upon the Children's

Room, which was the children's section of the library. It was filled with dozens of children. Most of them girls dressed in little princess outfits. They sat in a large group circle, enthralled by one of the female librarians reading to them the classic fairy tale, *Cinderella*.

Cinderella, not wanting to be seen, moved slowly behind a row of books and listened. She couldn't believe what she was hearing. It made her feel sick inside listening to each word this woman was reading aloud. It was her life! Cinderella leaned forward to hear better, putting her hand on a small stack of books. As she did this, she noticed the books were all titled, *Cinderella*, and sat under a spectacle of stars and glittering streamers that dangled from above. She quickly took her hand off the books and shook her head in disgust.

Just then, a little blonde-haired girl came over, grabbed one of the books and skipped down an empty aisle between a row of bookcases. She plopped herself on a stool, opened the book and turned the pages, looking longingly at the illustrations. Cinderella saw this and gingerly approached her.

"Hello," she started out sweetly. "You don't really want that book, do you?"

The little girl looked at Cinderella and responded with a flat "Yeah, I do."

Cinderella, believing the little girl didn't know any better, told her that she didn't believe she did, and went to take it from her. The little girl quickly held it away. Cinderella tried to remain calm and told her that the story wasn't real as she took hold of one end of the book. The little girl held tight to the other end and shouted, "No, I want it!"

Cinderella tugged at the book saying in a stronger tone, "No, you don't. It's filled with lies."

The little girl looked scared, but tugged harder. "Quit it!"

Cinderella wasn't able to control her anger any longer. "Give me the book!" she shouted, and a full on tug of war ensued.

The little girl screamed, "No! Stop it," then shouted, "Mommy! Mommy!"

Appearing suddenly out of nowhere was the little girl's mother, an overweight, protective type. She marched down the aisle, angrily grabbed the part of the book that her daughter had, and successfully yanked it away from Cinderella.

"What the hell?" asked the Mother.

Desperate, Cinderella exclaimed, "She shouldn't be reading that. I'm not happy. My life *isn't* perfect!"

The mother looked at Cinderella with zero sympathy and said, "That's not my problem," and handed the book to her daughter. She then looked back at Cinderella and asked, "Who do you think you are anyway?"

"I'm Cinderella, and that book is a *lie*!"

"You're whacked," said the mother, defiantly.

Overcome with anger, Cinderella began knocking all the books off the bookcases as she moved down the aisle. The mother held her daughter back, and stepped out into the open area where the librarian was reading to the other children.

"There's a crazy woman in here!" shouted the mother.

The librarian stopped reading and stood when she saw Cinderella go over to the display table and begin tossing all the books to the floor. She ripped down the streamers and stars as well. The children stood and clung to their parents as they watched. The library security was quickly dispatched and within minutes, two male security guards charged into the Children's Room and grabbed Cinderella, restraining her.

"I *am* Cinderella! And everyone must know the truth!" screamed, Cinderella.

But these shouts only made her look insane, so the security guards tightened their grip, dragged her from the Children's Room and out into the open lobby.

The Head Librarian, a nervous looking gentleman, raced over to them making the "shhhh" sound as Cinderella continued her cries of protest, which now echoed off the hallowed halls for everyone to hear. Including me.

Now, I just happened to be at the library that day since I took the advice from my attorney, Gregg, and decided to see what other subjects on psychotherapy I might write about. I was in the lobby perusing the current self-help books written by other psychiatrists; jotting down titles for inspiration on a small note pad when I heard the shouts from Cinderella. Hearing her scream, "I'm unhappy, none of it is true," caused me to stop what I was doing and go see what the commotion was about.

I watched as the security guards began to pull Cinderella toward the door, but she resisted, and continued to yell out, "I'm *not* happy!"

The Head Librarian was by this time wiping his brow with a handkerchief and begging in a loud whisper to get her outside and call the police. Hearing this concerned me since it seemed such a drastic measure for someone who was obviously deranged. I've seen patients in this sort of hysterics before. The poor thing didn't need the cops; she needed compassion and a doctor's help. I was only too happy to oblige, so I quickly approached the Head Librarian and whispered discreetly that I was a doctor. I asked him not to call the police and that he should allow me to try to handle the situation.

The Head Librarian was too riled up to be thinking sympathetically, and told me that this was something for the police to take care of as he headed toward the main desk to make the call himself.

I followed, grabbed his arm and said with urgency, "Really, she needs special care. Just look at her!"

The Head Librarian looked at me, angry for grabbing him, but then looked at Cinderella's "turn of the century" style clothes and, though hesitant, gave in. He nodded to the security guards, and they let go of Cinderella. She was by now out of breath and rubbing her sore arms from the squeeze those guards had put on her.

I stepped forward and gently put out my hand to her. "Let's go and get some fresh air, shall we?"

Cinderella was taken by my kindness. All her anger and upset began to fade as she took my hand. I led her out of the library and down its front steps. Once we reached the sidewalk, I let go of her hand and Cinderella let down her defenses.

"I don't know what came over me. I see my name painted everywhere and hear people talking about me. They all seem to have the wrong impression of who I am."

I smiled, happy that she had calmed down enough to speak rationally, and asked who she was. When she answered that she was Cinderella, I knew she was disturbed and, having treated many patients in my career who have suffered from delusion, I responded softly with, "Actually, you're not."

"But I am!" she insisted.

I looked at her eyes in search for the dilated pupils seen in most patients with such an affliction, but, strangely, hers weren't. I tried to ease her out of her delusional state by asking her what Cinderella would be doing in Newark, New Jersey of all places?

"But this is New York," she insisted. "I've been sent to New York."

"Sent by whom?" I asked.

"The Fairy Godmother," she answered.

I froze at the mention of the Fairy Godmother, and stared at Cinderella as if this was a twisted joke. Did Helen set this up to rile me? Or was this a stunt pulled by Rodney Klein? He always did have a sick sense of humor. Cinderella didn't acknowledge my stare and continued talking.

"The Fairy Godmother told me I was to come to New York to find this doctor." She reached into her pocket and pulled out a small piece of what looked like parchment, which is like a fine sheepskin paper, the type that the Declaration of Independence was written on. In fact, it looked as old as the Declaration of Independence.

Cinderella handed it to me, and indeed it *was* parchment paper from that era. As if being perplexed by this paper wasn't enough, seeing the name on it perplexed me even further.

"This is the name of the doctor you're supposed to see in New York?" I asked her.

Cinderella nodded. "Yes. You have heard of him?"

"This is my name," I told her.

"You're Boris Berger?" she asked in delighted surprise. "I've found you!"

"You think this is funny?" I asked, not at all amused.

"No, it's not funny...it's *wonderful*!" she exclaimed.

"I don't appreciate being made fun of," I said as I tried to give Cinderella back her piece of paper. She wouldn't take it. "Who put you up to this?" I asked.

Cinderella looked at me, confused. I waited for her to give in, but she just continued to stare at me. I started to crumple the piece of paper, but Cinderella grabbed my hand and stopped me.

"Oh, please, don't," she pleaded. "I assure you this is not a joke. I really *do* need your help."

"So, no one paid you to do this? Not my wife or anyone else?" I asked, still suspicious.

Cinderella shook her head and said no. She seemed sincere, plus who would have known I would be at the library at that time? I looked again at the piece of paper. Seeing my name on it *was* an odd coincidence. Surely, there must be a Boris Berger in Manhattan, even though Boris is not a common name. But still.

"I think you've got the wrong Boris Berger," I told her. "And I don't think it's my place to help you."

My words seemed to have dashed all hope for Cinderella as I watched her face fall as if I just told her that her cherished pet had died.

"How can I return to the castle without being changed?" she asked in a sad whisper.

She looked so disappointed that I felt the urge to touch her arm out of sympathy, but I had to remember this was a woman deeply disturbed and encouraging any of her delusions would only worsen her disorder.

"Where do you live?" I asked.

"The kingdom," she responded softly.

"How did you get here?"

"The carriage brought me," she answered.

I looked at her. If she *was* Cinderella she sure was keeping with the story. "The pumpkin carriage?" I asked only to see if she was still delusional.

"Yes!" she exclaimed, happy that I finally believed her, but I didn't and told her so...gently.

She seemed more disappointed then angry that I didn't believe her. The sad look in her once sparkling blue eyes instantly made me feel sorry for her. I wasn't sure what to do. I couldn't leave her stranded on the sidewalk in this condition, and since I didn't have any other patients for the rest of the day, I suggested we go back to my office where I'd help her find her doctor, the other Boris Berger that was in the "Big Apple," as she kept calling it.

Twelve

I arrived back at my office about twenty minutes later with Cinderella. The ride in the elevator was a revelation to her. She called it the "moving room," and loved the ride. As I greeted my secretary, Rachel, a young woman in her early twenties, I opened the door to my office and motioned for Cinderella to enter. Once she did, I handed Rachel the piece of parchment paper and asked her to locate that Boris Berger in New York.

Rachel took the paper and studied it with a quizzical look on her face.

"I know," I said, somewhat amused, "Another doctor with my name."

"No," she replied, "This paper. What's it made of?" She held it up to the light, and then brought it to her nose. "Smells like…lavender."

I ignored her curiosity, and told her again to do her best to find that doctor in New York and not to disturb me with any calls. Rachel nodded as I entered my office and closed the door.

Inside, Cinderella was standing by a wall looking at my diplomas. I was flattered whenever anyone bothered to notice them, but made no comment since I needed to keep this strictly about her.

"Please, have a seat," I said as I grabbed a note pad and pen from my desk. Cinderella sat comfortably on the couch across the room, as I took a chair nearby and looked at her carefully. "OK, why don't we start by you telling me your name."

"Cinderella," she said innocently.

I gave her a slight smile. "All right, now your *real* name."

Cinderella looked at me with all sincerity and said, "Well, actually, my name is Ella, but because I spent most of my time as a young girl near the fireplace and its ashes, my stepmother and stepsisters called me Cinder-Ella."

I jotted down the words, "delusional" and "confused" in my notebook, and then asked in a very calm tone, "You don't really believe that, do you? That's a fairy tale. It's not real."

"Oh, but it *is* real," Cinderella said without hesitation, then sighed, "Actually, *too* real. Why don't you believe me?"

"Because I think what's happening is you're experiencing a breakdown in reality. Sometimes reality can become too overwhelming."

Cinderella responded adamantly, "But I *am* Cinderella. There must be some way to make you believe."

"There's not," I said, bluntly.

I thought my direct approach might upset her, but instead, Cinderella put her finger to her lips, thinking.

"But there must be something I can do to prove – "

"There isn't, and as a doctor, I cannot encourage you to even try."

"But – " she began to say.

Feeling we would only go around in circles with this, I used another tactic. "OK, look, unless you can get Snow White in here to back you up, there is absolutely no way –"

"Snow White! That's a wonderful idea!" Cinderella said, excited.

As I began to say something, Cinderella quickly closed her eyes, said, "I wish Snow White to appear!"

Cinderella then slowly opened her eyes. I looked at her. She looked at me. A moment of awkward silence passed between us. It was obvious Snow White wasn't going to appear, but I wanted to give it a moment to prove this point to her. Actually, it was more time than anyone in my profession should have.

"OK, now that that's out of the way, let's talk about whom you *really* are. Have you had any sort of head injury recently?"

Cinderella gave me an odd expression. "Head injury?"

"Yes. Perhaps you – " I began, when suddenly the intercom on my desk buzzed. This annoyed me since I specifically told Rachel not to interrupt. I stood, went to my desk and pressed the intercom button. The confused voice of Rachel was heard.

"I'm sorry, Dr. Berger, but there is someone here to see you." Then she then whispered, "She's kind of persistent."

After I asked who it was, Rachel hesitated then answered in an unsure manner, "Snow White?"

I looked at Cinderella, who was wearing an eager smile. Perplexed and confused, I told Rachel to send her in. Cinderella sat up in anticipation. When Rachel opened the door, to my surprise, in walked Snow White. She was dressed as only Snow White would be, wearing that familiar, colorful dress with the puffy sleeves.

Snow White saw Cinderella, and with sincere glee, exclaimed, "Cinderella!"

"Snow!" shouted Cinderella in return. She leapt from the

74

couch and they embraced. Apparently, it had been a long while since they'd seen each other.

Rachel shot me a baffled look as she slowly stepped back out, closing the door behind her. Cinderella pulled away from Snow White and asked how her prince was.

"He's fine, handsome as ever. How's yours?"

Cinderella lied at first and said, "Oh, he's fine. We're doing well," but then she looked at me and, unable to keep up the façade, said, "No, that's not true. I'm unhappy.

Snow White let out a sharp gasp, and held her hands to her mouth as if it was some sort of deadly fairy tale sin to say this. Cinderella sadly nodded her head in shame as she looked down at the floor. I stood there, dumbfounded. I didn't know what to make of any of this. Cinderella noticed.

"Oh, where are my manners? I'm sorry. Snow, this is Dr. Berger."

Snow White made a very polite curtsey. I stared at her, mystified, and asked, "How did you get here?"

"I was summoned," said Snow White matter-of-factly, and then looked Cinderella. "By you?"

Cinderella nodded and told Snow White she was granted three wishes by the Fairy Godmother. Snow White gleefully clasped her hands together, and held them to her heart. "Oh, I just love wishes."

"Me, too! I used one to prove that I am real," Cinderella said.

Snow White let out another sharp gasp, put her hand to her mouth again and stared at me as if this was a crime against all things fantastical. "You don't *believe*?" she asked in a dramatic whisper.

"With all due respect...no," I said, coming to the conclusion that now I had two mentally ill women on my hands.

"What is your name?" Snow White asked me, wanting to get to the bottom of why I was a non-believer.

"Dr. Boris Berger," I answered.

Snow White's eyes narrowed as she thought long and hard about this. "Hmm. Boris Berger," she tried to recall. "Boris Berger…Boris…Boris *Andrew* Berger of Trenton?" she asked.

"Yes," I told her.

Snow White looked at me carefully. "When you were six, your mother read to you my story."

I let out a chuckle, taking this as an unconvincing way to get me to believe she really was Snow White, and told her that mothers read "her" story to their children all the time. To which Snow White responded, "But you were confused why the mirror on the wall would tell the evil Queen that I was staying with the dwarfs. From then on, and for many years after, you had a fear of looking into any mirror thinking it would tell your mother what you were up to."

I stared at Snow White, dumbfounded. That was true. I asked how she knew this.

Snow White innocently replied, "Oh, I see inside the hearts of every child who reads my story. We all do."

She looked at Cinderella for confirmation. Cinderella nodded.

Although I was thrown by her knowing something personal about my youth, I had to keep my wits about me and told her that being afraid of evil queens and mirrors was a typical fear for most children.

Snow White, not wanting to insult me, turned to Cinderella and, in the sweetest voice, continued with what she knew about me. "When he got a little older," she began with a giggle, "he was forced to look into a mirror to see why there was a stiffness in his trousers."

"Hey!" I shouted, embarrassed and stunned. "How do you know *that*?"

Snow White ignored my question, but looked at me adding, "And when your mother never questioned you about it, you finally knew that no one would tell on you. Your mirror spell was broken, and pleasure reigned!"

I swallowed hard. All of this was true, but how did she know? In a tight whisper I said, "No one knows that. There's no way you could -"

But before I finished my sentence, Snow White said, "Unless I was *real*?"

I stared at her. This was all too strange and overwhelming for me to process. Snow White, seeing that I was close to maybe believing, drove the point home with the final memory.

"Then, as you got much older, you liked very much to stand in front of the mirror without clothing and shout, 'I am the Pleasure King'!"

My eyes grew wide in horror and embarrassment. "Hey, no one that knows about...*that*. What's going on here? Who *are* you?"

Snow White looked up at the ceiling as if waiting for me to "get it." I looked at Cinderella. Cinderella shrugged, as if to say, "How else would we know?" I suddenly felt dizzy and sat down.

Cinderella and Snow White looked at me, worried.

"Oh, dear. He looks ill," Snow White said. "Perhaps I should go."

"But I'm not sure if he still believes," said Cinderella.

They both looked at each other, wondering how to guarantee this. Then Cinderella looked at me, and asked me to make a wish. My head was spinning and I couldn't think. And even though all of this seemed like some sick joke or game, perhaps being played on me by one of my colleagues, again, most likely Rodney Klein since this reeked of his type of sophomoric humor, I was not going to engage with either of them.

"I don't have a wish," I muttered.

"Oh, don't be silly. Everybody has a wish," insisted Snow White.

"I don't," I said, annoyed.

Cinderella and Snow White shot each other perplexed glances, then Cinderella said, "I know! I'll take you to see the Fairy Godmother!"

Snow White looked at Cinderella, concerned. "Oh, I don't know, Cinderella. Is that safe?"

"Why not? They know each other," answered Cinderella.

"Know each other?" I asked, now really bothered. "Hey, wait a minute, what do you know about -"

"Wouldn't you like to see your old friend again?" Cinderella asked.

"What friend?"

"The Fairy Godmother," she answered innocently.

"Oh, this is absurd!" I shouted. "We need to end this right now."

"But you *must* believe," pleaded Cinderella.

"Yes. Just agree to see the Fairy Godmother so we can prove we're real," said Snow White.

I stared at both of them. Either they were crazy, or I was. At this point I honestly didn't know.

"Just say it," said Snow White.

"Say what?" I asked.

"Say you agree to see the Fairy Godmother."

How I hated Rodney Klein at that moment. I was sure he was probably recording all of this to play at the next APA meeting, but I was so confused and wanted this to end, so I said with much resignation, "OK, I agree to see the Fairy Godmother."

Cinderella smiled with glee and, after closing her eyes, said, "I wish to bring Dr. Berger to see the Fairy Godmother!"

Suddenly, there was a tremendous flash of blinding light that forced me to close mine. I felt my body swirling, then lift upward momentarily, then land again. When I opened my eyes I was astonished to find myself in what looked like a cottage right out of, well, a fairy tale. I was disoriented and unbalanced that I nearly knocked over a stand that had a large book on it. I clung to the corner of a mantle of a fireplace to steady myself. My eyes darted around the room, unable to focus on one particular thing. Where was I?

As I looked around I saw that the room in which I was standing was a mess. There were cobwebs on the furniture and empty wine bottles sticking out from under every chair and sofa. I felt panic setting in until I saw Cinderella standing next to me. That gave me a sense of momentary relief.

When I began to ask her where we were, she quickly held her finger to her lips indicating for me to stop talking. I did.

From another room we heard the sounds of someone moving about. Bottles and glasses clanked together, and a woman humming an unfamiliar tune. She sounded as if she was ready to enter the room, and she did, holding a large sized goblet filled with wine in one hand, and a large jug in the other. It was the Fairy Godmother. The moment she laid eyes on Cinderella and I, she let out a startled screech, dropping both the goblet and the jug.

"Cinderella! W-what are you doing here?" the Fairy Godmother asked, and then looked at me. "And who is this?"

"I wanted to prove that we were real," said Cinderella, beaming with happiness. "Don't you recognize him? It's Boris Berger!"

"Boris..? He's *not* Boris Berger!" insisted the Fairy God-mother, looking at Cinderella as if she'd lost her mind.

"Oh, dear," said Cinderella, bringing her hand to her lips.

I rubbed my eyes wanting to wake up from this weird nightmare.

The Fairy Godmother looked at me in terror, and moved quickly away. She went over near Cinderella and said in a hushed and angry whisper, "That is *not* Boris Berger!"

"W-where am I?" I asked, trying to collect my bearings.

The Fairy Godmother, ignoring me, asked Cinderella, "What have you done? Who else knows about this?"

"Snow White. Dr. Berger asked to see her to prove I was re-al, so I wished for her."

"Oh, no! Snow White knows?!" shrieked the Fairy God-mother, bringing her hands to her face. She quickly pulled them away and said, "Wait...it's OK. Snow White knows to keep her mouth shut. She owes me big after cleaning up her reputation with those dwarfs. I'll have a talk with her later."

"Will someone please tell me what the hell is going on here? Who are you?" I asked the Fairy Godmother, demanding to know.

She gave me a worried look, began wringing her hands, and then took a brave step toward me. "I am...the Fairy...Godmother," she said slow and deliberately. "You...have...been...brought here...by...Cinderella."

It was as if she was talking to a space alien who just landed on her planet. And although that's what I felt like, I wanted her to stop.

"I can understand you. You can quit talking like that."

"Oh, that's a relief," she said with a sigh.

"So, what is this? Where am I?"

"Obviously Cinderella has made a mistake. A *big* one," she said turning her head and shooting Cinderella an angry look.

"But I needed to prove that –" Cinderella began to explain in her own defense.

"No, you didn't need to do *anything*," the Fairy Godmother scolded her. "What were you thinking bringing that...*him*...here?"

"I suppose I wasn't thinking," answered Cinderella as she bowed her head, ashamed.

"No, you weren't. Now I have to figure out how to get him out of here," she said, sounding put out.

She walked across the room and saw the spell book that I accidently knocked on the floor. "Oh, come on!" she said, annoyed.

My manners kicked in and I quickly bent down, picked up the book and placed it back on its stand. As I did this, I glanced at a page and saw written in old English script what looked like recipes with some of the words upside down and some in bold lettering, as if it was written in some sort of code. I leaned forward to get a better look, but the Fairy Godmother quickly slammed it shut.

"Mind your business," she snapped.

"How did I get here?" I asked her.

"You ask too many questions," she answered as she opened the book and began flipping through the pages.

"But I'm not getting any answers," I said.

The Fairy Godmother let out a frustrated sigh. "All right, let me break it down for you. You got here on a wish made by that one over there," she said pointing angrily at Cinderella. "A wasted wish, I might add, to prove that she and I are real. So, see?" she asked as she held up her hands and waved them. "We're real, OK? I'm who she says I am and she's who she says she is. Doesn't get any clearer than that. Now give me a couple of minutes and let me figure out how to get you the hell out of here and back where you belong."

"Where is here? Fairy Tale Land?" I asked, still in disbelief, but matching her sarcasm.

"If you want to call it that, but we prefer the Kingdom. Now shut up and let me figure out this spell."

I looked over at Cinderella. She still looked embarrassed and sorry for this…mistake.

I watched as the Fairy Godmother turned pages in that large book, searching for, whatever, then began to look more closely at my surroundings. It was a cute little cottage, though it would have been much cuter if it were clean. I then began focusing on the nick-knacks that seemed to be in the dozens and placed everywhere.

Suddenly, a handsomely carved glass dove that was on the mantle above the fireplace caught my eye. The details of it were striking and familiar. As I leaned in to take a closer look, something else caught my eye.

On a nearby shelf, I saw a row of old thick leather bound books. Each one had Roman numerals etched in real gold on their spine.

"The books with the gold numbers," I murmured to myself, and went over to them. I grazed my fingers over the numbers. It was real gold, all right.

As I looked around the room more carefully, artifacts began to leap out at me as if I had seen them all before. The thick legs of the oak desk in the corner with its fine, detailed carvings of ivy leaves, the fireplace made of round ancient stones, the lace curtains made of silk with transparent imprints of large butterflies on them. Everything began to register in my mind. This was not a dream. I had read about this room many times as a boy and young man, but not from any book of fairy tales. Then suddenly, it finally dawned on me where I was.

I quickly turned and looked at the Fairy Godmother, studying her just as carefully as I studied everything else. "This can't be true," I muttered.

The Fairy Godmother looked up from her book. "What's that you say?" she asked.

"Y-you're the Fairy Godmother," I said staring at her.

"Yes, but you're not the Boris Berger I meant for Cinderella to find," she said, still sounding annoyed.

"I think I am," I said, and began searching for something with my eyes that would prove it.

The Fairy Godmother became alarmed and worried as she watched carefully where my eyes went.

"The music box!" I exclaimed upon seeing a beautifully carved, cherry wood box on an end table next to a large, comfortable rocking chair.

So eager was I to get to it, I nearly lunged for it. At the same time, so did the Fairy Godmother. She slapped her hand over it before I got to it, preventing me from looking inside.

"Let me open it," I demanded.

"No," said the Fairy Godmother, pressing her hand tighter on its lid.

I couldn't understand why she was doing this, until that, too, dawned on me. "You're afraid I'll recognize the song it plays, aren't you?" I asked staring deep into her eyes.

She stared deeply into mine. A look of recognition began to form on her face, but she still would not lift her hand from the box.

I stepped back and said, "I don't have to open it. I know the song."

Cinderella stepped forward looking perplexed yet intrigued. The Fairy Godmother said nothing, but her expression read fear. I cleared my throat and began to sing the song, admittedly off-key, that was in the box. It was a song written during the 1890's called "On The Sidewalks of New York."

"East side...West side...all around the town..."

The Fairy Godmother's face drained of its color. "H-how could you know?" she asked lifting her hands to her face in disbelief.

I took a step forward and gently opened the music box. From it played the song I had just sung. Cinderella let out a surprised gasp.

"It was my great grandfather you knew," I said.

"Your great grandfather...?"

"Yes. Boris Berger. I was named after him."

"Oh, my," said the Fairy Godmother as she swayed a little then slowly took a seat.

I have to admit, I swayed a little too, still trying to take all of this in. "So, my great grandfather wasn't crazy after all," I said.

"No, he wasn't," said the Fairy Godmother. Then, very quickly, she asked with great trepidation, "What do you know?"

"Everything," I answered.

"Oh, geez," she moaned, as she shook her head and stared at the floor. She then slowly looked up at me. Her expression changed from worry to appreciation. She smiled.

"Welcome to the kingdom, Boris Berger. Your great grand-father was a very good man, and a smart man. Without him, I wouldn't be here...and neither would Cinderella."

"And without *you*, he would never have gone insane," I said staring at her with blame and anger.

Thirteen

The year was 1899, if you're counting in earth's time, but to the Fairy Godmother it was just another day. She was close to getting her Fairy Godmother degree from some sort of fairy tale academy that would make her an official fairy godmother, however she began to have doubts. Was she good enough? Could she handle the responsibility it took to be in charge of the wishes and dreams of others? With the wand came great power and responsibilities, and she wasn't sure she was up for the job.

There were several candidates vying for this particular position of Fairy Godmother, but only one could be chosen, so each was given a specific case as their final academy qualification exam. They were assigned a lonely girl or boy with seemingly impossible dreams. The Fairy Godmother was given Cinderella, but before she even met her, the insecure Fairy Godmother developed what we psychiatrists call Social Anxiety Disorder. This is a phobia that involves overwhelming worry that centers on a fear of being judged by others, or behaving in a way that might cause ridicule.

Being the smart woman that she was, the Fairy Godmother did some research about her anxiety and came upon an article in the New York Tribune (how she got a hold of that newspaper, I'm not sure) that mentioned a doctor by the name of Sigmund Freud. Freud was considered the "Founding Father" of psychoanalysis, and upon reading about his cases and the successes of most, the Fairy Godmother decided to find Dr. Freud and ask him to help her.

In the same article, she read that the American Medico-Psychological Association was holding their 55th Annual meeting in New York City. In her naiveté, she thought Dr. Freud would be there. Being a psychiatrist, why wouldn't he be at such a meeting, was her thinking, and if she traveled to New York and found him, she was convinced he would help her.

It was on a late evening in May when the Fairy Godmother arrived in New York City. Not knowing what the weather was like in New York during that month, she wore a long winter coat just in case it was cold. It wasn't. But she wore it anyway. The annual meeting was held in the Myrtle Room at the Waldorf-Astoria Hotel, and the Fairy Godmother arrived just as it came to a close. Most of the doctors had already left, or were in the hotel bar for a drink and discussion.

The Fairy Godmother wandered through the lobby of the Waldorf, passing doctors, college professors and others who had been in attendance, looking for the famous doctor from Vienna. She stopped several people to ask if Sigmund Freud was at the hotel, or where she might find him. Seeing her in a long winter coat in springtime, she appeared a woman clearly in need of therapy herself, but instead of helping her, they ignored her.

This didn't stop the Fairy Godmother. When she saw doctors going into the hotel bar, so she followed them. The men in the bar shot her odd glances when she entered since it was somewhat unconventional back then that a woman would be in there, especially without a chaperone, but then turned their attention back to their drinks and company.

At a table near the bar sat three doctors who were in a heated discussion about psychoanalysis. Two of them agreed that not everyone could be cured of mental illness while the other, who puffed lazily on a pipe, was adamant that psycho-analysis was the cure all for any psychological disorder. That doctor was my great grandfather, Boris Berger.

"If a patient is seriously deranged, Boris, there can't be a cure since there is no way to even get through to such a pa-tient," argued one of the doctors.

"With patience and understanding, I believe one can," replied my great grandfather. "It is unethical for any of us to not even try, and I don't mean simply with one or two sessions, I mean weeks, months – even years, if need be. The point is to never give up."

"I would only be committed to such a patient if the inflict-ed, or his family, had deep pockets to pay for that length of time," said the other doctor with a chuckle.

"That attitude is disgraceful," my great grandfather said angrily. "It is our duty to supply proper care to anyone who needs it, money or no money."

"Oh, don't get all riled up, Boris. I agree that all who suffer from madness or lunacy deserve proper care, but the time, what you are suggesting is just impossible. You can't guaran-tee a cure, it's plain and simple."

"I believe where there is a will, there is a way. There has to be," my great grandfather told them.

The other doctors glanced at each other and exchanged slight smiles. They knew my great grandfather was passionate about his work, but at times, maybe too passionate.

"Then perhaps you need to prove it. Otherwise, there can be no agreement," replied one of the doctors. "You'd need to find the worse case of delusion or hysteria, and give it your best," he added, and then took a sip from his beer.

Just then, the Fairy Godmother approached a serious looking professor who was standing not too far from the table where my great grandfather and his colleagues were. Having been trying to get the attention of someone who might help her, and looking exasperated, she put her hands on the professor's lapels and asked, "Kind, sir, I have come far to speak with a Dr. Sigmund Freud. I am in great need of his service. I cannot spend much time here since it is of utmost importance that I get back to the kingdom before anyone notices my absence. You see I am on only a temporary leave from the land of fairies. Can you please tell me where I may find Dr. Freud?"

The professor delicately removed the Fairy Godmother's hands from his lapels, let out gruff, "He is not here!" and marched away.

Discouraged and tired, the Fairy Godmother wandered over to a wall and leaned against it. As she did this, her wand fell from inside her coat. It hit the floor, bounced, and then rolled, making an odd clanking sound.

The two doctors and my great grandfather saw this, having overheard the exchanged she had with the professor. They watched as the Fairy Godmother chased the wand under an occupied bar stool, getting on all fours, and crawled to retrieve it.

Once she did, she crawled back to an open space, stood and gave the wand a good shake, hoping it still held its power. To be sure, she slapped it hard against her right arm, then her left, then opened her coat and gave it a few hard slaps across her thigh. The tip of the wand gave off a strange, pinkish glow that satisfied the Fairy Godmother enough to hide it back into her coat.

The two doctors chuckled at the sight of her, then one, getting an idea, turned to my great grandfather and said, "Well, Boris, I think you found your candidate. Not only is she mad, but obviously beyond recovery. If you want to prove to us, and all in our profession, that anyone can be cured, have a go."

The doctor laughed along with his colleague. My great grandfather, angered and bothered by their callous humor stated nobly, "All right, I will."

He rose from the table, straightened his suit and made his way over to the Fairy Godmother.

"Excuse me," he said politely, "I couldn't help but overhear you were in search for someone. Might I help?"

The Fairy Godmother sighed with great relief and said, "Oh, yes! Thank you. I am looking for Dr. Sigmund Freud. You know, the famous doctor who helps people with their problems?"

My great grandfather nodded and said, "Yes. I know who he is, but he isn't here. He's in Vienna."

"Oh," said the Fairy Godmother. "Then would you be so kind as to take me there? It is very urgent that I see him."

My great grandfather heard the chuckles of his colleagues nearby, who obviously overheard her request. He glanced back at them. They both raised their drinks in comical encouragement.

Not amused, my great grandfather turned to the Fairy Godmother and said gently, "My good woman, Vienna is in Austria, in Europe. We're quite far away from there."

"Oh, dear," said the Fairy Godmother, discouraged. "I haven't time to look for him in another city. I was so hoping he could help me with my problem."

"Perhaps I can help," offered my great grandfather. "I am far from Freud's level of expertise, but I am in the practice of psychoanalysis. I am an alienist – a doctor."

"Oh, splendid!" the Fairy Godmother exclaimed. "You see, I left the kingdom because I'm not sure if I can handle the responsibility of the wishes of so many."

My great grandfather, seeing that this poor woman was seriously disturbed, and not wanting his colleagues to be privy of what she was saying, gently took her arm and said, "Why don't we go somewhere private to talk. We'll go to my office downtown."

"Yes. Thank you, thank you so much," said the Fairy Godmother as my great grandfather led her out of the bar and out of the hotel.

Less than an hour later, they arrived at my great grandfather's office, having gotten there by carriage. My great grandfather brought the Fairy Godmother into his small office and, of course, she had a difficult time convincing him of who she was, as well as the "kingdom" where she was from.

My great grandfather began to doubt the conviction he made just an hour earlier with his colleagues – that psychoanalysis could cure anyone, until the Fairy Godmother suggested she bring him to the kingdom to prove it. Much like me with Cinderella, my great grandfather agreed thinking this was only part of her delusion until, of course, the Fairy Godmother gave a few waves of her wand and they were transported to her cottage.

Again, since there is no such thing as time in the kingdom, it wasn't until much later that, what only seemed like a day spent by my great grandfather at the Fairy Godmother's cottage, was in fact, ten days in earth's time. When he returned to New York after using psychoanalysis on the Fairy Godmother, and curing her of her doubts and worries, no one knew or understood where he was during that time.

He tried to tell friends and family members of his journey, but they, of course, thought him mad. So adamant was my great grandfather about what he knew, he wrote of his experiences in papers, papers he had hoped to be published in medical journals. However, they were never published. Instead, they were kept locked up, and some burned, by his family for fear of embarrassment and retribution. This only made my great grandfather more determined to tell the world of this "other world," so he published a book – a small volume that, unfortunately, became sort of a popular manual, to be made fun of, among those in his profession, on what can happen to a psychiatrist who becomes "burnt out."

My great grandfather went on a short speaking tour with his book, talking about the time he had spent with the Fairy Godmother and this magical kingdom that he had visited. This, of course, caused his colleagues and patients alike to turn on him. He was stripped of his license to practice and spent nearly a year in a sanatorium.

Although he was found perfectly sane with only terms such as "eccentric" and "overactive imagination" put onto his record, he spent the rest of his days at home with his wife and son (my grandfather) in their new house in Trenton, New Jersey. My family was forced to move out of New York due to the constant reminder, and humiliation, of my great grandfather's book and tarnished reputation.

However, I was told by my grandfather many times that great grandfather was a very intelligent and decent man, and died happy because he understood that what he knew to be real could not possibly be accepted by those with no imagination, or of open mind, or of things beyond science.

His book is out of print, and has been for over a century, but it is still well known among psychiatrists, and often quoted when one is writing about, or discussing, severe delusion within patients. Or, as in Rodney Klein's case, what happens when a psychiatrist becomes overwhelmed in dealing with mental illness day in and day out.

Most of my great grandfather's papers were lost over the years, but some survived and were handed down from my grandfather to my father, and then to me. I have them stored in a box in my garage. Although my great grandfather was a man very much loved and respected, his "tall tales" of the Fairy Godmother left a stain on our family name.

Growing up, if, or when, his name was spoken, it was usually in hushed whispers. People would somehow find out about my great grandfather, and from time to time a kid at school would toss out a snide, hurtful remark to me about my "nut job" great grandfather.

I hated the fact that I was named after him because of his reputation, but had learned to accept it. Although, I admit, it still burns me when a colleague asks about him. I usually brush off any inquiries about great grandfather's delusion with a remark like, "that was over a hundred years ago," and walk away.

So, you can imagine how shocked and alarmed I was when I found myself to be in the presence and home of *the* Fairy Godmother. It validated my great grandfather, and proved that he was not insane. However, I nowhere near prepared for what this new revelation was about to do to me.

Fourteen

➻ BACK AT THE COTTAGE ❦

Cinderella and the Fairy Godmother listened intently as I told them the fate of my great grandfather.

"Well, everything you told is true," sighed the Fairy Godmother. "Except the part about my coat. Yes, it was spring, but it *was* a very cool evening."

"I'll be sure to correct that part next time I tell the story," I said sarcastically.

Not appreciating my tone, The Fairy Godmother said, "Listen, I told Dr. Berger not to tell anyone about what he saw here."

"I wish he'd listened," I said. "He became the laughing stock of his profession."

"And you're sorry about what happened to him?" asked the Fairy Godmother, surprised by my anger.

"Yes!" I said. "Of course."

"Oh, but you shouldn't be. He wasn't. In fact, he was most grateful."

"Grateful? How would you know?"

The Fairy Godmother smiled, and then rose from her chair. She walked over to a shelf and pulled out a book. It was a familiar looking, thin hardcover volume. She walked over to me, held it out and said, "Read the inscription."

Unsure of what this was all about, I took the book. When I opened it, it gave a crunching sound. The spine was tight with age. I turned to the first page and saw the inscription.

"Read it aloud," encouraged the Fairy Godmother.

My Dear Friend, my world is all a-buzz, and in a fit, about what I've written in this book, what you and I know to be true. Let them squeak and squawk. No matter. If I were to be granted just one wish, it would be that my son, and his son, and his son to follow will believe and forever know the happiness that I've acquired from our short time together. From my deepest – I thank you. Regards, B. Berger.

Cinderella held her hand to her cheek, touched. I looked at the Fairy Godmother.

"How did you get this?" I asked.

"He *wished* for me to have it," she said with a smile. "It came long ago wrapped in brown paper."

"Have you read it?" I asked her, holding up my great grandfather's book.

"No need to," she replied.

"Well, I'm not making the same mistake my great grandfather made," I said as I handed it back to her. "I'm not telling a soul about any of *this*. It all ends here! Now if you'd get me back, we'll just pretend none of this ever happened."

"But what about me?" Cinderella anxiously asked.

"I can't help you," I told her, unable to look her in the eye as I did.

"Oh, but you can!" insisted the Fairy Godmother. "You are an alienist just like your great grandfather. You are quite capable."

"But why do I have to do it? Why don't you wave your wand and just help her yourself?"

The Fairy Godmother looked at me with soft, wise eyes. "My dear, there is only so much my wand can do. Spells only work for problems of the kingdom."

"Then get someone else to do it...Tinker Bell or Red Riding Hood."

"Oh, no. Another of this world cannot use a wish or spell on another unless granted, and even then must be only for good, never for malice, for they would perish in the kingdom by stroke of midnight. Plus, what I had, and what Cinderella has, goes much deeper. Only your kind, the physicians of the mind, can fix her problem."

"Fix? Fix what?" I asked, and then turned to Cinderella. "What's wrong with you anyway?"

Before Cinderella answered, the Fairy Godmother shot her a hard, threatening look. Her eyes defying her to say the word, "unhappy."

"I...uh...I-I'm afraid," she said, keeping one eye on the Fairy Godmother.

"Afraid of what?" I asked.

Cinderella glanced at the Fairy Godmother then quickly replied, "That I'll kill my husband!"

The Fairy Godmother rolled her eyes at her response. *That's the best she could come up with?*

I was taken aback. "You mean, Prince Charming?"

Suddenly there was a knock at the door. We all froze at the sound of it. Looking exceptionally worried, the Fairy Godmother put her finger to her lips indicating for us not to make a sound as she tiptoed over to the window, drew back the curtain ever so slightly and peered out. A look of alarm came across her face.

"Crap!" she whispered to us. "It's Sleeping Beauty. I bet she's back for more slumber dust."

She tiptoed back over to Cinderella and me. "Ever since that spell, her sleep pattern has been all messed up," she explained, and then looked at me. "She can't find you here. You must go. And take Cinderella with you."

"Go where?" I asked.

"From whence you came," she answered as she made her way across the room and grabbed her wand from the shelf.

"Oh, no. Send me back alone. I told you I can't help her," I insisted.

"You *can*...and you *will!*" demanded the Fairy Godmother. "And one more thing," she said as she went over to her desk, grabbed something from it and put it in my hand.

"That belonged to your great grandfather. He left it here. You should have it."

It was a pipe, a Briar pipe, to be exact, and in mint condition, from the late 1800's. The shape of the bowl was full-bent with a short stem and mouthpiece. Engraved in small letters, where the shank of the pipe met the stem, were my great grandfather's initials: "BB."

It felt strange to be holding something so personal of my great grandfather's, something he had left behind well over a hundred years ago. But in that moment, I felt a sense of connection. My great grandfather was here, and now I was, too. Suddenly I felt nostalgic for an era long gone, and a little proud of him. That was something I'd never felt toward him at all.

As I was caught up in my reverie, studying the pipe, I heard the Fairy Godmother say, "Cinderella, keep to the plan...a fortnight. And don't ever bring anyone back here again!"

"Hey, wait a minute..." I started to say just as the Fairy Godmother waved her wand several times.

"May Cinderella and Boris be/Back to where they cure crazy."

Suddenly gold dust surrounded Cinderella and I. It was so thick I had to close my eyes. I felt my body swirl and lift again, and when I opened them, I was back in my office with Cinderella. I had to steady myself, feeling a moment of vertigo, as she flopped on the couch, exhausted from our "trip."

Stunned and disoriented, I asked, "D-did that really just happen?"

"Yes," said Cinderella with a smile.

"I – I don't believe it," I muttered as I slowly sat down in my chair.

"Still?!" came a voice from across the room. It was Snow White who was sitting in a corner with an open book on her lap.

Surprised to see her, I let out a startled gasp and leapt from my chair. "You! You're still here?" I asked in shock and dismay.

"Yes, and I picked up this book while you were away. It talks about the "Pleasure Principal," the "Id" – that which seeks instant gratification. Reminds me of the Evil Queen. She's totally run by her Id."

"I-I can't believe this," I said as I felt my head begin to pound.

"Well, you *should* by now," said Snow White. "Especially with that souvenir you brought back," and pointed to the Briar pipe that was still in my hand.

I let out another frightened gasp and threw it on the floor. Snow White stood, placed the book back on the shelf and said it was time for her to go. Cinderella got up and gave Snow White a hug.

Snow White then turned to me, and with a mischievous glean in her eye said, "Fair well, Boris...King of Pleasure," and with that, she disappeared in a cloud of blue and purple smoke.

Rattled, I rushed to the door to look in the waiting room to see if that's where she went. I opened it and looked around, gasping like a lunatic. I asked Rachel if she had seen anyone come out of my office. Rachel looked at me with concern, and shook her head no.

Before I went back in my office, she said, "Doctor, I've searched the Internet and there is no Boris Berger in New York."

"Never mind about that," I said and went into my office slamming the door behind me. Cinderella was again sitting on the couch.

"Where did Snow White go?" I asked.

"Home," she answered looking at me, worried that I still might need convincing. "Oh, please say you believe now."

I stared at Cinderella, trying to take it all in. "Is this a trick, or am I losing my mind?"

"Perhaps reality has been too...*overwhelming*?"

Stung by my own words, I shot her a frazzled look. It was all too much to comprehend, but since there was no other explanation, I studied Cinderella hard, then sat down and rubbed my forehead.

Cinderella sat forward and said, "I know this is confusing. It is to me as well, but I came to the Big Apple to see you. You know now that it wasn't a coincidence that we found each other...it was magical fate."

"This isn't the Big Apple," I groaned.

"But this is New Ark, is it not?"

"It's Newark, yes, but not the Big Apple. That's *New York*. You're in New Jersey."

Cinderella thought for a moment. "Oh, that's right! Your great grandfather was in New York, but your family moved here. The spell knew where to find you. It was the Fairy God-mother that got it wrong!"

"The Fairy Godmother got *a lot* of things wrong," I said. "I'm not my great grandfather. I don't know how to help you."

"But are you not a doctor?"

"I'm a therapist," I replied.

"What is a therapist?" she asked innocently.

I explained, in simple terms, that I help people with their problems, mostly by talking things out.

Cinderella's face lit up and exclaimed, "Ooooh! So, you *can* help me!"

She must have read resistance in my face since her smile began to disappear. "You will help me, won't you?" she asked. "I have no one else to turn to."

She looked at me with her big, hard-to-resist, pleading eyes. In that moment, although I was still flushed with confu-sion, my mind trying to settle on what just happened, and knowing my life had just taken a most bizarre turn, I felt sorry for her. I saw the burden of being *the* Cinderella. The weight of that came across clearly in her tired expression.

I stood and slowly paced the room. My thoughts raced in so many directions. Most of them questions. How can I help her? Why was this happening to me? Fairy Tales *are* real? Am I to pick up where my great grandfather left off? Who would believe any of this? What if I *can't* help her? Am I losing my mind?

As I paced I would glance in her direction, and every time she would stare up at me with those helpless eyes. If I said no, then where would she go? Would that deem me a failure? Would she find help with someone else? Would someone else even *try* to help her, or simply commit her?

She was here with me for a reason, though I honestly didn't understand why. But right now that wasn't important. I was a professional and she was a patient that needed help. It was my duty. This, I knew, is what I had in common with my great grandfather...a sense of responsibility.

I rubbed my forehead again, knowing the huge commitment I was about to make, and said, "OK. I'll help you."

Cinderella was beyond thrilled, and expressed this by leaping from the couch and giving me a big hug. My body stiffened to her embrace since I'd never been so close to an icon...of literature, that is. Her body felt warm and real. It surprised me. Cinderella then pulled away and thanked me profusely.

"I must go now to buy food. Shall I return tomorrow?" she asked eagerly, as if wishing tomorrow was already here.

I nodded, suggested she return at ten o'clock the next morning, then reached for one of my business cards and handed it to her.

"This is my address and phone number. In case you get lost...again," I said.

Cinderella looked at my card, then smiled as she repeated the hour and grabbed her burlap sack.

"One more thing," I said before she opened the door to leave. "Do you have a place to stay?"

"I do," she answered with the brightest smile. "I am staying with a woman and her two daughters, and I really must be going since I have their home to clean and their dinner to prepare." And with that Cinderella repeated the time, "Ten o'clock," opened the door, then did the strangest thing...she gave me the finger!

"Whoa! What's *that* for?" I asked, shocked and offended.

Cinderella lowered her hand. "I was just saying 'hey' – like everyone does here."

"People have been giving you...doing that at you?"

"Yes! I think it's marvelous!" she exclaimed.

I slowly closed the door behind her and said, "Yeah, well…that's not a salutation. It means something else."

"Oh? What does it mean?" she asked innocently.

I struggled to find a way to delicately explain it. "Uh, well, it means…it means they don't like you. Kind of like, "get lost"-that sort of thing."

"Oh," said Cinderella, looking embarrassed. "Then all those people out there were not being friendly after all."

"No, they weren't. But don't feel bad. Everyone gets one of those from time to time."

I opened the door and she walked out, still looking a little disillusioned. Welcome to reality, I thought, as I closed the door and began making my way toward my desk. I stopped when I saw my great grandfather's pipe on the floor. I picked it up and stared at it as took my seat. I was still trying to process everything. *Reeling* from everything, was more like it when Rachel knocked, and then entered.

She glanced around and asked, "Where's that…where's Snow White?"

I had no answer. The truth was too bizarre. The best I could say was, "She went home."

"Oh," said Rachel, who gave the room one more look-over then walked out, utterly baffled.

I put my grandfather's pipe on the desk and starred at it for a long while, then picked it up and held it to my nose to smell the still faint smell of tobacco. I looked again at the engraved initials. They were mine, too, I thought, as I gently rubbed them with my thumb. I couldn't resist taking a small cloth that I had in a desk drawer, and vigorously wiped the mouthpiece. After I felt it was clean enough, I slowly brought the pipe to my mouth and bit on the stem.

In my mind I pictured my great grandfather in his office, leaning back in his chair after a full day of seeing patients and puffing away on this pipe that was now in my possession. I wanted to do the same, so I began to lean back in my chair, then stopped and pulled the pipe from my mouth. Staring at the small relic from history, I knew in that moment that my life was never going to be the same.

Fifteen

That evening, Mrs. Mortadella, Nikki and Angelina were sitting at their dining room table, having just finished their dinner. In between burping and unsnapping the top button of their jeans to breath, they all shared how good the meal was and how "stuffed" they felt.

Mrs. Mortadella was the most impressed and said, "She must have taken classes. *That* was amazing."

When Cinderella entered the room wearing an apron, over the dress she was still wearing since she arrived, Mrs. Mortadella and her daughters quickly sat up acting unimpressed. Cinderella asked if they enjoyed her meal, and looked at them in eager anticipation for their answer.

"It was adequate," said Mrs. Mortadella sounding bored.

Nikki and Angelina followed suit by tossing out mutually unimpressed "whatever's." Cinderella looked downcast at the table, as if trying to figure out where she went wrong, then tried to brighten their moods by suggesting dessert.

"I made a crumb apple pie, a cherry cake with homemade

103

frosting and a vanilla cream custard. I wasn't sure what your tastes were."

Nikki stared at her in disbelief. "You made all of *that*?"

Cinderella nodded, as if it was effortless. It was. Angelina held her stomach. "Gawd, I couldn't eat another bite."

"Yeah, I'm done," added Nikki.

They both got up and left without even a "thank you." Mrs. Mortadella stood and ordered Cinderella to put it all into the refrigerator, hinting that they might have it later, then walked out of the room. Cinderella let out a heavy sigh and began cleaning up the sloppy mess they left behind. A moment later, Mrs. Mortadella returned carrying a pile of clothes and dropped them on the table.

"Here are some things that the girls were going to get rid of," she said. "Ya gotta start wearing something more up to date 'cause you're starting to creep us out with whatcha got on." She then turned and left the room.

Cinderella was embarrassed for a brief moment, and then happily began sorting through the pile of clothes. If it would get her out of that tight corset, she thought, she was ready to wear anything.

That same night, I was home, tired and exhausted from my "trip" to the Fairy Godmother's cottage. I sat in my bathrobe, staring at my computer. I was doing a Google search about the Cinderella tale. Actually, I had been at it for hours, reading every article on the Internet I could find about her. It was nearing midnight, so I began printing the articles for my session with Cinderella in the morning. That is, if she were to return. My mind kept switching from wondering if I had imagined the whole thing to, how in the world was I going to help her?

I clicked on one article after the other and printed them all. As the sheets came out of the printer, I rubbed my eyes and stood. Once they were done, I collected the pages, put them in my briefcase, turned off my computer and left the room.

I made my way down the hall and stopped by an open door. It was the door to my son's bedroom. I peered inside and saw my 7-year old son, Walter, asleep in his bed. I loved Walter more than anything, and wanted so much for him to have a happy childhood, but I felt a failure in this regard due to the break up of my marriage. Walter had always been closer to me, which is one of the reason's why he chose to stay with me instead of his mother, although it wasn't much of a choice since Helen had pretty much left both of us, but still, it was wrong that Helen wasn't with us. It hurt on so many levels, but seeing Walter always made me smile. He was a bright, and good kid. I was lucky in that regard. I whispered a "good-night" to him, then closed the door and headed down the hall.

Once in my bedroom, I took off my robe just as I passed a full-length mirror. When I caught a glimpse of myself in just my boxers, I remembered what Snow White had said and quickly covered my chest with my hands, and ducked away from it. Feeling unsure and afraid, I slowly peered into the mirror. When I realized what I was doing, I immediately came to my senses.

My reaction to the mirror bothered me as I climbed into bed. Strange how a long forgotten childhood trauma could still haunt me, I thought. I then kept reviewing in my mind what occurred at the Fairy Godmother's cottage, as well as the details of it. And how all of it was true, just as my great grandfather wrote and said it was. But look what happened to him when he told everyone. He was an alienist who only alienated himself. It was imperative that I make sure that didn't happen to me. I made this pact with myself as I turned out the light and stared up at the ceiling. Sleep did not come easy to me that night.

Sixteen

In the beautiful kingdom far, far away, an orchestra played inside the castle. Guests were dancing as pretty maidens stood along the walls chatting, and keeping an eye out for any available squires. The Prince was on his throne looking bored and anxious. Next to him were his parents, the King and Queen. The Queen had a worried eye on her son. Finally, she leaned over to him and said gently, "You should dance."

"With whom?" he asked in lost desperation.

"Surely, any one of those maidens would be more then happy to oblige," encouraged his mother.

"I want only to dance with my wife," insisted the Prince angry that his mother could even suggest such a thing. "How would it look if I were to dance with another?" he asked expecting her to agree.

"Better than it looks to be stood up," she retorted, keeping in mind that appearances were everything, even in the magical kingdom.

The Prince glared at his mother. "She will be here!" he insisted, although, for the first time ever in his life, he had doubts.

The Queen looked at the King, unconvinced.

Suddenly, the Prince saw something from across the room. Cinderella's Stepmother and two Step Sisters were making their entrance. The Prince leapt from his throne and eagerly made his way across the ballroom. The maidens along the wall sighed as he passed and approached the Stepmother.

"Hello, Stepmother – so nice of you to come," he said with true politeness all the while looking over her shoulder for Cinderella.

"We've been waiting a long time for you to throw another ball," she said, and then whispered, "I'm still trying to marry them off."

She motioned with her eyes at her two daughters who were pathetically unattractive and abrasive in attitude as they had always been. The Prince managed to throw them a smile, and then looked quickly back at his Stepmother.

"Is Cinderella with you?" he asked anxiously.

"You mean she's not here?" the Stepmother asked, her mind racing with delight at the possibility of unhappiness between Cinderella and the Prince.

"She has not been herself lately," he confided sadly. "I'm afraid she's left me." He lowered his head, ashamed.

The Stepmother tried hard to hide her smile, but it was a struggle. She looked at her daughters and, with a quick jerk of her head, motioned for them to come forward. They did, like two obedient dogs, loving gossip and perhaps another shot at the Prince.

The Stepmother then motioned for them to "comfort" him. They each took a side of him.

"That's terrible," said the first Step Sister. "You must be *so* sad."

"And lonely. *Really* lonely," said the other as she began to stroke his arm. "All alone in this big castle. In your big empty bed."

The first Step Sister saw this and became competitive. She began stroking his other arm. "It's so typical of Cinderella to take off. She always was so flighty."

The second Step Sister interjected, "What you need is a *real* princess. Someone who will treat you right."

"*Really* right," said the first Step Sister suggestively.

The Prince grew uneasy with their creepy attention. He politely pulled away and walked briskly across the ballroom, back toward the King and Queen.

As he was about to pass, the King stopped him. "Where are you going, Son?"

The Prince snapped angrily, "To find my *wife*," and stormed away.

Seventeen

❧ NOT YOU AGAIN ❦

I arrived at my office early the next morning. I wanted to be sure I had all my notes in proper order before Cinderella arrived. Rachel came in a few minutes after me and was surprised to see me there. I explained that I felt it was going to be a long day and wanted to get a good start.

As she was turning on her computer and setting down her coffee from Starbucks, I heard the elevator door open out in the hall. I peered out, expecting to see Cinderella; instead, it was Rodney Klein. A wave of disgust came over me. He was the last person I wanted to see, but I figured I'd give him a few minutes, and then get rid of him.

Rodney entered the reception area wearing his usual obnoxious grin. He really held the belief that everyone was thrilled by his presence.

"Hi'ya, Boris. Got a minute?"

My expression said no, but I waved for him to come into my office anyway. Before he did, he leaned over Rachel's desk.

In that swarthy style of his he said, "Morning to you, too, Sweetheart."

I couldn't see Rachel, but I'm sure she was thinking the same thing I was – Bleh!

Rodney entered my office like a confident alley cat as I closed the door behind him.

"What do you want, Rodney? My first patient will be here any minute."

"I've come for information," he said as he rubbed his hands together like an excited gold miner.

"What information?" I asked, already bothered by this.

"About your great grandfather. I've decided to write a book about him."

I felt my stomach turn and my chest tighten. The blood boiling in my body made it hard for me to say anything. I could decide whether I wanted to kick him out, or strangle him.

"That lecture I gave was such a huge hit, it made me realize that I was really on to something. Everyone knows about...well, what happened to, your great grandfather, but not about the man himself. I thought it would make the perfect book – maybe even another best seller!"

I shot Rodney a tense glare as I moved over to my desk. I figured having the desk to separate us would curb my urge to slug him. My glare got through...a little.

"OK, I can see that you're not thrilled with the idea. And I was kind of expecting that, so...I'll let you write it with me," he offered as if *that* would make me want to jump on board.

"No," I said flatly.

"But why not? Your great grandfather was famous!"

"For all the wrong reasons," I replied.

"But his book – "

"The one I wish he'd never written," I snapped angrily,

then instantly felt embarrassed for my outburst. I busied my-self by shuffling the papers on my desk.

"Aw, you have nothing to be ashamed of, Boris," Rodney said as if he was speaking to a child. "In fact, I've already done so much research in preparing for my lecture that I came upon a lot of interesting tidbits about your great grandfather that I'm sure *you* don't even know."

"There isn't anything I don't know about him," I said in a tone to convey my disinterest.

"Did you know that he knew Houdini?" he asked.

I shot him a surprised look. The greatest magician who ever lived? I *didn't* know this, and was stunned to hear if from him, of all people.

"Didn't think so," Rodney said, making me feel stupid that I hadn't. "Apparently, he spent a weekend with Houdini and Sir Arthur Conan Doyle at a hotel in Atlantic City back in 1922. Doyle was heavily into spiritualism and was trying to convert Houdini. Houdini had read your great grandfather's book, as did Doyle, and they wanted to meet him."

For a brief moment I was in awe of my great grandfather, but was sickened that I was finding it out from this clod.

"How do you know this?" I asked, thinking perhaps this was a fabricated ploy of his to persuade me to approve of his book idea.

Rodney reached into his pocket and pulled out two docu-ments. He laid the first one on my desk.

"Here is a copy of the hotel ledger that your great grandfa-ther signed. Notice the name right above his is signed by Houdini, and eight names above his is Doyle's."

I looked carefully at the document. It seemed authentic. Then Rodney placed down a second document.

"A signed dinner ticket by Houdini and your great grandfather.

Note the hotel's name on the bill. Apparently, they both fought over who would pay, then decided to split it."

I looked at the bill. This, too, seemed authentic.

"And lastly, this photo…"

He reached into his jacket pocket, removed an old photo and placed it on the desk. I picked it up for closer inspection. There, in that grainy photo, was Harry Houdini standing near the water's edge in a one-piece bathing suit. Nearby, sitting on beach chairs, was Sir Arthur Conan Doyle and his wife, both smiling and wincing from the sunshine, and in the water, near the shoreline, was indeed my great grandfather, lying on his stomach with his head up as a small wave splashed his body. Again, I was amazed and felt a sense of pride, but my stomach turned that Rodney knew this and I didn't.

"That's a month and half of intensive research right there. Man, did I have to really dig for those. Facts no one knows. Not even you. I was going to mention this in my lecture, but knew I should save it for my book."

His book? I wanted to punch him. I looked at him angrily and said, "I don't care if my great grandfather knew the Queen of England, I can't be a part of anything that is going to bring a new wave of embarrassment to me and my family."

"You're not seeing the bigger picture here, Boris," Rodney said in a way that hinted we were close friends. We weren't.

"Oh, I see the bigger picture all right. I get letters and emails *still* from crackpots all over the world who either *think* I'm my great grandfather, or looking for more information about something he wrote over a hundred years ago," I told him. "For God's sake, there's even a Facebook page dedicated to him. *Boris Berger Believes!*"

"That's why there should be a book!" Rodney insisted again, wearing that stupid grin.

I looked him square in the eye and through gritted teeth said, "I will be no part of *any* book, at *any* time, in regard to my great grandfather."

"Will you at least endorse it?" he asked.

"Get out!" I shouted.

This turned his mood to resentment. "Well, whether you're involved or not, I'm writing the book!" he shouted back with entitled arrogance. "This is why you'll never get any farther than where you are, Boris. You're a loser."

He quickly collected the documents off my desk and left my office. He stormed past Rachel, without even a swarthy goodbye, and headed toward the elevator. I stared down at my desk, seriously bothered by his last remark.

Rodney paced in anger, wondering how he was going to get his book idea off the ground without my help, when suddenly the elevator door opened and out stepped Cinderella carrying her burlap sack. Never to pass on a pretty face, he made his usual wolf eyes at her and watched as she approached Rachel's desk.

He took one step into the elevator when suddenly he overheard Rachel announce, "Cinderella is here to see you, Dr. Berger."

Rodney quickly took a step back out of the elevator, holding its doors from closing, and watched Cinderella enter my office.

If only he had left thirty seconds earlier, or Cinderella hadn't arrived on time, all of our futures would have been a lot different.

Eighteen

It was exactly ten o' clock when Cinderella stepped into my office. She was now dressed in "normal" clothes, at least by today's standards. She wore sweatpants and a t-shirt with an obnoxious printed slogan about New Jersey on it, but I said nothing. What she had on was the least of her problems, as well as mine, but I was happy to see her looking refreshed and eager to start.

Once again, I told her to take a seat on the couch, while I grabbed my notepad and sat in the same chair across from her. I have to admit, I was nervous to be working with a fairy tale princess, but decided to treat her as I would any of my other patients.

"So, why don't we start with what brought you here," I began.

"The Fairy Godmother turned a pumpkin into this wonderful carriage –"

I held up my hand to stop her. "No, no. I'm talking about when you first realized there was something wrong?"

115

Cinderella though for a moment then answered, "Well, I don't really know. I've never been able to sleep very well..."

"How long have you had trouble sleeping?"

Cinderella answered matter-of-factly, "Oh, centuries ago."

"You haven't slept in centuries?"

"I mean, yes, I sleep, but I wake up in the middle of the night filled with such dread and fear," she answered.

"What time of night do you wake up?"

"Midnight. It's always midnight."

As I jotted this down on my notepad, I muttered, "That makes sense."

Cinderella heard this, and asked why. I looked up feeling guilty for having let that slip and said, "Well, according to the story –"

Cinderella quickly cut me off, "You mean, my *life*. It's *not* a story.

I apologized, and went back to the issue at hand. "Wasn't midnight the hour when everything would change back? I mean you had until midnight to return home from the ball, right?

Cinderella nodded and answered yes.

"That must have been quite stressful, being on the clock like that. Sounds like you may be suffering from PTSD."

Cinderella looked at me not knowing what that meant.

"PTSD. It stands for Post Traumatic Stress Disorder. Perhaps you have a fear that you'll turn back to your former self."

Cinderella thought about this. "My former self. Well, I'll admit, my life before the Prince was hard, but it wasn't terrible," she said with sincerity.

"Maybe not, but perhaps there are unresolved issues?"

Cinderella looked at me, perplexed.

"Here, I've done some research," I said as I reached over, grabbed the printed pages from my desk and began sorting through them. "I've gone over some of the stories that have been written about you. There are a lot of different versions, but the story is basically the same. From what I can tell you went from rags to riches, kind of like winning the lottery. You weren't prepared for the new lifestyle you married into, and you went in without resolving issues from your past. It's one thing to wish for a Prince Charming to come and rescue you, but a whole other to have it actually happen."

Cinderella quickly sat forward. "Wait – did you say wish for Prince Charming to come and *rescue* me?"

I nodded yes.

"I *never* wished for that," Cinderella said adamantly.

"You didn't?" I asked, surprised to hear this.

"No. Never."

"But that's at the core of the Cinderella Complex."

"There's a *complex* named after me?" she asked with a sour expression.

"Yes. Oh, but you're not alone. They've named complexes after other well-known figures. For instance, Napoleon has one...and Peter Pan..."

"Peter has one?" she asked, surprised. "I wonder if he knows," she whispered to herself.

I was taken aback. Did she know Peter Pan? Does this mean Peter Pan is *real*, too? I wanted to ask, but needed to keep the focus on her, so I jotted down a note to ask her later.

"What is my complex?" she asked.

"Well, it's when a woman fears independence and has an unconscious desire to be taken care of. They want, or expect, their partner, or 'prince charming' to rescue them."

Cinderella became enraged. "Oh, no! No, no, no, no, NO! That's all wrong! I was not wanting, nor expecting, the Prince, or *any* man, to rescue me."

"But you went to the ball –" I began.

"To get out of the house!" Cinderella cried. "I spent all my days slaving for my stepmother and stepsisters. I needed a break. I wished for one night out. Just one night!"

"And you met the Prince..."

"Yes, we met, and liked each other," Cinderella explained. "But I didn't expect it to amount to anything. I was a commoner. I knew my station. I never thought he would *marry* me, and I sure didn't sit around hoping that he would. In fact, if you read "the story" more carefully, the Prince came looking for *me*," she huffed. "Who wrote these stories anyway? What are their names?"

I looked through my papers and read off several names. "Charles Perrault, The Brothers Grimm, Hans Christian Andersen –"

Cinderella rolled her eyes. "All men. Typical. Who else? Continue, please," she said, irritated.

I cleared my throat. "Well, there were the writers of the Disney movie."

Cinderella looked at me confused. I had to explain what a movie was. She found the whole idea of films fascinating until I told her about the Disney movie that was based on her.

"It was written by eight -" I hesitated, not wanting to say.

"Men?" she asked.

I nodded. Cinderella rolled her eyes again.

"OK, so maybe they missed the point, but that aside, what did you *want* before you met the prince?" I asked.

"Want?"

"Yes. Everybody wants something," I said anxious to hear what her answer would be.

Cinderella looked upward as if trying to think.

"Were you happy at home?"

"No. My stepmother wasn't very nice. Neither were my stepsisters. They worked me to the bone, but again that was my station," said Cinderella hating this truth.

"A station you were able to get away from in a very big way."

"Yes, I suppose," said Cinderella. "But I was never a princess."

"But you did go off to live happily ever after," I reminded her.

Cinderella looked sad after I said that.

"What's wrong?"

"That never happened," she said with her eyes cast down to the floor. She then looked up at me and asked, "Maybe you can tell me, Dr. Berger – how does someone live happily ever after?"

I wanted to answer this, but couldn't. What did I know about happily ever after? She looked at me, discouraged.

"Let's talk about your friends," I said, wanting to pull her out of her gloom and keep it moving forward.

"Friends?" she asked, as if were a foreign concept.

"Yes. Surely, you have friends. For instance, the other princesses that you lean on for support. Like, Snow White. "

"The other princesses? No. I mean, yes, they are quite lovely, but no, this isn't something I can go to any of them about. Nor them to me."

"Why not?"

"We're all *perfect*, remember?"

"You say that sarcastically."

"Well – " she began, but stopped and nervously nibbled on her fingernail.

"If you have something to say, you can say it here. This is what therapy is all about...not holding anything back. Saying

119

what you really need to say without any ridicule or judgment. You're safe here."

Cinderella, never having had the opportunity to do this before, began slowly. "Well, first of all, as you know, I'm supposed to be 'perfect.' Heaven forbid any of us are *imperfect*, though we most certainly are. Take Ariel for instance..."

"Ariel? The Little Mermaid?" I asked for clarification.

"Yes. The girl is from the sea, but no matter how hard she tries, she *still* smells like low tide. It's disgusting, but no one would ever dare tell her."

I was surprised by her bluntness, but encouraged her to continue.

"And Jasmine? The girl is the daughter of a Sultan, and yet she marries a street hustler, and we're all are supposed to treat him as a prince? I mean, come on! Who knows what he did before they met. A thousand and one nights...of what? Can't be good. And that Genie of his! No one can say the word "wish" without that smoky monstrosity appearing. It's goodbye privacy and beyond annoying, especially at parties. But everyone just smiles and acts like he's not an intrusion." She shook her head in frustration. "It's just a world where everyone is so nauseatingly polite. *Urrggh*," she growled.

I realized I had opened the floodgates for Cinderella because once she got started it was as if there was no stopping her.

"And then there's Mulan," she said quickly, sounding a bit gossipy. "She *says* she only impersonated a man out of fear of her father, but we all know she liked doing it a lot more than she should have. *A lot* more, if you know what I mean."

Cinderella then leaned forward and whispered, "It's in the way she looks me and the other princesses. We can tell."

Was she hinting that Mulan is a lesbian?

"And *don't* get me started on Aurora."

I shifted uneasily in my seat. "So, basically what you're saying is, you have no support system," I said, getting back to my initial point.

"Aside from the raccoons, mice and squirrels? No. I have no one."

I began jotting down a few notes. Cinderella watched, concerned.

"Is this helping at all?" she asked, concerned.

"Well, it's a good start," I assured her.

"Do you think I'm...curable?" she asked with doubt in her voice.

I paused momentarily, wanting to do my best to encourage her. "We're just getting started. It's going to take some work. But let me ask you something. You said back at the Fairy Godmother's home..."

"Cottage," she corrected me.

"Cottage, right. You said you wanted to kill your husband?"

Cinderella's mood suddenly became sullen. She sat back on the couch. "I've had thoughts," she admitted.

"Why? Isn't he supposed to be perfect?"

Cinderella's eyes narrowed at the mention of "perfect." I hit a nerve.

"He's *perfect*, all right," she said, bitterly.

"You seem angry," I said.

"You would be, too, if all day long you had to deal with *that* guy."

"He's *too* perfect?" I asked.

"For my taste, yes."

"What exactly *is* your taste?"

"I don't really know. That's my problem. All I know is, according to these stories everything about my life is supposedly wonderful and glorious."

"Stories aside, it's safe to conclude that not everything is perfect, or you wouldn't be sitting here with thoughts of murder swirling around in your head."

"Yes, that's why I'm here," she said.

"So, you get that you're imperfect." I stated, gently.

"Yes!" she said sitting forward. "But everyone expects me to be otherwise, even those men who wrote those awful lies about me. They expect it of me, as do all the children who read and believe those books. Why, I'm not even allowed to say aloud that I'm un-"

She stopped herself, frozen, with a look of fear in her eyes.

"Un..?" I asked, sitting forward.

"Well, you know," she said, waving her hand as if brushing it off.

"No, finish what you were going to say."

"I'm..." she began, and then stopped herself as if some invisible force was preventing her from speaking. Her eyes darted around the room terrified that someone might hear.

"Go ahead," I said gently.

She leaned forward and whispered, "I'm unhappy."

I thought I'd be playful with her, so I looked around the room, acting nervous, and pretending I heard something. "Do you *hear* that?"

"What?" Cinderella whispered with fear in her eyes.

"Nothing," I said, smiling. "See? The world didn't come to an end."

Cinderella looked at me for a moment, still unsure, then let out a happy, relieved giggle.

"Oh, Dr. Berger. You really had me frightened."

"I saw."

"So, are you saying that it's OK to be unhappy?" she asked.

"It certainly is," I assured her. "In fact, most people are."

"But I want to be happy," she said.

"Welcome to the human race," I sighed.

"Then I'm not alone in my feelings," she said, it was finally sinking in.

"No. You're not."

After she ponded this, she asked, "Do you think the Prince is unhappy?"

"I wouldn't know. What do you think?"

"I doubt it. He's always so...so..."

"Perfect?" I asked.

"Yes," she snarled.

"Which is why maybe you have thoughts of killing him. You want to destroy in someone else what you, yourself, don't have."

"You make it sound as if I'm jealous."

"Are you?" I asked.

"Jealous of him?" she asked, as if the concept was absurd.

"It's something to think about," I told her, as I closed my notepad and began to get up from my chair. "Let's stop here."

"Are we done?" she asked.

"For today, yes."

"May I return tomorrow?" she asked as she grabbed her burlap sack and stood.

"Yes. Same time. We'll meet every day at this time, if that works for you."

"Oh, yes," she said with a smile.

"By the way – where are you staying?"

"The Castle Condos, the home of Mrs. Mortadella and her two daughters. They're very kind."

"Do they know you're...?"

"Yes, I've given them my name."

"Oh," I said, concerned. "Well, look, maybe it's best you not tell them who you really are."

"Why not?"

"Well, I doubt they would believe you. I didn't, remember?"

"I honestly don't understand your people," Cinderella, shaking her head. "You believe a book – a story that isn't at all real – yet not believe me, who is."

"Well, nobody's perfect," I said.

That made her laugh.

"Thank you, Dr. Berger. You've given me a great deal to think about. That post-traumatic thingy, and that complex I've apparently given to so many. I will see you again tomorrow. Ten o'clock," she said and went to the door. I opened it and Cinderella walked out.

I watched as she made her way out of the reception area toward the "moving room," then closed the door and began collecting my papers.

As I sifted through them, I took a seat at my desk. Cinderella was unhappy. This was quite a revelation to me. If *she* was unhappy then was there such a thing as true happiness for anyone? My thoughts caused my hand to write in my notes the question she asked: *How does someone live happily ever after?*

Nineteen

⇒ A WOLF IN WOLF'S CLOTHING ⇐

When the doors of the elevator opened on the main floor, Cinderella stepped out. Unbeknownst to her, Rodney was there, waiting for her. He had lingered in the lobby the past hour hoping to find out who she was.

As Cinderella headed to the door, Rodney quickly stepped in front of her and gallantly opened it. Cinderella smiled, thanked him and walked out. He followed.

"Excuse me, Miss..." Rodney said, stepping up behind her.

Cinderella stopped and turned around.

"Is your father a thief?" he asked.

This took Cinderella by insulted surprise, until Rodney added, "Because he stole the stars from the skies and put them in your eyes."

Never having heard this corny pickup line, or any for that matter, flattered Cinderella. She smiled. Rodney grinned. His line worked.

"My name is Rodney...Rodney Klein. I think I saw you earlier upstairs."

"I didn't see you," said Cinderella.

"I had just left. I was visiting my good friend, Dr. Boris Berger."

"Oh! You know Dr. Berger?" asked Cinderella. Her eyes lit up.

"Yes. We've been friends for years. Colleagues, even. I, too, am a doctor. I didn't catch your name."

"I'm Cinderella," she answered.

Rodney smiled, smitten with her innocence. "As in the fairy tale princess?" he asked, playing along.

"Yes. That's me," Cinderella responded.

"Uh, no, I meant 'as in' the fairy tale princess. Not the actual Cinderella," Rodney corrected her.

"Yes. I *am* the actual Cinderella," she said, and then quickly remembered what I had asked her. "Oh, dear. I shouldn't have told you that."

"It's all right," assured Rodney, again playing along. "Your secret is safe with me. Sometimes I like to pretend I'm Prince Charming."

Cinderella's eyes narrowed. "Now why on earth would you want to be like *him*?"

Her sudden and sour demeanor took Rodney aback. "Well, I was just – "

"My husband may be a prince, but, trust me, his charm becomes grating after some time," she told him in a curt tone.

Rodney looked at her confused. "Wait – you're married?"

"Yes. To the Prince."

Rodney looked at her carefully. Was this a joke? "How do you know Dr. Berger?" he asked.

"Since you're his friend, I trust I can tell you. His great grandfather knew the Fairy Godmother. She sent me to him."

"His great grandfather, Boris Berger?" asked Rodney with piqued interest.

"That's right. The Fairy Godmother thought I should come here to see Dr. Berger for help."

Rodney stared at her, unsure what to make of all of this. He had just heard me say earlier how I had struggled to avoid the many "nut cases" out there who were trying to get in touch with me, so this made little sense. Why would I see anyone posing as Cinderella and telling such a wild tale?

"So, you know all about Boris' great grandfather and his book?"

"Oh, yes," said Cinderella.

Rodney pondered this and, wanting to gain more information about me, my practice and this so-called Cinderella, asked, "Can I buy you lunch?"

Cinderella smiled with glee. "Oh, you're most kind! It's good to make new friends, especially one of Dr. Berger's."

Rodney smiled. The bait was hooked. He linked his arm with hers and off they went down the sidewalk.

A couple of hours later, after Rodney and Cinderella finished their lunch, he sat back and said, "Well, this was one of the most enjoyable and insightful lunches I've ever had."

"Do you really mean that?" asked Cinderella, not used to having this sort of attention from a man outside of the Prince.

"I really do," answered Rodney, as he leaned forward and smiled at her again. "You have quite the imagination."

Cinderella looked at him, perplexed. "I don't know what I said that was so imaginative since everything I've told you was simply the truth."

Rodney was removing a credit card from his wallet when she said this. He paused and looked at her. "So, all that talk about the kingdom, the Fairy Godmother, and you taking Boris to meet her was true?" he asked.

"Yes. Why would I make that up?"

"And you came here because you needed time away from your husband – because of too much perfection?" he asked.

"Yes. As well as to spend time on my own and discover who I really am, not just this princess, that I feel nothing like deep inside."

What a troubled, delusional girl, Rodney thought as he placed the credit card on the small tray that a waiter came and quickly took away. That was until Cinderella said something that led him to think that all of this just might be true.

"I'm so glad the Fairy Godmother found Dr. Berger for me. She told me he is just as good as his great grandfather, who was well respected by other great men, such as that magician and the one who wrote those famous novels about Sherlock Holmes."

Rodney froze. He stared at Cinderella in stunned silence.

"Is everything all right?" she asked.

"Y-you mean Houdini and Arthur Conan Doyle?" he asked.

"Yes. Those are the men," she replied.

"Boris told you that?"

"No. The Fairy Godmother did. I doubt Dr. Berger knows anything about those men. Or maybe he does," she said with a shrug. "I'll ask him."

Rodney stared at her, unsure. Cinderella noticed.

"Are you all right?" she asked, concerned.

"Y-yes. I'm...all...right," he muttered as the waiter came back and gave him the receipt for lunch.

He collected it and slowly stood. Cinderella stood, too. As they left the restaurant, Rodney kept glancing at her with a perplexed expression. How did she know about Houdini, he wondered. It took him so long to discover that information that *nobody* knew.

He was silent during most of the ride home with Cinderella. When they arrived at The Castle Condos, Cinderella opened the car door to let herself out.

"Wait – " Rodney said just before Cinderella closed the door. "I think it would be a good idea if you didn't tell Dr. Berger that we've met."

"Why not?" Cinderella asked innocently.

"Well..." Rodney began, trying to think fast. "Well, you see, there is a rule among doctors that they not see each others patients."

"But I'm not your patient," said Cinderella.

"Right. But, it's just this rule, and I'd like very much to see you again. Of course, that is, if you want to see me."

"I'll do as you wish," Cinderella said, then she giggled and played with her hair. "And, yes, I'd like very much to see you again, too, Dr. Klein."

"Rodney. Please," he said smiling, knowing he had her under his slimy spell.

"All right...Rodney."

"When do you see Dr. Berger again?" he asked.

"Tomorrow and every day at ten o'clock," she answered.

"Good. Then why don't I meet you outside his building, the day after tomorrow? I'll be parked right out front. We'll have lunch again," he said.

"Oh, I'd like that very much," squealed Cinderella.

Rodney chuckled. "You're delightful...and very, very pretty."

This made Cinderella blush.

"OK, I'll see you the day after tomorrow. And remember..." he said putting his finger to his lips to signify secrecy.

Cinderella did the same, then closed her door and watched him drive off. Smitten herself, and as if floating on a cloud, she entered The Castle Condos and made her way through the lobby. As she passed a large mirror that hung close to the staircase, she stopped abruptly. Seeing what she was wearing made her cringe in embarrassment.

Wearing secondhand sweatpants and a t-shirt made her look like a sloppy wreck, she thought. She held her hands to her face in horror, and quickly made her way up the stairs.

Twenty

❧ TAKE ME TO HER ❧

Still angry after leaving the ball, the Prince rode at great speed up to the cottage of the Fairy Godmother. He dismounted his horse, approached the door and pounded on it with his fist.

Once again, bottles were heard being knocked about from inside before the Fairy Godmother heaved open the door. She looked just as she did with Cinderella – wearing a ratty bathrobe and slippers. She was startled to see the Prince.

"Oh! Uh, hello, your Highness. Uh, sorry I didn't make it to your ball. I was actually going to go, but –"

"I need to speak with Cinderella," the Prince demanded.

The Fairy Godmother was relieved he had no interest in her not attending the ball.

"She's not here."

"Do you know where she is?" he asked.

"Yes, but, don't worry, she'll be back. I just forgot to let you know," the Fairy Godmother said sheepishly.

"Back from where? I must see her," he said with authority.

The Fairy Godmother stepped back shaking her head. "I don't think that's a good idea."

"But she's my *wife*," the Prince said, raising his voice. "I must go to her. What if she's in danger?"

The Fairy Godmother said, "Oh, she's not. She just needs her space, your Highness."

"Space? But she has all the space she needs right here!" he exclaimed with open arms, motioning the kingdom.

"Not *that* kind of space. Just…trust me, when a woman says she needs her space – let her have it. She'll return in a fortnight."

"A *fortnight*!" the Prince shouted in outrage.

The Fairy Godmother gently motioned for him to lower his voice. He did, but only a little.

"Then I shall stay here until she returns!" he said, folding his arms stoically.

That idea sickened the Fairy Godmother. The last thing she wanted to do was baby sit this guy and lose out on her desperately needed sleep…and drink.

"All right, all right. I'll send you to her," she said, as she pushed open her door and let him inside. "Come out to the back and help me find a pumpkin."

Twenty-One

❧ CAN IT BE TRUE? ❧

After dropping off Cinderella, Rodney cancelled all his appointments and drove quickly into Manhattan. His head was so filled with questions about his lunch with Cinderella; he felt he had to go talk it out with someone. The only one he knew to share this with was his friend, Billy, who was a nerdy, mild-mannered, bespectacled young man in his early thirties who worked in the commercial sales department of The Lancet, the medical journal that is second to the world renowned New England Journal of Medicine. That was the journal Rodney would have given his right arm to be in, if it were possible.

Billy wasn't so much a friend, but someone Rodney merely befriended because he worked at The Lancet. Rodney was always trying to get as close as he possibly could to either of these prestigious medical journals, and Billy understood well why a best-selling doctor would have anything to do with him other than that fact. Billy had low self-esteem, and it made him feel better about himself that someone of Rodney's stature trusted him.

Rodney caught Billy while he was on one of his breaks. As Billy sat at a small table in an empty break room eating his tuna salad sandwich, he listened as Rodney told him all the details of his time with Cinderella. Every once in a while, a co-worker of Billy's would enter to buy a soda from the soda machine. Rodney would immediately stop talking, approach the co-worker, who was usually a young, entry-level employee equally as nerdy as Billy, stick out his hand and introduce himself along with a short list of his accomplishments. The co-worker would be startled at first, then suspiciously shake Rodney's hand and make a quick exit.

"Ya gotta stop doing that, Rodney," said Billy with his mouth full. "That's not gonna get you published. We're in commercial sales. They can't do anything for you."

"You never know," said Rodney, and then asked eagerly, "So, what if this girl really *is* Cinderella?"

Billy chuckled after taking a sip from his soda. "Yeah, right. And I'm Superman."

"No, seriously. Let's just say that she is. Would that get me into the New England Journal of Medicine?"

"It would get you into that journal and every other journal in the world, not to mention every news outlet," said Billy as he crumpled up the plastic wrapping of his sandwich and tossed it at the trash bin several feet away. He missed.

"What would I need to do? Write a paper about her?" Rodney asked.

"Well, yeah, but you need proof first," said Billy.

"I can't prove it," said Rodney, discouraged.

"Then no paper," said Billy as he rose from his seat and took the last sip from his soda. He walked over, picked up his plastic wrapping from the floor and tossed that and the soda can into the trash bin.

"I need to get back to work. It was great seeing you, Dr. Klein. Good luck with the girl," he said, raising his eyebrows in a knowing fashion, and walked out of the room.

Rodney lingered, pacing the room slowly. "Proof," he murmured several times over as he wondered how to get it.

Twenty-Two

❧ DÉJÀ VU ❧

The next morning, Cinderella was curled up asleep on the small futon in her closet bedroom. When she awoke, she slowly sat up and tried to stretch, but her arms were blocked by a shelf overhead. When she stood, she was wearing shorts and a tattered, faded t-shirt with the words, "*Jersey Girls Don't Pump Gas*" printed on the front. This was one of the "generous" throwaways from one of the sisters. Cramped as she was, Cinderella began to dress to prepare breakfast on time for the three women she lived with.

An hour later, Mrs. Mortadella and her daughters were finishing their breakfast of eggs, bacon, toast, waffles, roasted potatoes, French toast with fruit, along with milk and orange juice that Cinderella had laid out for them. Once again, the women were stuffed with such wonderful food, and hid their gratitude when Cinderella entered from the kitchen wearing an apron and started to clear the table.

Angelina looked at her sister, Nikki, and asked if she wanted to go shopping with her. She needed a new dress for a party that night and wanted help picking something out.

Upon hearing this, Cinderella exclaimed in excitement, "A party?"

"Yeah, it's downtown," said Nikki.

Cinderella's eyes sparkled at the thought. "Oh, it sounds like fun. May I go?"

Nikki and Angelina gave her "you've got to be kidding me" looks and ignored her.

Mrs. Mortadella struggled to stand, having eaten too much, and said, "It's the girl's night, Cinderella. Anyway, you have a lot to do here. The bathroom still needs cleaning, and the kitchen, too." She then addressed her daughters with a slight burp, "Come on, Girls. Let's go shopping."

They all sluggishly moved from the table, gathered their purses and happily walked out the door. Cinderella watched, feeling left out, and looked at the mess they left behind. All she could do was sigh and collect the dishes.

Later, after Cinderella finished cleaning the kitchen and bathroom, she decided to clean the fireplace. Seeing that she still had time before she was to come see me for our session, she thought she'd get it out of the way. She put her hair up in a kerchief and began doing what came so naturally to her, clearing out the soot and grime from a fireplace.

I was on my way to the office when I decided to swing by The Castle Condos. I felt it important to see just where Cinderella was staying and with whom. I suppose my paternal nature had kicked in. It wasn't hard to find the condo complex since they had fake turrets on the roof to make it look somewhat like a castle, although instead it only cheapened it. There was nothing regal about it at all.

Cinderella had just begun sweeping out the ashes when I

rang the doorbell. You can imagine my surprise when she answered the door covered in soot.

"Dr. Berger!" she exclaimed. "What are you doing here?"

"I thought I'd give you a lift to the office. What are you doing?" I asked, staring at the ashes that were smeared on her cheeks and hands.

"Cleaning the fireplace," she said, as she wiped her forehead with the back of her hand, leaving a charcoal trail across it. "Come in."

As I entered, Cinderella went back to the fireplace and began sweeping soot into a dustbin. "I'm almost done. Then I'll wash up and we'll go," she said cheerfully.

I glanced around the place. "Where are – "

"Oh, they all went shopping. There's a party tonight and they wanted to buy new clothes," said Cinderella, getting that I was talking about the others who lived there.

"Will you be going?"

"No," she answered looking sad, and then went back to her cleaning.

I watched her. She was once again playing out a role she was being forced into and yet, was oblivious to it. I asked, "Does any of this seem familiar to you?"

Cinderella looked about the room, and then shook her head.

"Not even a little?" I asked hoping for some sort of recognition to set in.

She giggled and said, "Dr. Berger, I've never been to New Ark before, so how could any of this be familiar to me?"

Was she really that un-self aware? I wondered, and then suggested she hurry with what she was doing so we could get to my office as soon as possible.

Twenty-Three

❖ THE SECOND SPELL ❖

The Prince plopped the large pumpkin down next to the mice and rats, then took a step back, but the Fairy Godmother pushed him forward, saying, "No, you get in there, too. We're going to get this in one shot."

The Prince took his place next to the pumpkin. The Fairy Godmother cleared her throat and lazily raised her wand.

"OK...here goes nothing...*Too many words I don't care to mince/Turn all of this into transportation for the Prince!*"

She waved the wand. Suddenly, a huge burst of bright colors sparkled everywhere. As the sparkles settled, the pumpkin had turned into a handsome carriage. The mice had become horses, and the rats were the same two coachmen. The Prince was now dressed in jeans, boots, a white dress shirt and a leather sports jacket.

"Hmm," said the Fairy Godmother, "Interesting look you got there."

The same coachman who checked out Cinderella was now checking out the Prince. He gave him a seductive smile and

139

asked, "How *you* doing?"

The Fairy Godmother glared at the coachman and snapped, "You! Back in the driver's seat!"

The coachman grudgingly climbed up onto the carriage. The other coachman stepped up to the Fairy Godmother, looking pissed off.

"Hey, the last time we came 'this close' to not making it back. I hope you've fixed that."

The Fairy Godmother gave him a guilty look, but spoke as if she knew what she was doing. "This time I used extra power. You should be fine."

"Are we going to New Ark again?" he asked.

The Fairy Godmother looked at him, perplexed. "New Ark? What do you mean, New Ark?" Suddenly it dawned on her. "Newark? I sent Cinderella to *Newark*?! "

The Prince overheard this. "Is there a problem?"

Trying not to sound panicky, though she did anyway, the Fairy Godmother insisted, "Yes, you must go and help Cinderella. I sent her to Newark, New Jersey!"

"Is that a place of danger? Risk? Peril?" he asked.

"'Yup, that about sums it up," said the Fairy Godmother.

"Then we must leave immediately!"

"Wait!" shouted the Fairy Godmother as she approached the Prince and looked him square in the eyes. "I need to tell you where you are to go to secure your safe return. Once you find Cinderella, the two of you get to New York City. It's in New York. You got that? *Newwww Yorrrrk*," she said, enunciating it slowly for him to understand. "There is a big forest area there – it's called Central Park. In a fortnight, be at 75th East and Central Park at midnight."

The Prince stared back at her with great intent and repeated back to her, "A fortnight. New York. 75th East and Central Park. Midnight. I will."

As the Prince opened the carriage door, about to get in, the Fairy Godmother pulled on his jacket.

"Wait, one more thing – you are very charming, and where you are going they treat people like you *very* special."

"I *am* special," he replied without even a hint of modesty.

The Fairy Godmother bit her tongue, not wanting to make a snide comment. "Right, but you're a little bit *too* special. They're not used to perfection. Don't be surprised if you're – hard to resist."

"I will take head," he assured her as he climbed into the carriage and closed the door.

The Fairy Godmother stood back and muttered, "Oh, I hope this all ends well," then she held up her wand and waved it twice.

The carriage slowly began to move. It got off to a bumpy start like the last time, but as it gained momentum down the path, it climbed up into the night sky and eventually disappeared.

The Fairy Godmother watched, and then let out another exhausted sigh. As she schlepped back into her cottage, she muttered, "I'm way too old for this," then stepped inside.

The early morning sun shone over the same open field where Cinderella first landed. It was empty with only the muffled sounds of traffic in the near distance when suddenly, the carriage carrying the Prince landed hard and bounced several times before it came to a complete stop.

The Prince opened the door and stepped out. He looked around, confused by this strange, desolate looking property. One of the coachmen climbed down and stood next to him.

"This is where we landed the last time. Cinderella went through those bushes and out onto the main road," he said.

"Show me," ordered the Prince.

"Nope. You're on your own," said the Coachman.

"I *command* you to show me," the Prince said with authority.

The Coachman looked at him with snide resignation. "What are you going to do? Throw me jail? I'm a *rat*," he said as he shook his head and got back on the carriage.

The Prince looked at him, confused, then cautiously walked toward the shrubbery and found his way through it. He stepped cautiously out on the gravel road next to the interstate highway. The traffic at that hour was evenly paced, yet heavy. The Prince was a bit frightened, yet enthralled by the action of it.

"Metal monsters!" he whispered to himself. "But there are people inside them." Then he realized, "Ah, they are coaches!"

He looked up and saw the sign for Newark. Filled with courageous anticipation, he stepped out closer to the road and held up his arm to flag down a car. Suddenly, several cars quickly pulled over, one behind the other. Unable to resist his magical charm, the drivers opened their doors, men and women alike, and called out in willing succession, "Need a lift?"

The Prince grinned as he made his way to the first car.

Twenty-Four

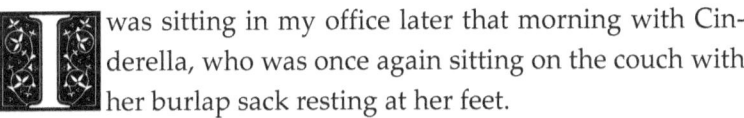 was sitting in my office later that morning with Cinderella, who was once again sitting on the couch with her burlap sack resting at her feet.

"All they do is make me clean up after them. 'Scrub the bathtub', 'Pick up my clothes', 'Don't forget to wash the dishes' – it's endless," Cinderella said, sounding overwhelmed and fed up.

"Sounds vaguely familiar," I said, giving her a knowing glance.

"What do you mean?"

"A mother with two selfish daughters? See the pattern?" I asked.

Cinderella stared at me, confused.

"You've recreated your past."

Cinderella thought for a long moment, and then exclaimed, "You're right! I'm doing it all over again!"

"Yes. It means you never worked out those years of frustration and anger in your youth. That part of your life is incomplete. You're angry."

Cinderella gave me a perplexed look. "Oh, but I'm not," she said sincerely.

"*That's* called denial," I told her.

Cinderella, again, took her time and thought about this. "How can I be in denial when..?" she began to ask, then stopped to think about this more. Finally, it registered. "Oh...I *am* angry!" she declared, and then quickly asked, "But what do I do about it?"

I leaned forward and said, "You voice it. You stand up for yourself."

Cinderella frowned. "But it's their home."

"Are you paying rent?" I asked.

Cinderella nodded.

"Well?" I asked.

She looked at me, not getting it.

I thought about this for a moment, wondering how to put it in terms she would best understand. "OK, when you were a child living with your stepmother and step sisters, you deserved to be there. It was your home, too. *You're* the one that allowed them to bully you, but now you can break that pattern by telling these women that you deserve better treatment."

Cinderella looked at me, doubtful.

I continued, "You've got to stop repressing that anger. It's just festering inside you. And it's most likely the underlying cause of your unhappiness. Anger turned inward causes depression."

"Depression," whispered Cinderella, struggling to understand.

"Yes. If you have all that anger inside of you, but you don't let it out, it stays in you. It then manifests into depression, rage...thoughts of killing someone even."

Cinderella looked at me. She was beginning to understand.

"So, saying how I feel – how I truly feel – will make me less angry?" Cinderella asked.

"It's a healthy release, yes. And will help you to see that you deserve better," I said.

Cinderella pondered this. "So far you've told me that I am suffering from post-traumatic stress, depression and now...anger?"

"So far...yes," I said.

"Is there more?" she asked.

"I don't know. This is only our second session."

"How many will I need?"

"As many as it takes," I answered.

Cinderella sat back, not pleased by this. I suppose she was used to a wave of a wand to fix any problem.

"But I have only a short time here," she said, discouraged.

"Well, I'll get you to understand a lot of your feelings, and give you some books and exercises to do before you go, so when you're back home...or the kingdom, rather...you can do some things for yourself, especially if you ever feel like you're falling back into certain patterns."

"But will I be cured?"

"Cinderella, therapy is not a quick fix, but you'll know enough to get you through whatever issues come up. Awareness is key."

"But awareness doesn't make me feel any better."

"You will," I assured her.

Suddenly, to my surprise, Cinderella quickly sat up, changed the subject and asked, "Would you do something with me? I need to buy new clothes, and I want you to come with me."

"You want me to go shopping with you?"

"Yes," she said. "Don't worry, I'm not in denial, I'm just

tired of wearing someone else's clothes and…well, it will make me feel better."

"Sounds like you're avoiding the therapy," I told her.

"Sounds like you don't understand that I need to do something nice for myself…for once," she answered back with a smile.

She had me there, plus I thought it might be interesting to step out with *the* Cinderella. It would give me more insight to who she was and how she interacted with others. I asked her if she had any money to buy clothes.

"I have a lot of cabbage," she said, smiling as reached for her burlap sack and opened it. She motioned for me to peer inside. My eyes grew wide at the site of all that cash. It was stuffed with hundred dollar bills.

"Wow. That is a lot of…cabbage," was all I could say.

"Will you take me shopping?" Cinderella asked, beaming with enthusiasm.

Her innocence and excitement was infectious. Yes, I told her, but it would have to be after several other appointments I had, so we agreed to meet at four o'clock later that afternoon. When she left my office, I found it a little hard to concentrate on much else except the fact that I would be going shopping with Cinderella!

Twenty-Five

he Prince stepped carefully out of a silver Toyota and onto a sidewalk in downtown Newark. He looked at the middle-aged woman inside. She had big, mall hair and was chewing gum, as a cow would chew cud. She looked at him as if she were undressing him with her eyes.

'Thank you again M'Lady. You've been most generous and kind," the Prince said to her.

"Ya got my numba?" the woman asked giving him a drooling stare.

The Prince rolled up his sleeve exposing a large phone number written in black pen on his arm. "Yes," he said to her. "You've made it quite prominent."

"I'll be expecting your cawl," she said, and then blew him an ugly air kiss.

The Prince smiled, politely bowed, and then closed the door. After the Toyota pulled away, the Prince started down the sidewalk. As he passed people, especially women, they turned their heads and paused to look at him. Yes, he was *that* charming.

Twenty-Six

❧ THERAPY WORKS! ❧

When Cinderella entered the condo after her session with me, she noticed immediately that Nikki and Angelina had made a mess in the living room with their purchases. Bags, boxes and clothes were strewn everywhere. Nikki came out of her room, followed by Angelina.

"Where have you been?" snapped Nikki, "I need this blouse ironed."

"And my new dress needs to be taken in some in the back," ordered Angelina.

They tossed the blouse and the dress at Cinderella. She barely caught them. Cinderella politely handed them back and said, "I'd like to help you both, but I have to be someplace at four o'clock."

Just then, Mrs. Mortadella entered holding a piece of apple pie that Cinderella had made. She wiped crumbs off her blouse letting them fall to the floor. Angelina rushed to their mother's side.

"Mom, she won't help us!"

148

Cinderella was taken aback by this untruth. "No, I said I would, but –" she began, until Mrs. Mortadella cut her off.

"Help the girls, Cinderella, and make sure you sweep the floor, too. There are crumbs everywhere."

The girls gave Cinderella snide, twisted smiles and flopped on the couch with their mother, kicking their feet up on the coffee table. Ever obedient, Cinderella bowed her head and began to go into the kitchen when she soon recalled what we had discussed just a short time earlier. Her confidence building, she turned around, walked back into the living room, stood in front of Angelina and Nikki and said definitely, "No! Do it yourselves! "

She tossed the blouse and the dress back at them, and then looked at Mrs. Mortadella. "And you can get a broom and sweep up your own crumbs! I said I have someplace to go and I'm going!"

They stared at Cinderella in stunned disbelief, as she spun around and headed to her bedroom closet. Cinderella entered and slammed the door behind her. Inside, she staggered for a moment, shaken by what just happened. She held her chest and sat on the futon, trembling.

After Cinderella took several deep breaths and let them out slowly, she realized her victory. A big, buoyant smile came across her face. She was getting "cured."

Twenty-Seven

❧ SHOPPING WITH A PRINCESS ❧

That afternoon, I took Cinderella to the mall in Short Hills, New Jersey, which is about twenty minutes outside of Newark by car. Cinderella, having never been in a mall, loved the ambiance, the shopping and especially the escalators.

"A moving staircase! How ingenious," she squealed was we rode on one the first time.

People gave us odd glances since, well, adults don't usually peer over the railings pointing at the crowds below shouting, "Wheeeeee," but I didn't care. She was having fun and that's all that mattered.

When I led her into Nordstrom's, a stylish department store, she was even more animated and excited as she told me about how she stood up to Mrs. Mortadella and the girls that morning.

"I said, 'sweep up your own crumbs!' Just like that! Can you believe it?" she asked, boasting.

I nodded. "Yes. You've told me four times already. I'm proud of you."

"I'm proud of myself! For the first time!" she beamed, then saw several evening gowns displayed on statuesque mannequins that quickly caused her to let out another squeal of delight. She rushed over to one very elegant gown and glided her hand along the material. I stepped up next to her.

"It's so beautiful. I want it," Cinderella said half asking, half insisting.

"Uh, I think you want to go with something more subtle. You're not in the castle," I reminded her, giving her a look of reason.

Cinderella's excitement faded a bit. "Yes. I suppose you're right," she said trying to be practical. Then she blushed and whispered, "But I do need some...under garments."

I smiled. She was behaving quite adorable, as she glanced around and saw the lingerie department nearby. As we walked together toward the racks of bras and underwear, I realized this wasn't my place, so I slowed down my steps as Cinderella quickened hers until she reached the racks and soon disappeared behind them. I decided, as most men would, to stay on the outskirts to give Cinderella her privacy. It's funny how a women's underwear department can make men feel like a degenerate if they are in any sort of close proximity to it.

Cinderella was taking quite some time with her shopping, and I was getting a little bored, so I lazily leaned on a rack of brassieres, although I wasn't paying attention at all to what I was leaning on. I wish I had because it wasn't more than a minute when suddenly I heard the sound of a woman's voice calling out my name. I turned and saw it was Helen, my estranged wife, and she was fast approaching in my direction.

Although she had that stern, determined look on her face, she still looked like the woman I married, and still loved. Walter looked more like her than me, which I was happy about. I could see the Helen I loved, and who once loved me, in his face forever.

"What on earth are you doing *here*, of all places?" she asked in a surprised yet bothered tone.

I stood at attention upon hearing her speak. It was a natural reaction since I was familiar with that tone and knew she wanted a straight answer. I guess I was so surprised to see her that I actually forgot where I was. It soon dawned on me once I turned and saw the rack of lacy bras of all sizes and colors surrounding me. This made me stumble awkwardly in my speech. I always stumbled with my words when I was caught off guard.

"Oh, I'm...I was...uh –" was all that came from my lips.

"Where are the papers? I still haven't gotten them," Helen barked, bored with my stammering.

"Right. Uh, to be honest, Helen...I, I haven't looked at them –"

Helen rolled her eyes, tired of me dragging my feet. "Boris, this is getting ridiculous. I've been more than patient with –"

Just then, Cinderella stepped out from between the racks of lingerie and approached me, holding up a pair of pink, silk panties with small roses embroidered on the front.

"Do you think these are too much? I want to treat myself to something special...to celebrate my performance today."

Suddenly I felt ill when I saw Helen staring at Cinderella in angry disbelief, then she looked at me.

I managed a weak smile and whispered to Cinderella, "Uh, yeah...those are fine. Get whatever you want."

Cinderella squealed with delight, "Oooh, this is so much fun!" Then she smiled at Helen sweetly and said, "hello" before she spun around and returned to her shopping.

Helen never kept her eyes off of Cinderella when she asked in a very displeased tone, "Who is *that*?"

I nervously responded, "Uh, no one. She's really no one."

Helen looked at me, unconvinced and suspicious. "Boris, what's going on?"

I took Helen's arm and led her away. Helen cranked her head back in Cinderella's direction as I did this.

"She's awfully young, Boris," Helen said, sounding bitter.

"No. Not really," I said clearing my throat, and then in a whisper added, "She's just a friend."

Helen stopped. "A friend? Then why are you whispering? And why didn't you introduce me?"

"You don't need to know each other," I said with weak authority.

"What are you hiding, Boris?"

I began to sweat. "I'm not – nothing. I'm not hiding anything," I said as I wiped my forehead with the palm of my hand.

"Then why are you sweating? You always sweat when you're nervous."

I let out a nervous chuckle. "I am? It's warm in here. You feel that?"

I was trying to distract Helen, but failing. Helen looked in the direction of Cinderella. "She's pretty…and *half* your age. I'm surprised."

I didn't like what she was implying, and became more straightforward. "Look," I told her, "I'm not – it's not what it looks like. There's no girl, er, woman – I'm not seeing anyone."

Helen looked at me, not buying it. Just then, Cinderella approached holding a shopping bag.

"I got the silk pair. I bought two."

She beamed again with delight. Helen shot her a competitive look. I quickly took Cinderella's arm and looked at Helen.

"I'll sign the papers and get them to you as soon as possible," I said as I led Cinderella quickly away. I glanced over my shoulder just once, enough to see Helen still watching me with a look of interest and suspicion on her face. Somehow I knew this was far from over with Helen.

Twenty-Eight

⋙ DOWNTOWN NEWARK ⋘

The Prince had been wandering for a long time, but wasn't tired. There was too much activity for him to take in to even notice that time had passed. He was startled, awed and, at times, disgusted by all that was around him. The obnoxious sounds of the cars, buses and trucks that passed on the street caused him to flinch in panic at first, but he soon got used to it.

Something else the Prince had never seen or heard before was an airplane. That is why he hit the pavement face down covering his ears, when one, flying out of nearby Newark International Airport, appeared in the sky overhead. The people passing were kind enough at least to step over him and continue on their way when he did this. A few stopped out of curiosity, probably to see if he was alive or dead. But once the plane flew away, he got up from the sidewalk and watched it fly away in amazement.

One of those times, after a plane flew overhead and the Prince "took cover" on the pavement, he stood, brushed the grime from his clothes and noticed a thin, homeless man wearing dirty jeans and an open dirty shirt sitting against one of the buildings. He was African-American with very dark skin. He smiled a toothless grin at the Prince. The Prince smiled back and approached him.

"Good day, Sir," said the Prince.

"How ya doing?" asked the homeless man.

"I'm afraid I am lost."

"I can see dat. I been watching you," said the homeless man. "You just get here? Where you from?"

"The kingdom," answered the Prince. "I just arrived, and am new to your city."

"You never been to Newark before?"

"I have not," replied the Prince.

"Ever been to Jersey before?" the homeless man asked.

"I have not," repeated the Prince.

The homeless man let out a chuckle. "You better watch yo 'self den. People will getcha if you don't watchit."

"Who are these people?" asked the Prince as he cautiously looked around.

"Anyone and everyone. What is yo name?"

"I am the Prince," answered the Prince, regally.

The homeless man looked at him, perplexed, then nodded his head vigorously and said, "OK, OK, dat's cool. You da prince. I'm Tyrone."

"Tyrone. A noble name," said the Prince as he extended his hand to Tyrone. Tyrone wiped his hand on his jeans then shook the Prince's hand, appreciating the respect.

"You all right, Prince. Yeah. You all right," said Tyrone, again nodding his head vigorously.

"Tell me, Tyrone…who is your king?"

Tyrone looked at the Prince, puzzled. "My king? Uh…well, I guess that would be Martin Luther."

"Ah," said the Prince. "And your queen?"

Tyrone thought it over and said, "Latifah. Queen Latifah."

"King Martin Luther and Queen Latifah," said the Prince, as if committing the names to memory.

"Oh, and we got a chairman of the board. His name is Frank. He was from Jersey," offered Tyrone.

"Frank. I see," said the Prince.

"And a boss, too. His name is Bruce," said Tyrone.

"I will have to meet all these royals while I'm here, but first I must find Cinderella."

Tyrone let out a chuckle that sounded more like a cough. "We all looking for her," he said giving the Prince a knowing wink.

"Are you?" asked the Prince, astonished.

"Every man dat I know is," said Tyrone.

The Prince looked around the street, paying close attention to the men. "That's good, Tyrone. Good to know every man is in this with me."

Tyrone, again, looked at the Prince, puzzled.

The Prince, seeing men moving in every direction, asked, "These men seem to have this area covered. Where shall I look for her? Lead me to the best region."

Tyrone scratched his head, confused. "Uh, I guess just take MLK all the way up toward the school. There should be a lot a' hot Cinderella's up thata way."

"MLK?" asked the Prince.

"Martin Luther King…straight that way," said Tyrone, pointing north.

"Ah, a street named after your king! That's magnificent!" said the Prince. "Many thanks to you, Tyrone. Perhaps we will meet again."

"See ya," said Tyrone, giving a wave as the Prince headed north on Martin Luther King Boulevard.

Twenty-Nine

➤ THE BURDEN OF HAPPINESS ❧

I was unlocking my front door as Cinderella stood there holding her bags filled with her new clothes. Before I opened it, I said to her, "My son, Walter, is seven. I think it's best if we just tell him you're a friend."

Cinderella looked puzzled by my request as I opened the door and we entered. I told her to set her bags down on the hall table. As she did this, she glanced around taking in the humble ambiance of my home. I could tell she liked it from her smile and how she said it reminded her of her own when she was a child.

Suddenly, from down the hallway, came Jessie, my reliable 15-year old babysitter. She was the daughter of one of my neighbors who got along well with my son. She was a sweet teenager who appreciated earning money and understood responsibility. In other words, she was a rarity.

"Hi, Dr. Berger," said Jessie with a smile, as she approached me. "Walter's in the living room. I gotta get back home. My mom's waiting, and I have some homework I gotta finish for tomorrow."

As I was pulling out several bills from my wallet, Jessie looked at Cinderella. A look of faint recognition came upon her face.

"Do I know you?" she asked.

Cinderella smiled warmly, but did not answer. After I handed Jessie her money and thanked her, she took one last look at Cinderella, still wondering how she knew her, then shrugged, said "good night" and walked out the door.

Just then, Walter, my bright, sensitive, dark-haired boy, rushed from down the hallway, shouting, "Daddy!"

As he was ready to leap into my arms, he came to an abrupt stop when he saw Cinderella and stared up at her in awe.

I smiled and began to say, "Walter, this is -"

"Cinderella!" Walter said without taking his eyes off her.

I looked at my son, stunned. Cinderella extended her hand and leaned down to Walter.

"Hello, Walter," she said in a very warm and friendly tone.

Walter shook her hand, still in awe. I was confused.

"Walter, why don't you go wash up. I've ordered Chinese food. It should be here any minute."

Walter reluctantly headed down the hall, but kept turning back to check out Cinderella. Before he turned a corner, he peered back one last time. Cinderella watched and gave him a little wave. Walter crinkled his nose with a grin then skipped away.

I looked at Cinderella, confused. "H-how did he know?"

Cinderella smiled. "Children with open hearts know. They always do."

"What about those children in the library?" I asked.

"I was not myself," answered Cinderella simply.

"And Jessie?"

Cinderella let out a sad sigh. "She's growing up and starting to forget. It happens." She then changed the subject. "Your home is lovely."

I was very perplexed by all this, but said nothing and gently led Cinderella toward the kitchen.

Hours later, after having enjoyed a delicious Chinese dinner with Cinderella and Walter at the kitchen table, Cinderella put on a mock fashion show. She was gleefully displaying the clothes that she had bought earlier that afternoon. She reached in one of her shopping bags, pulled out a lovely linen blouse and held it up to her chest.

"How about this one?" she asked us.

"I like it. It's pretty," said Walter, thrilled to have a princess ask for his opinion.

"I agree," I chimed in, smiling at her.

"You've said that about everything I've shown you so far," she said, half mocking me.

"That's because you're *pretty*," said Walter, with no fear in expressing himself.

"I agree," I said again.

Cinderella looked at me, then we all broke out into laughter. I glanced at the clock and noticed it was late. "The fashion show is over. It's time to say goodnight."

"Noooooo," whined Walter.

"Yesssss," I said, imitating him. "You have school tomorrow."

Walter got out of his chair, but before he left the room he looked at Cinderella and asked innocently, "Are you dad's new girlfriend?"

Cinderella giggled. I was mortified.

"*No*, Walter," I said, embarrassed.

"Oh. I thought that's why mom called today," he said.

"Your mother called?" I asked, surprised and alarmed.

"Yeah. Four times. She said she misses us."

Misses us? Was this some sort of joke? I sat there stunned and baffled. Cinderella looked at me, confused. Seeing the look on her face, I tried to explain.

"Walter's mother and I…we're sort of…separated."

Cinderella stared at me, pondering what I just said, and then asked, "And you help married people?"

Her question made me feel small, as if I were a fraud. I was too embarrassed to respond.

"Are you still married to the Prince?" Walter asked Cinderella, again, innocently.

"Yes," answered Cinderella with a sad smile.

"Why didn't he come with you?" Walter asked with a slight tilt of his head.

"He's not here because…uh, because…" Cinderella, uncomfortable, struggled to answer.

I couldn't help myself and whispered loud enough for her to hear, "And you're the symbol of happily ever after?"

Cinderella shot me a startled look, but Walter, oblivious to the meaning of our exchanges, broke the awkward moment by saying, "I wish I could meet the Prince."

"Maybe one day you will," Cinderella told him, although she knew it probably would never happen.

Before any more embarrassing questions or statements came out of Walter's mouth, I quickly stood. "Come on, Kiddo. Bedtime."

"Good night, Cinderella," Walter said with a wave, as we headed out of the room.

Cinderella gave him a little wave back. Walter left and I followed. But before I stepped out of the room, I looked at

Cinderella. We gave each other a knowing "relationships are tough" look, and then I smiled faintly and went to tuck in my son.

Thirty

❧ My Prince Has Come ❧

The Newark nightclub scene was just as you'd picture it to be -lots of dancing, music and sexual energy. In one such club, two attractive women were standing near a crowded bar.

Woman #1 shouted above the obnoxiously loud music to Woman #2, "I found him wandering around. He said he's on some quest, but whatever. Look at him, he's *gorgeous*."

As she collected drinks from the bartender, Woman #2 asked, "Which one is he?"

Woman #1 motioned with her head, "Over there –"

At the other corner of the bar, the Prince was standing by a wall. A small group of women had started to circle around him, vying for his attention. One young woman who was standing uncomfortably close to him shouted seductively, "So, what are you doing tonight?"

"I'm looking for Cinderella," the Prince shouted back.

All the women giggled and sighed at his romantic reply. At the bar, Woman #1 saw this and became angry and jealous.

Woman #2 warned, "You better get over there."

Woman #1 darted quickly through the crowd toward the Prince carrying a drink in each hand. She soon arrived, but was having a hard time getting through the small group of women. Frustrated, she started to "accidentally" spill the drinks on several of them, causing the women to step aside. When she got next to the Prince, she put the empty glasses down and possessively took his arm.

"Let's get out of here. I know another place we can go to," she shouted at the Prince.

"Will Cinderella be there?" he asked, hopeful.

"As soon as you get you've already found her," she said with a smile, hoping he'd get what she was saying. He didn't. She led him away anyway, to the dismay of the other women.

Throbbing dance music played at the next club that was much like the last one. This one was packed with wall-to-wall "Jersey Shore" types enjoying themselves. Nikki and Angelina were on the dance floor grinding to the music. Several sweaty, hot men with thick muscles grinded right along with them.

Across the room, the Prince was standing with Woman #1, and watching the people on the dance floor. Woman #1 was moving her body seductively as she kept her arm on the Prince. The Prince was overwhelmed by the atmosphere and loud music. So much so, that he repeatedly put his hands to his ears and winced.

Woman #1 shouted to him, "Wanna dance?"

The Prince looked at her, unable to hear.

She shouted again, louder, "Ya wanna dance?"

The Prince still couldn't hear. Frustrated, she pulled him to the middle of the dance floor and started to seductively grind on him. The Prince watched, somewhat amused. Several of the muscle boys eyed the action and honed in on Woman #1, gradually pushing the Prince out of the way. Woman #1 was too into the dance, and herself, to notice.

As the Prince stepped back, he accidentally bumped into Angelina who spun around angrily, ready to lie into the jerk. When she saw the Prince, her eyes widen and her body went limp.

The Prince, feeling bad for stepping into her, said politely, "Pardon me."

Angelina was barely able to speak. She managed to stutter, "N-no – no, my fault, totally."

The Prince bowed, then made his way off the dance floor. Angelina followed him like a lovesick puppy. When the Prince found an empty corner, he stopped and turned. To his surprise, there was Angelina looking up at him.

"Oh. Hello again," he said with a smile.

Angelina stared dreamily into his eyes and managed a love struck, "hi."

Just then, a muscle guy wearing a tank top with greased back hair, danced up to Angelina.

"Hey, Angie, I thought we was dancing –"

Without even turning to look, she shoved him away hard with one hand. He went barreling backwards.

"Y-you're gorgeous," she gushed to the Prince.

The Prince grinned and said with confidence, "So I've been told."

Angelina saw this as her "in" and asked, "Ya wanna hook up?"

The Prince looked at her, perplexed. "Hook up?" he asked just as Nikki approached them.

"Angie, why'd you shove Ronnie -" she began, then took one look at the Prince and forgot everything around her. "Wow! You're *hot*. You look like a prince."

"I am," said the Prince, matter-of-fact.

Nikki and Angelina looked up at him and asked in unison, "Really?"

The Prince nodded. Angelina asked, "What's your name?"

"Prince," said the Prince.

Both Nikki and Angelina laughed, thinking his response was funny and cute.

"That's a good one," said Nikki, being flirty with her smile.

Suddenly, several women began to approach, eyeing the Prince. Nikki and Angelina became territorial, and each took one of his arms. They gave each other a knowing glance, and quickly led him through the club. As they pulled him forward, they pushed people out of the way, shouting obnoxiously, "Coming through, outta the way...hot guy with us...coming through!"

Once outside, the three of them stood on the sidewalk. Nikki looked at the Prince and asked, "Whatda'ya wanna do now?"

Angelina chimed in, "We can go to *your* place."

"I have no lodgings. I've been walking all day, and..."

"You can come home with us!" Nikki quickly offered.

Angelina added, "Yeah. We have lots of room."

The Prince considered this. "Well, it *is* late –"

"Come on, we'll get a cab," said Angelina.

She then grabbed Nikki by the arm and they both stepped off the curb away from the Prince to hail a taxi.

"Remember, I saw him *first*," whispered Angelina, marking her territory.

"I'll take sloppy seconds of that *any* day," said Nikki as they both started waving their arms wildly to flag down a cab as fast as possible.

Thirty-One

❖ DO I KNOW YOU? ❖

ater, a taxi pulled up in front of The Castle Condos. The door opened and out stepped Cinderella carrying her shopping bags. She was tired from her long day as she entered the building, and climbed her way up the stairs. She balanced her bags in one hand as she put the key in the lock, opened the door and entered.

She went straight down the hall to her bedroom closet and tossed her bags on the small futon, then lazily headed for the kitchen for a glass of milk. As she passed the living room, she made a quick side glance and saw Nikki and Angelina sitting on the couch with the Prince. It didn't register at first what she saw, so she continued into the kitchen. She stopped suddenly.

Wait – was that the Prince? Cinderella quickly walked out of the kitchen and stood staring into the living room with a look of anger and surprise on her face.

"What are *you* doing here?" she addressed the Prince, still stunned to see him.

The Prince, just as startled, quickly rose from the couch. "My darling –"

Nikki and Angelina gave each other confused looks. *Darling?* They quickly stood up, too. The Prince made a fast dash toward Cinderella, but she put up her hand to stop him.

"How did you get here? How did you find me?" Cinderella asked, her anger growing, and feeling that urge once again to clobber him.

As the Prince was about to speak, Nikki stepped forward. "Wait, youse two know each other?" she asked in a tone demanding an answer.

Cinderella saw the jealousy in her eyes and thought fast.

"Uh, yes – we met long ago," she answered.

Angelina stepped up next to Nikki, and just as inquisitive, asked, "Did you two hook up?"

The Prince let out a frustrated sigh and whined to Angelina, "What *does* that *mean*?"

Cinderella answered quickly, "Yes. We hooked up, but a *very* long time ago." She, too, had no idea what it meant, but went along with it.

"So, he's still, like, your boyfriend?" asked Nikki shooting her a snide, jealous look.

"*Was*," said Cinderella. "He was my boyfriend."

"Yes," chimed in the Prince, "And soon we mar –"

Cinderella cut him off. "Soon we realized it wasn't working out, so I left."

The Prince looked at her, perplexed. Cinderella noticed and said to him, "Can I speak with you in the kitchen?"

The Prince replied obediently, "Yes, my love."

She tugged hard on his arm and led him away. Nikki and Angelina watched, and then looked at each other, confused and bothered.

Cinderella, livid, pulled the Prince into the kitchen and whispered in a stern tone, "How did you get here?"

"My darling, you weren't at the ball and I became worried that –"

"I told you I needed time away. *Alone*," Cinderella hissed.

"Yes, but I thought you might be in danger, so the Fairy God-mother helped me find you." He looked down at her modern clothes, and made a sour face. "Oh, my beloved, your dress is so –"

"Fitting for here," she said quickly. "As are yours," she said as she looked at his and made a sour face, too. "Though, I do prefer you in your – wait! We're not here to talk about clothes. You must leave at once," she said adamantly.

"But I've nowhere to go."

"I don't care. This is my break, and you shouldn't have come. And I don't want them to know we're married."

The Prince looked wounded by this. "But why?" he asked.

"They'll throw us both out! We'll say you were once my boyfriend, but we're no longer together."

The Prince tried to protest. "But my love –"

"You *must*," demanded Cinderella and wouldn't take no for an answer.

The Prince sadly gave in. "Yes, my princess."

"Now go out there and tell them you have to leave."

The Prince lowered his head. "Yes, my darling."

"And stop with the 'my darlings', 'my loves', 'my princess'," She said as she shook her head in frustration and walked out of the kitchen.

The Prince followed behind her. They both walked back in-to the living room where Nikki and Angelina were waiting.

"My friend has something he wants to say," announced Cinderella. She looked at the Prince. He looked back at her, hating this, but did what he was told.

"Yes. Sadly, I must go."

Nikki and Angelina rushed to his side.

"No, you can't," insisted Nikki.

Angelina added, "You don't have a place to stay." She glared at Cinderella. "Are you throwing him out?"

Cinderella tried to reason, "No – no, I –"

"You're *not* leaving," barked a determined Nikki to the Prince. "You can sleep in my room," she said slipping her arm into the Prince's.

Angelina slipped hers into the Prince's other arm. "He can sleep in mine!"

They began an angry tug of war, pulling the Prince in each direction until Cinderella could stand no more.

"No! He'll sleep on the couch!" she announced.

"I will?" the Prince asked, pleased.

Cinderella rolled her eyes and gave in. "Yes. But just for the night. You'll leave in the morning."

"I'll get some sheets for you," shouted Nikki, enthusiastically.

"I'll get the pillows," added Angelina, as they both rushed out of the room, ecstatic.

The Prince looked at Cinderella, "They seem to want me to stay," he said with a sheepish shrug.

"They want more than that from you, trust me," Cinderella said with a snide smirk.

The Prince moved closer to her. "My darling – how I've missed you." He went to put his arm around her, but she pushed him away.

"Stop it! Just go to sleep."

She walked out of the room annoyed. The Prince watched, rejected. Nikki and Angelina raced back in with blankets, sheets, pillows and comforter, and busily started to make up the couch for him. He feigned a smile, and then looked forlorn in the direction of where Cinderella went.

Thirty-Two

❖ HELEN AGAIN ❖

The next morning, I was getting Walter ready for school. I packed his lunch, and then started to put papers in my briefcase. Walter was tying his shoes when the doorbell rang. He shouted, "I'll get it," and dashed for the front door, taking off with one shoe still untied. I quickly followed him. When he opened it. Standing there was Helen.

"Mom!" Walter said with surprise and excitement.

He rushed to her and threw his arms around her waist. She hugged him back and closed her eyes, obviously missing the unconditional love from his small embrace.

"Helen," I said, although it sounded more like as a stunned question.

"Hello, Boris. I was in the neighborhood and thought I'd come by and take Walter to school. Is that all right?"

She looked at me as she used to. The look that said she still cared. This threw me off. I could only answer in the affirmative and motioned for her to enter. She smiled warmly at me, a smile that utterly confused me, so I quickly made my way back into the kitchen. Helen and Walter followed.

"I have Walter's lunch ready. I just have to find his back-pack," I told Helen, it being a typical morning for us. "Walter, go get your backpack," I said, and watched Walter skipped out of the room.

Where he was happy, I felt blind-sighted, though I didn't want Helen to notice.

"I'm kinda in a rush. I have an early appointment," I said as I finished shoving papers in my briefcase and grabbed Walter's lunch.

Helen stepped closer and took the lunch from my hand. "I can do that. Don't be late for your appointment," she said sweetly.

I looked at her, suspicious of her kindness. It was what I've always wished would happen, but still didn't trust her motives.

"Why are you in the neighborhood at this hour?" I asked.

Helen looked caught for just a second. "Uh...oh..." she fumbled, obviously searching for a lie to tell me. "I found a new dentist nearby. I need a crown put in, but I'm early. You know me, always early. If this isn't OK – "

"No, it's fine," I said. "I'm happy you're here. Walter's happy, too, of course."

Then there was an awkward silence. Helen glanced around.

"Everything looks the same," she said breaking the silence.

"Yeah. Nothing's change. Except, of course –"

We looked at each other. In that moment I missed her, but couldn't say it. Instead I blurted out, "I better get going."

I hurried, snapped shut my briefcase, and looked at Helen. She was still staring at me in some kind of "hoping to rekindle what we had" sort of way. At least I think that's what I saw. I wasn't even sure anymore. Thankfully, Walter came back in carrying his backpack.

"Kiddo, I'll see you after school," I said, then leaned in and kissed him on his head.

"Thanks, Helen. Good to see you," I added, it sounding like an afterthought, and headed for the door. Helen followed me.

"Boris –" she said, as she seductively walked up and gently straightened my tie.

I watched, hating that I liked the gesture, and then she kissed me on the cheek. I tried not to melt.

"Have a good day," she said with a smile.

When she walked slowly back into the kitchen, I stood there, touching the side of my face where Helen kissed it. I couldn't even remember the last time she did that. I wondered when that time was as I opened the front door and walked out.

Outside, I took several steps to my car and stopped. Again, I touched my face where Helen kissed me. I have to admit, an optimistic smile came to my face. I glanced back at the house, wanting terribly to forget about my appointments and be with my wife and son again, but I knew I couldn't, so I went and got into my car.

I learned from Walter later that, after I left, he was inside the kitchen tying his shoe while Helen looked around. More like snooping, I'm sure. She slid her hand across the counter top, looking nostalgic.

"So, Walter – how are you and Dad getting along?"

"OK. Are you coming back home?" he asked, hopeful.

"We'll see," she answered warmly.

"I miss you, Mom," Walter admitted in a shy way, although he meant it with all his heart.

Helen went over to him and got on one knee. "I miss you, too, Sweetie," she said as she hugged him tight.

Suddenly, she saw a woman's blouse under the kitchen table. She pulled away from Walter, crawled under the table and grabbed it. Crawling back out and standing, she looked at it and asked, "Walter…whose shirt is this?"

"Cinderella's."

"Cinderella?"

"Yeah. She's dad's friend. Cool, huh?" He looked at his mother expecting her to thoroughly agree.

"Her name is Cinderella?" asked Helen. Walter nodded his head, smiling. Helen saw this and asked gingerly, "And you like *her*?"

"Who doesn't?" asked Walter as if the question was stupid.

Helen checked out the size of the blouse. It made her eyes bulge. She muttered to herself, "Size two. I hate her."

Thirty-Three

✦ Annoyingly Charming ✦

That same morning, Nikki, Angelina and Mrs. Mortadella were at the table having breakfast with the Prince. He was wearing one of Nikki's t-shirts, though, being a girl's shirt, it was exceptionally tight on him. Across the front of it were the words, *I'm From Nork*.

Cinderella decided she'd rather be in the kitchen cooking than sit with any of them, and that is what she did. The Prince sat wedged between Nikki and Angelina who were fawning over him. Nikki grabbed a plate of pancakes that Cinderella had placed down just moments earlier and started to pierce a stack with her fork

"Here, have some more pancakes," she said as she slapped the stack on his plate.

Angelina, not to be out done, grabbed a plate of French toast and started doing the same.

"No, have some more French toast," she insisted as she held the plate to the Prince's face.

Struggling to be gracious, the Prince held up his hand. "No,

I've had enough. Thank you."

Just then, Cinderella entered the room. The Prince's eye brightened at the sight of her.

"It was a fine breakfast, my –"

He was about to say "my love," but caught himself and said with great emphasis, "*Friend*." He then added, "I had no idea what a fine chef you are."

Cinderella shot him a bothered look. "There's a lot about me you don't know," she said, trying to hold back her anger.

Angelina grabbed her napkin, brought it to the Prince's face and dabbed around his lips. "Ya got some sugar on your face."

Nikki, not to be beaten, jealously straightened his hair with her fingers. Cinderella rolled her eyes seeing this pathetic competition over her husband.

Mrs. Mortadella then spoke to her daughters in a passive/aggressive tone, "Girls, go clean your rooms since Cinderella's made it clear she's not gonna help us anymore."

Cinderella, offended, shot her a look that read, "I just cooked your breakfast, bitch" and stormed back into the kitchen. Nikki and Angelina grudgingly got up and left the room.

As soon as they were gone, Mrs. Mortadella seized the moment and moved seductively next to the Prince. "So, how long are you in town for?" she asked batting her eyelashes.

"A fortnight," replied the Prince.

"Oooh. You speak French. Love that," she said as she placed her hand on his thigh, close to his crotch, and gave it a squeeze.

At that moment, Cinderella walked back into the room. She saw Mrs. Mortadella's hand on the Prince's thigh and, in an abrupt tone, called out, "All right – time to go!"

She grabbed the Prince's hand and yanked him out of his chair. He stumbled as she pushed him out of the room.

"Get your things. You're coming with me," she demanded.

The Prince went in the living room to collect his jacket as Cinderella went in her bedroom closet to grab her burlap sack of money. Nikki and Angelina came out and saw the Prince preparing to go.

"You're leaving?" Nikki whined.

"I must. Thank you for your hospitality," he said, flashing her a perfect smile.

Just then, Cinderella came out holding the burlap sack, ready to go.

Angelina asked the Prince angrily, "Are you leaving because of *her*?"

Cinderella, ignoring her, said to the Prince, "Let's go."

The Prince feigned a smile at the girls and followed Cinderella out the door. The girls paced the room, angry and upset, and then Mrs. Mortadella entered. Nikki rushed to her side and wailed like a spoiled child, "Mom, she took him away!"

Angelina took a more bitter tone. "Let's kick her out."

"No! She's paying for everything. Plus, if we did that, we'll never see *him* again," said Mrs. Mortadella. She then added, "He's perfect for one of you."

Nikki chimed in, "Or both!"

Mrs. Mortadella and Angelina shot Nikki an odd look.

Nikki looked at them, surprised. "What? I can share."

Mrs. Mortadella stepped away from her daughters and began pacing the room herself contemplating the situation.

"We'll think of a way to get him away from her," she murmured. "We'll think of a way."

Thirty-Four

⇒ MARRIAGE IS NOT A FAIRY TALE ⇐

 was sitting comfortably at my desk, quietly review-ing a file, when suddenly Cinderella stormed into my office and announced dramatically, "He's here!"

Behind her stood Rachel, looking embarrassed and perturbed that Cinderella obviously ignored her request not to intrude on me. She gave me an, "I'm sorry" look, but I gave her a nod that it was OK, and waved her on to leave. Rachel shook her head, still annoyed, as she closed the door behind her.

"Who is here?" I asked Cinderella in a soft tone, hoping she'd lower her voice as well.

"The Prince. He followed me when I told him that this was *my* time to get away. This is *my* break! He never *listens*!"

The Prince was here? I thought, surprised, in Newark? I was just getting used to having Cinderella here, but now there were two of them? My thoughts began to race. What was he doing here? What does he look like? Will there be more like them to follow? Am I going mad? I stood and walked around my desk, interested for myself, yet also concerned for Cinderella.

"Where is he?" I asked.

"Right outside. Will you talk to him?" she asked exasperated.

I looked at the door. It was strange to know *the* Prince Charming was right behind it. I hesitated, and looked back at Cinderella. She looked at me, helpless. Putting all of my own thoughts aside, I said diplomatically, "I'll talk with you both together."

Cinderella let out a heavy, discouraged sigh. I recognized that sigh. I've heard it from previous patients. One partner wanting me to say all the things that they themselves couldn't, but this was therapy. It doesn't works that way.

"It's going to be all right," I said, as I patted her shoulder.

Cinderella looked at me with trusting eyes, and then went to the door. She opened it and called out in a pissed off tone, "Get in here."

I stood waiting for the Prince to enter. Cinderella and I both waited. She peered out, let out an annoyed huff and threw up her hands. Perplexed, I went and stuck my head out the door.

There he was, the Prince. He was very handsome and oozed charm, yet wearing the silliest t-shirt I think I'd ever seen, which was too tight for him. I also saw Rachel unable to control herself. She was shamelessly pressing herself against his chest and outlining the lettering on his shirt. In the two years that Rachel had been my secretary, I'd never seen her behave in this manner.

I let out a loud "ahem," but that only caught the attention of the Prince. He looked at me with friendly, inquisitive eyes and flashed a brief smile. Then he gently did his best to step away from Rachel, but she wouldn't let him.

"Rachel!" I said loudly. Rachel stopped and looked as if she was coming out of a trance. She straightened her skirt and stepped away from the Prince.

"Would you please come inside?" I asked the Prince. He nodded and approached the doorway.

He peered in at first, not knowing what to expect. When he saw Cinderella standing with her arms folded, fuming, he hesitated entering.

"Please, come in. Have a seat," I said as I stepped in first and carefully checked him. So, this was the famous Prince Charming. It was like meeting a rock star…but not.

"Interesting shirt you have on," I commented.

"Yes. However, I am not from Nork. I am from the kingdom."

"Well," I chuckled, "Nork is slang for Newark. That's how it sounds when people from here say it, hence –"

"Hence what?" asked the Prince.

I was taken aback a bit. He didn't get it?

"It's not important," I said, and then pointed to the couch. "Won't you have a seat?"

The Prince sat down slowly and cautiously. Cinderella sat next to him. I grabbed a note pad and pen from my desk and sat in the chair across from them. I couldn't help but stare out of curiosity, and then realized I was staring.

"OK – So, you understand that I'm a psychiatrist?" I asked the Prince.

The Prince replied in a stiff, royal manner, "Yes. Cinderella has told me of your profession. You counsel."

I nodded, and was about to speak when the Prince said with great conviction, "I do *not* have a problem."

Cinderella rolled her eyes. I saw this and asked, "You have something to say to that, Cinderella?"

"No," she replied flatly.

I looked at her, knowing she did, but didn't press it, and thought about how to proceed. I had a clueless Prince and an angry Princess in front of me. This was new, and I wanted to be sure I handled it very carefully.

"All right," I began, "Well, obviously Cinderella came here because she has a problem that needs addressing." I addressed the Prince. "And it's good that you're here to listen and maybe help." Then I addressed Cinderella. "I think where to start is to look at what is making you so unhappy."

Cinderella replied, "I don't know what that is."

"OK, then let's look at your life prior to meeting the Prince. Let's start from the beginning. Tell me...tell *us*...about your childhood."

"You know. You've read the stories," she said sounding bored.

"Yes, but I'd like to hear it from *you*. You said yourself the stories are inaccurate."

The Prince looked at Cinderella, then at me. "I don't know the stories," he said, perplexed.

I was dumbfounded. "You *don't*?" I asked.

The Prince looked at me deadpan and replied, "I don't read fairy tales. I live them."

"Oh," I said, having to think about that for a moment. "Then it's even more important that you hear this from Cinderella."

I looked at Cinderella and motioned for her to share with a slight wave of my hand toward the Prince. Cinderella was hesitant.

"It's OK. Go ahead," I encouraged her.

"Well...I was born to loving parents," Cinderella began. "My father adored me, as did my mother. She and I were very close. I loved her so." She fought back tears, then continued, "But then she died when I was nine, and that left my father and I so lonely and heartbroken.

I grabbed a tissue box and handed it to her. She took one then continued. "Then my father remarried my stepmother. She had two daughters from another marriage."

I interjected, "How was that for you? A new mother?"

"I didn't mind at first," Cinderella answered simply. "I saw it brought great joy to my father, and seeing him happy made me happy."

"Yes, but – how was it for *you*?" I clarified.

Cinderella struggled to remain polite. "It was...it was awful. No one could replace my mother. Certainly not that woman and those two –"

She stopped herself. She had never spoken a bad word about anyone and couldn't bring herself to do so now. I leaned forward and gently urged her to speak. "It's OK. Say what you really feel."

Without hesitation, Cinderella blurted out, "Those two selfish, haggard wenches!"

"Oh, my!" gasped the Prince having never heard Cinderella, or anyone for that matter, speak so harshly.

Cinderella held her hand to her lips, ashamed, and said, "I'm sorry."

I quickly defended her. "No, it's OK. It's how you feel. Get it out. Keep going."

Cinderella looked at me, about to shake her head no, but I nodded yes and said, "It's really OK."

Cinderella sighed, "Yes, they were...*are*...wretched girls of the worst sort. Spawned by the Queen of Hades herself!"

The Prince shifted in his seat, uncomfortable. Hearing his wife speak like this was unsettling. Cinderella continued.

"They put me in rags and made me cook and clean from morning till night, and berated me at every turn. They were mean and evil and cruel. Vile, despicable, foul, nasty, revolting, offensive, malicious –"

"OK. We got it. That's good. Good job," I said gently.

The Prince looked at Cinderella with sympathy. I noticed this and asked him, "How does it make you feel to hear this?"

"I did not know any of this," the Prince replied.

I shot Cinderella a confused look. "You've never shared this with him?"

"He lives in a perfect world. He would never understand," Cinderella said with a frustrated sigh.

The Prince took offense. "You've never given me the chance."

"You never *asked*," snapped Cinderella.

"That's because I thought everything was –"

"*Perfect*?" Cinderella shot back, then shook her head and let out a huff.

The Prince looked at me for help.

"OK, let's continue," I said. "Do you have any children?"

The Prince and Cinderella looked at me, confused by the question. I was confused that they were confused. There was an awkward silence, so I decided to change the subject.

"OK, tell me how the two of you met."

The Prince answered immediately. "At the ball."

Cinderella shot him an angry look. "No," she said, "We met at my house."

The Prince looked at her, perplexed.

"Remember? You stopped by for some water? You were parched from your long journey? I came out and drew water from the well?"

The Prince thought hard, trying to recall.

"The water...the *water*..." Cinderella repeated, her rage building.

Then it hit him. "Oh, yes! Yes, the water. I remember now."

"And what was your first impression of her?" I asked him.

The Prince thought again. Nothing was coming to him.

"You barely looked at me," Cinderella said sadly.

The Prince defended himself. "I had just returned from my long journey, and –"

"You would never look at a girl in rags. That's why. It's called being shallow," said Cinderella.

The Prince, trying to omit his guilt, stammered, "No, I – I was..."

Cinderella looked at me. "It wasn't until I was in a gown and looked like a princess that he took notice."

"OK, but I'm sure once he got to know you..." I began, and then looked at the Prince, hoping to save him. "Tell us what it was that made you want to marry Cinderella."

"She fit the slipper," he replied, matter-of-fact.

I winced. Cinderella went livid.

"I fit the slipper?! Did you just say that? I fit the *slipper*? So, you're saying our entire marriage is based on a shoe size?"

"Cinderella – " I began, hoping to calm her.

"That's so stupid...and ridiculous...and mindless...and shallow!" She then looked at me, exasperated, "See what I have to deal with?"

The Prince, feeling remorse, reached out to touch Cinderella. She shot him an icy stare, and hissed, "*Don't!*"

"Cinderella, perhaps you're being –" I began, but she quickly cut me off, too.

"No!" she shouted as she stood and turned to the Prince. "I regret the day the Fairy Godmother helped me go to your stupid ball. You're not a dream...you're a nightmare! My *worst* nightmare! I'm done!"

And with that, she charged toward the door, swung it open and stormed out. The Prince was stunned and embarrassed at first, then sat forward and stared at the door.

I sat back and said calmly, "What I suggest is that you learn more about where Cinderella *came* from, so you can be more understanding of where she's *coming* from."

The Prince continued to the stare at the door.

"She has been through a great deal, long before you met her, so it's important that you give her some time, and space, to find herself," I continued, but noticed that he wasn't listening. He kept staring at the door. "What are you doing?" I asked him.

"Waiting for Cinderella to return."

"Uh...she's not coming back."

"She will. Of this, I am sure," said the Prince.

I was now more worried for him then Cinderella. He was obviously in denial, as well as delusional, but that was to be expected given he was raised in a fantasy environment. I leaned forward and put it as gently as I could, "She isn't coming back...at least not today."

"But she always returns. Everyone *always* returns," he said as if my suggesting otherwise was the most absurd thing he'd ever heard.

"Where you are from, I'm sure that may be so, but not here. Cinderella will not be coming back to you...not today."

The Prince looked at me confused and wounded. He sat back contemplating this, then said sadly, "She said I am a nightmare."

"She was upset. People say things like that in the heat of the moment."

He considered this, and then said, "I should have asked her about her life before me."

"Yeah. That would have helped," I told him, "But don't be so hard on yourself. This can be worked out."

"Maybe I should go find her. She is my wife, and we

should work this out immediately," he said ready to rise from his seat.

"No. That's exactly what she *doesn't* want," I said, and motioned for him to remain seated. "Look, I get she's your wife, and you feel you have a certain amount of say in how she acts and behaves – maybe even thinks, but if you want this to work out you need to stop treating her like she's a possession. Marriage doesn't mean ownership. It means two people wanting to be together. She's never had the chance to figure out who she is – so allow her the time to do that."

The Prince thought about what I said then asked, "Do you think she loves me?"

I was taken aback by his question. Considering who he was, that he would show any lack of confidence. "I don't know," I answered. "Probably, or she wouldn't have married you. But right now she just needs to be by herself."

"What shall I do in the meantime?" he asked. "I haven't any lodgings or currency."

"Oh," I said, unsure what to do with this classic fairy tale figure. "Well, I suppose you can stay with me," I offered.

"You're most kind, sir," said the Prince in a stately manner.

"You can call me Boris," I told him.

"Boris it is!" he nearly shouted, flashing the whitest teeth I'd ever seen, and said it in such a manner that made me feel sworn in to his imaginary royal family.

"And what is your name?" I asked.

The Prince let out a chuckle. "You amuse me, Boris," he said as he stood.

How was I amusing him? I was confused. I stood and asked him his name again.

He grinned and said, "I am the Prince!"

"So, that's your *name*?"

"It always has been, and always will be," he said as he put his fists on his hips proudly, and flashed once again those pearly whites.

Suddenly, I began to have second thoughts about having offered him to stay with me.

Thirty-Five

☆ THE PICK-UP ☆

Cinderella stormed out the door of my office building and found Rodney conveniently parked in front waiting for her. She jerked the passenger door of his car open, got in and sat back in a huff.

"Something wrong?" Rodney asked.

"Drive," ordered Cinderella, staring ahead.

"OK," replied Rodney, unsure, as he started the car and slowly steered it away from the curb. They drove for a long while until Rodney gingerly asked, "I take it the session didn't go well?"

"The Prince is here," Cinderella fumed.

"The – what?" asked Rodney, surprised.

"The Prince. My husband. He's here."

Confused, Rodney pulled over and stopped the car. "He's *here*?"

"That's what I said," replied Cinderella, still angry.

"Wait, but…I mean, how…I mean…he's here? The Prince…your Prince…*the* Prince Charming…your…"

189

"Yes! Why are you acting so strange?"

"Well, it's not every day that –"

"He came to find me. He couldn't bear one minute without me."

"I can't blame him. You're so beautiful," said Rodney, doing his best to win her favor.

"It's not because of that," Cinderella said, dismissing his come-on. "He really *can't* be without me. It's so annoying. It's suffocating. I can't stand it!"

She let out a frustrated growl as she raised her fists and shook them. Then she began her tirade. "I told him I needed to get away. I need to be by myself for once. I need to figure out who I am. I can't do any of that with him in the way. Why doesn't he ever listen?!"

"Well – " began Rodney, ready to give his professional opinion.

"Everything has to be done *his* way. It's *his* castle, *his* parents, *his* kingdom…what's mine?"

Rodney was about to answer when Cinderella barked, "Nothing! I've got nothing!"

"That's not true," said Rodney.

Cinderella stared at him as if defying him to contradict her, yet wanting him to keep talking.

"I mean, your name alone –"

"Isn't mine. My name is Ella. The cinder part came from my stepmother."

"Oh," said Rodney, stumped.

"I may as well give up. This was all a big waste of time. I'm trapped forever in this life," Cinderella said, discouraged.

"No, no…it's no time for defeat. I'm gonna help you."

"How?"

"Well, first I need…proof," said Rodney, cautiously.

"Proof?"

"Yeah, to know that what you're saying is, you know…"

"Real?" asked Cinderella, growing annoyed.

"Yeah."

"Why does everyone need proof around here?" she lamented. "You don't see me asking everyone if they're real, do you?"

"Well, no, but…"

"Why can't people just *believe*?" Cinderella said, bothered.

"Not everyone is claiming to be Cinderella," said Rodney, thinking this would make her understand.

Cinderella glared at him. "Take me home."

"But I was only trying –" Rodney began, but Cinderella wasn't interested.

She folded her arms and made it clear by staring away from him. Rodney started his car and drove off. When they arrived back at The Castle Condos, Rodney pulled up in front and Cinderella quickly reached for the door handle.

"Wait," said Rodney. "Look, I do believe you, OK? It's just getting others to. That's the problem."

"I'm tired of having to convince everyone," Cinderella argued.

"I understand, but just give me proof and I'll do the rest," suggested Rodney.

Cinderella looked at him. It would be nice to finally not have anyone asking if she was real anymore, she thought. "Well, I do have one wish left."

"Great, we'll use that," said Rodney, happy to be getting somewhere.

"I don't know -" said Cinderella, hesitant.

"You don't have to do anything now. We'll think about it, but in the meantime…where is the Prince?"

"I left him at Dr. Berger's office. Why?" she asked suspiciously.

"I was thinking maybe we can go over there and see the Prince –"

"No!" snapped Cinderella. "He has nothing to do with this. I thought you were helping *me*."

"I am!" said Rodney, moving closer to her. "I just thought meeting him would…"

"I no longer feel comfortable about any of this. I don't trust you. I don't trust anyone," said Cinderella as she opened the door and stepped out.

As she was about to close the door, Rodney said, "Cinderella, I was only…"

"Good day, sir," she said and slammed the door shut.

Rodney, defeated, watched her go inside.

Thirty-Six

❧ BACK TO REALITY ❧

inderella entered the condo, aggravated and exhausted. Nikki and Angelina rushed to her and started berating her with questions.

"Where's the Prince?" asked Nikki.

"Yeah, whatd'ya do with him?" demanded Angelina.

Cinderella said nothing. She went in the kitchen to get a glass of water. They followed.

Nikki said in a snarky manner, "You treat him like crap."

Cinderella stood at the sink and drank her water, too tired to care what they were saying.

Angelina made a disgusted face and said, "Gawd only knows what he sees in you."

Nikki added, "All I know is once he's with a Jersey girl, he ain't ever going back!"

Angelina and Nikki then gave each other a "fist pump." Cinderella put the glass in the sink and walked out. They followed her.

"I know if he was *my* man, I'd treat him like a king," said

Angelina.

"Or a prince," said Nikki.

Angelina shot Nikki a stupid look.

"Same difference," Nikki said with a shrug as they both followed Cinderella down the hallway to her bedroom closet where she stopped.

"You know, we have way more to offer him than you do," bragged Angelina.

"Yeah, like looks," said Nikki.

"And brains," added Angelina.

"Right," agreed Nikki. "And these -" she said, as she and Angelina both proudly cupped and lifted their breasts with their hands at the same time.

"Whatd'ya have to say to that?" asked Angelina.

Cinderella remained silent as she walked into her bedroom closet and slammed the door in their faces. The girls "dropped" their breasts, looked at each other, insulted, and then went into the living room. Angelina flopped down on the couch. Nikki flopped down next to her.

"We can't let her get away with that," she said angrily.

"We can't let her get away with *him*," Angelina corrected her. "We can totally get him. We just gotta get some time alone with him," plotted Angelina.

"If only we knew where he was," Nikki sighed.

Angelina, getting an idea, sat up. "I got it! We'll follow her! You know they gotta be hanging out together. Then, the first chance he's alone, we'll *grab* him."

Nikki leapt from her seat. "We'll pull a robbery!"

Angelina stood up, too. "A total robbery!"

They smiled victoriously at each other, and then gave each other another "fist-pump."

Thirty-Seven

❧ FOLLOWING THE LEAD ❧

odney couldn't resist meeting the Prince, so after he was done with his afternoon appointments, he came to my office. When he got off the elevator, he walked cautiously toward my secretary, Rachel, who was at her desk "working hard" posting on Facebook.

"Hello, again," said Rodney, sounding a bit more professional with her than the first time.

"Hi," Rachel replied, taking her eyes off the computer screen momentarily.

"Is Dr. Berger in?"

"No, he's gone for the day," Rachel told him, then went back to staring at her computer.

"Thanks. I'll catch him at home."

As Rodney began to turn away, Rachel said, "He's not home...or won't be for a while. He went out to dinner."

"Oh, well, it's kind of urgent that I see him," Rodney told her.

"Call his cell phone," Rachel suggested in a blasé manner, engrossed in her Facebook page.

Rodney knew he couldn't. I would never have answered, but that didn't stop him from faking it. He pulled out his cell phone and pretended to call me. He made sure to speak loudly so Rachel would hear.

"Hey, Boris! Yeah, it's me. You know those important documents I showed you the other day? Yeah, those...well, I have someone interested, but I need to see you tonight before the deadline. I know...I know...and I usually wouldn't bother you this late, but you know how deadlines are."

Rodney paused for a moment, pretending that he was listening to my "response," then he said, "Right. Sure. Great, I'll meet you there. Thanks...I'll see you soon."

He got off his phone and thanked Rachel. She gave him a disinterested nod. Rodney then began to walk toward the elevators when he said aloud, "Oh, damn. I didn't get the address of the restaurant."

He pretended to call me back, and then pretended that I had turned off my phone. He walked back over to Rachel, looking at his watch, giving his performance that extra "effect" as if he was in a hurry.

"Do you have the address to the restaurant? Dr. Berger turned off his phone. It's in the Ironbound, right?"

Rodney took a wild guess where the restaurant was, though it wasn't so wild since that's where most of the better restaurants are in Newark.

Rachel punched several keys on her computer keyboard, found the address and gave it to Rodney. That was way too easy, Rodney thought. He smiled his swarthy smile and thanked her.

"You're the best," he said to Rachel with a wink, and happily made his way back to the elevator.

Thirty-Eight

➤ TO THE RESCUE ❧

I did take the Prince to a nice restaurant in the Iron-bound section of Newark. It was located on Ferry Street where they specialize in Portuguese influenced cuisine. The Prince seemed to enjoy the ambiance while the wait staff apparently enjoyed him. His charm was infectious, causing waitresses, and several waiters, to fawn over him. While at first it was an interesting phenomenon to watch, and even at the time, comical, but after a short while it became intrusive, and I had to ask the manager to rein in his employees.

The Prince was happy to have food in front of him. I ordered us both the Paella Marinera, which was paella marinated with saffron rice, lobster, shrimp, clams, scallops and New Zealand mussels. He was unfamiliar with our order and moved the food around on his plate with his fork, eyeing it suspiciously. As he did this, I did my best to explain Cinderella's need for some independence.

"She didn't have a very happy upbringing, you know."

The Prince didn't look up. He just continued to rearrange the food on his plate.

"From servant to princess. That's quite a leap. The pressures were not easy for her. It may appear on the outside as if she has it all, but...she doesn't."

The Prince pushed a small portion of rice to the side of his plate and put his face closer to see what seasoning was on the fish. I assumed he was listening, and kept talking.

"She, of course, was OK at first, but as time wore on, the happy veneer that she was showing began to tarnish...crumple even."

The Prince jabbed a scallop with his fork and held it up. "What is this?" he asked.

"A scallop," I told him. He looked at me, puzzled. "It's a bivalve mollusk. A type of shell fish."

"Ah," said the Prince, finally understanding, though he put it back on his plate and continued to dissect something else.

"Are you listening to me? Did you hear what I said about Cinderella?"

"I did. You say my wife has pressures from being a princess."

"Yes!" I said relieved to know that he wasn't as clueless as I had initially thought he was. "So, you understand that is why she is acting out?"

The Prince decided at that moment to take a bite of shrimp from his plate, but didn't know to remove the tail. I heard the crunch and was about to warn him not to swallow it, but he did and began to choke. Seeing his face turn red and his eyes watering, I quickly handed him my glass of water and he gulped it down. When he was finished, he let out little spastic coughs, tugged at his neck and said, "That felt sharp going down my throat."

I told him it was the tail of the shrimp, which should have

been removed. He wiped his eyes with his napkin and sat back. "I think perhaps I would much prefer some mutton."

"Mutton?" I asked.

"Yes. Surely you have mutton…hogget?" he asked.

"Yeah. I don't think they serve hogget here," I said. It never occurred to me what exactly the Prince ate.

"Well then, I will be happy to enjoy this bread with butter and wine," he said, as he happily dug his knife into the butter dish on the table and slapped it heavily onto a dinner roll.

He took a large bite and grinned as he chewed, then followed that with several gulps of wine. I liked that he was so easy going and accommodating.

"So, getting back to what I was saying, you do understand why Cinderella has been acting out?"

"What do you mean 'acting out'?"

"Her erratic behavior," I said, now back to believing this guy *was* clueless.

"She said she needed a break," he said casually.

"Then why are *you* here?"

"I was told she was in danger."

"So you raced over here to *save* her?" I asked, giving it a snide undertone.

"She's my wife," he said getting a tad defensive.

"OK…so you're here, you see she's all right, why don't you go back to the kingdom?"

"I must stay a fortnight until the carriage returns," he said. "That is how the spell was cast."

"Two weeks," I said to myself as I sat back in my seat. I wondered what to do with this guy for two weeks, and if that would be sufficient time to "fix" whatever it was that was making Cinderella unhappy. I had no choice, I thought. I would have to do all I could.

I sat forward and said, "Let's go back to my house. If you're still hungry, I'll make you something there – and you can meet my son, Walter."

"That sounds grand!" said the Prince as he pulled the napkin off from around his neck.

As soon as he did this, the wait staff charged at our table, one trying to beat the other, to get there first. They all shouted over one another saying things like, "Anything else I can get you?" and "How about dessert?"

The Prince was oblivious to all of this strange attention, of course, but not the other diners. They all stretched their necks to see who the "celebrity" was. The manager had to come over and break up the scene. The wait staff slunk disappointedly back to their other tables, but not before slyly dropping off napkins and strips of paper with their phone numbers written on them. The Prince looked at each one, perplexed.

"Why is everyone here so obsessed with numbers?" he asked me.

I didn't answer, but stood, took them from his hand and crumpled them as we headed out of the restaurant.

The Prince and I walked across the parking lot to my car. Unbeknownst to me, Rodney was slunk down in his car seat and peering at us over his dashboard. He had arrived earlier, parked and sat in his car waiting for us.

I don't think he heard me explaining to the Prince how he needed to be more mindful of Cinderella's feelings and what she had gone through before they met. The Prince told me that this was never anything he considered, and that, again, he knew nothing about whom she was prior to their meeting. That's when I explained that in Newark, as well as in most of the rest of the world, people got to know each other by talking and learning about each other before they got married. Then I suggested that it might be a good idea if he and Cinderella went on a date.

The Prince stopped. "A date? What is a date?" he asked.

"It's a special time set aside to spend with the one you're interested in romantically," I told him. "For instance, like going out to a restaurant for dinner."

"Cinderella and I eat at the castle," he said.

"OK, but, the point is to take her someplace nice and romantic...to sit across from each other and talk. Really get to know each other."

"Are there such places here?" he asked me.

"Yes," I assured him.

"Wonderful! Then I will write her a letter immediately requesting a date!" he nearly shouted.

"Or you can just call her," I suggested.

"You mean shout her name aloud and she will hear?"

"No, no," I said as I reached into my pocket and pulled out my iPhone. "This is a cell phone," I began, as the Prince leaned in closer to get a better look. "You can just scroll down like this and pull up the person's number. Then press it, and once they hear the ring on their phone, they pick up and then you're talking."

"Astounding!" said the Prince as he stared at the lights on my iPhone, mesmerized. I handed it to him and he held it close to his face, studying it.

"What is Cinderella's number? I will call her now," he said, excited.

"Oh. Well, I don't think she has a number."

The Prince looked at me, disappointed. "Then it is of no use," he said handing the iPhone back to me.

I took the phone. "No," I said. "I guess maybe you should write that letter. I'll make sure she gets it."

"Thank you," said the Prince as we headed toward my car.

I took the clicker out of my pocket and unlocked the doors to my car. I motioned for the Prince to go around to the passenger side and get in, which he did. I then opened my door.

As I was about to get in, two young men, muggers, both in their mid-twenties, rushed up to me out of the dark shadows. One slammed my door shut as the other pushed me up against the car. I was too startled and stunned to think about anything except for the knife that one of the muggers held close to my face. Both spoke fast, as if they were in a hurry, and demanded I give them my cell phone, all my money and credit cards. My hand shook as I began reaching into my pocket.

Suddenly, I heard a voice come from behind the two muggers. It was the Prince. I noticed he was holding my briefcase.

"Gentlemen!" he shouted.

The two muggers turned their heads. One of them was soon on the ground, since the Prince wielded the briefcase across his face. The one with the knife quickly let me go and went to stab the Prince. The Prince blocked it with my briefcase, causing a deep gash into its leather.

The Prince then swung the briefcase, as if it were a weapon, hard against the mugger's head. He fell to the ground, but it didn't knock him out. Then the Prince stood over them and said, "I wish you men toads!"

To my shock and surprise, suddenly, the young men instantly turned into two frogs on the pavement! They made "ribbit" sounds to each other, as I stared in disbelief.

"There!" the Prince said to me, "They will bother us no longer."

"Wait! You can't do that! Turn them back!" I insisted.

The Prince looked at me, confused. "But they are criminals. They meant to do you harm. This is their punishment."

"I get that, but you can't turn humans into frogs. They may be criminals, but they have family and friends and...never mind, just turn them back!"

The Prince gave me a serious look, then grinned and slapped his hand on my shoulder.

"You are a good man, Dr. Berger...a kind and compassionate one, as well. Yes, if it is your wish, then I will turn them back at once."

With that, the Prince picked up both frogs and tossed them several feet away. Actually, in close proximity to Rodney's car who was, by the way, watching all of this in utter disbelief.

"Hey!" I shouted.

"Better they be at a safe distance," he said.

He was right. I didn't think of that.

"I wish you toads to be turned back into men," he declared, and within a second, both frogs became the young men they were before.

The muggers were flat on their backs on the pavement. They both sat up in surprise. They looked at their bodies, then at each other, then at us, with shock and fear on their faces. The Prince approached and stood over them, as only a fairy tale prince would, and went into a righteous speech.

"Coward is the man who uses weapon and force against one who is without arsenal! Back to your kingdom, knaves, and tell all others like you to take heed before using evil on those who stand in justice!"

Both muggers swayed as they stood, giving each other confused looks, then ran off into the night. I have to admit, I was still shaken, but also impressed by the Prince and his actions. He came back over, stood next to me and asked if I was all right. I was. He then lifted my briefcase and looked at the jagged rip caused by the mugger's knife.

"I found this large piece of boxed leather in the backseat. It came in most handy until I remembered the Fairy Godmother gave me three wishes," he told me as he handed me my brief-case.

His cool demeanor after such a violent assault peaked my interest. "You really can't help yourself, can you?" I asked.

"What do you mean?"

"You saw I was in trouble and just jumped right in. I didn't even hear or see you. You just came out of nowhere, and you...rescued me."

"Yes. That's what I do," he said, matter-of-fact.

"Just as you rescued Cinderella."

"From what?" he asked.

I looked at the Prince. He had no idea what I was referring to. That's when it dawned on me that indeed, there was no "rescuing" in the Cinderella story at all, and that coming to someone's rescue was something just innately ingrained in him. It was something he instinctively did. He was never out to save or rescue Cinderella as the storybook let on, or was misinterpreted. I believed he truly did love her, and now it was just getting Cinderella to understand this fact. The Prince and I got into my car and I drove out of the parking lot, heading home.

Seeing my car leave, it was now safe for Rodney to sit up. He quickly rolled down his window for fresh air, then got out of his car and walked over to the spot where the frogs, I mean, men, were just minutes earlier. He stared at the spot, then out at the open intersection.

"My God," he said in shocked surprise. "It's true...it's all true."

Thirty-Nine

➤ BACK HOME ◆

Later, the Prince was in my home sitting comfortably on the couch with Walter. I sat across from them, enjoying watching the two of them interact. Walter was completely engrossed by what the Prince was telling him.

"So, I took my sword and held it close to the dragon's neck and said, 'By my troth, if ye should breathe fear into one other maiden, I shall come back and finish what here I've granted ye pause'."

Walter's eyes grew wide. "Whoa! And did he ever do it again?"

The Prince gave Walter a slight grin. "No. My sword gave him silence."

"And you saved the girl?" asked Walter.

The Prince let out a chuckle. "Of course. That is our responsibility as men – to be kind, and protect the fairer sex."

"Is that how you got Cinderella?" Walter eagerly asked.

The Prince gave a cocky grin. "No, it was my charm that won her heart."

Walter looked at him quizzically. "Are you and Cinderella gonna get a divorce?"

I sat up, embarrassed. "Walter, don't ask questions like that."

"But when Cinderella was talking, she sounded a lot like mom before mom left us."

Walter's words stung. As adults we tend to forget that kids hear and know everything…even down to the last detail. Plus, it was heartbreaking hearing the sadness in my son's voice.

"You are divorced?" the Prince asked me, looking concerned.

"Uh…no. Separated," I told him.

"But separated is like divorced, right, Dad?" Walter asked innocently.

There was suddenly an awkward silence. I tried to find a good, protective answer for my son, but I didn't have one. I felt on the spot. I could have explained the difference between separation and divorce, but I had done that already for him, in so many variations, but obviously my son was smart to know better. It was me who was trying not to face what was the truth.

The Prince looked crestfallen, but not for me, for himself.

"I don't wish the same to befall me and…" he began to say.

"Don't worry," I blurted out. "You and Cinderella will be fine."

As soon as those words left my mouth I regretted saying it. I knew it was a promise I shouldn't have made. And I think both Walter and the Prince knew that, too. Suddenly, there was a heavy weight in the room, so I quickly changed the subject.

"Walter, it's getting late. Time for bed."

"Can't I hear one more story?" Walter whined.

"I think the Prince may be tired, too," I answered, again, speaking for myself but diverting it to someone else.

Thankfully, the Prince's instinct to "save" the situation kicked in. "Nonsense, I love to talk about my adventures," he said giving me a wink. "But just one more," he said to Walter, "As I carry you to bed."

The Prince got off the couch and turned his back to Walter. Walter stood on the couch, hopped on his back and the Prince began yet another story.

"This is the tale about the time I met the evil ogre who was twenty times my size –"

Walter, happy to be riding on the back of such a legend exclaimed, "Wow!"

"Wow, indeed," said the Prince as he happily carried Walter out of the room.

I stood and smiled although it faded as soon as they were out of sight. Walter's words still disturbed me. I had tried everything to save him, as well as myself, from the pain of a divorce. I had been stalling on signing those divorce papers, but I couldn't let that continue. Divorce was inevitable for me and Helen and the sooner I faced that fact, the sooner Walter and I could get on with our lives. I told myself that perhaps *my* "wish" had been answered by finally letting Helen go. Something better would be in my future, and Walter's as well.

I never felt so defeated as that moment when I went over to the desk in the corner of the room and removed the divorce papers from its drawer. I opened them slowly and glanced over the legal wording one last time before finding where my signature went. I then took a pen and signed them.

Forty

✦ FICTION TO FACT ✦

arly the next morning, Rodney rushed into the offices of The Lancet, found Billy and shouted excitedly, "It's true! It's all true!"

Embarrassed when his co-workers looked up to see what all the commotion was about, Billy led Rodney into a private conference room and closed the door.

"What are you talking about?" he asked, as he craned his neck looking out of the glass windows to make sure his superiors weren't around. "You can't just barge in here acting like a maniac!"

"It's true...she's real! I saw it with my own eyes! Cinderella is real!"

Just then, a co-worker of Billy's entered the room. Rodney did his best to contain his excitement as the co-worker made a quick apology, grabbed a folder from the conference room table and left. Billy noticed that Rodney did not make a play to introduce himself to his co-worker, and began to wonder if maybe what Rodney was saying was true.

"That's the first time you didn't throw yourself at someone here," said Billy.

"Who? That guy?" asked Rodney, acting superior. "Forget him. Forget all of them. Peons! I'm going for the top brass now. Cinderella is real…the Prince is real!"

The Prince? There's a Prince? Billy was confused.

"I am going to prove it and be famous. And rich. Rich and famous!" Rodney exclaimed.

"Where's your proof?" asked Billy.

"I don't have it…yet. But I've figured out how to get it," said Rodney with an evil glean in his eyes.

"Who's this prince?" Billy asked.

"Prince Charming, who else?"

"Oh. So, now Prince Charming is here," chuckled Billy, believing now this was all a joke.

"Yes. I saw him turn two guys into toads," Rodney said as he paced the room. "Cinderella is pulling back from me, so I've devised a plan get her to trust me. She has one wish left, so I know she'll be able to make anything happen, make anything come true…and it will blow the minds of every doctor and scientist on the planet!"

"You saw the Prince turn two guys into toads?" asked Billy, bewildered.

"Yeah. It was amazing. Oh, to have that kind of power," Rodney said, envious. "I am going to prove to the board of the APA and the heads of the New England Journal of Medicine that *I've* discovered the key to a whole new universe. Fairy tales are real!" He shouted as he continued to pace the room in excitement.

"A-are you *sure* you want to stick your neck out like that? I mean, you're sounding kind of like you're losing your grip. No offense."

Rodney stopped pacing. "I've never had a firmer grip, Billy. And you're going to help me get Cinderella to give me her last wish."

Billy swallowed hard. He was no longer worried about Rodney's reputation or career, but now his own.

Forty-One

❧ DO YOU LOVE HIM? ❧

Cinderella sat on the couch in my office, still angry about the Prince's arrival and his cluelessness to her feelings. I, myself, was still feeling depressed after signing the divorce papers, but was able to set it aside and focus on Cinderella and her needs.

"He's never really done anything for me outside of buying me things," she complained. "He's never proven that he loves me."

"He married you," I responded.

"Without knowing who I really am."

"Who are you?" I asked. "Tell me."

Cinderella thought for a moment. "I'm a simple girl with no ambition who got lucky."

"Is that all?"

"I'm still working on it," she said with a sigh.

"The prince is, too," I told her.

"I can't go back to how it was," she said, shaking her head.

"You're that tired of perfection?"

"Yes," she answered.

I sat forward to make sure she was listening. "I'll let you in on a little secret...*nothing* is perfect, or you wouldn't be here. You'd be happy, as people expect you to be, but happiness is an illusion. What you want is peace of mind. The prince is working to understand you better. I know this because I've been spending time with him. You left him and the kingdom without trying to talk it out."

"I did, but he was too self-absorbed to listen!"

"He's listening now," I said as I reached over to my desk and grabbed the letter the Prince had written requesting a date. He had stayed up all night working on it. I handed it to Cinderella.

Cinderella took it. Looking puzzled, she opened it and read it to herself.

"What is a date?" she asked.

"It's when you go some place alone together — such as a quiet dinner," I told her. "I've made reservations for the two of you for tonight."

"No. I don't want to see him," she said, dismissive.

"Cinderella, I know you want me to help you figure out why you're unhappy, and I will, but pushing your husband away isn't going to make it easier. He may be annoying at times..."

She rolled her eyes as if to say "that's an understatement," but I continued. "He's noble and honest...and a gentleman. There aren't many of those left. If you stayed here in Newark long enough you'd see that. You need to give him another chance."

"What – to *rescue* me? He couldn't rescue a cat from a tree."

"Oh, you're so wrong about that," I said.

Cinderella huffed. I stood, went to my desk and got my briefcase.

"I went out with the Prince last night, and was attacked by two thugs."

Cinderella gasped. "Oh, no!"

"Oh, yes. Look what they did to my briefcase."

I turned the briefcase around to show her the large gash on the side of it. She gasped again.

"Are you all right?" she asked, genuinely concerned.

"I'm *alive* because your husband saved me."

Cinderella shot me a startled look.

"There were two of them, but he was fearless and scared them off. The Prince rescues people because he cares. He's not trying to show off, or thinks you're helpless. He does this any time he sees someone in danger or in trouble. Like he did with me. And, believe me, I am very grateful."

Cinderella gave a look that expressed she was proud of her husband, but that soon faded. She was brought back to the fact that she was unhappy and didn't want to have him interfering with why she was here, which I completely understood, but suggested that she go on the date anyway, at least to tell him what she needed and why. I knew this would be a good way for Cinderella to work on her regaining her "voice." That's when she told me the success she recently had in ignoring the two young women with whom she was living with.

"You're really getting the hang of not letting people run all over you, aren't you?" I asked.

"I am. If I only knew how to do it when I was younger, I would have told my stepmother that she could take her fireplace poker and shove it up her – "

"Yes," I quickly interrupted. "I see you really *are* getting the hang of it. That's good."

Cinderella looked down at the letter from the Prince again. "It's strange, some of this doesn't sound like him at all."

"What do you mean?"

"This part here – 'I would like to see you alone without any agenda, so we can just talk and just be ourselves.'"

"I helped him a little," I admitted.

"But the rest is all him," she said, and read the rest of it aloud. "'It is my sincerest request that you attend a date at my most humblest request to feast on words and supper.'"

I grimaced and said, "He's trying."

"I don't want to be 'saved'," she warned.

"He knows that," I assured her.

"And this doesn't mean I'm going to just fall into his arms and everything is going to be fixed," she insisted.

"You're just going to have a nice dinner and talk," I promised her.

Cinderella looked at me, suspiciously.

"You're a counselor of marriage, but it's not my marriage that I came here for. Perhaps the Fairy Godmother got the wrong doctor."

I was taken aback, hearing her doubt my ability. It actually kind of hurt.

"But I am willing to go on this 'date.' And after it is over, I want you to go back to helping me. Just *me*," she said, as if giving an order.

"I will," I told her.

With that Cinderella stood and headed for the door.

"I'll have a car pick you up and take you to the restaurant. I wish you both the best of luck."

Cinderella nodded and walked out. I closed the door and hung my head momentarily. She was right. I was a marriage counselor, and a bad one, I thought. My book was rejected because I couldn't even keep my own marriage afloat. Who was I to help the most famous couple in history save theirs? Maybe the Fairy Godmother *did* make a mistake. I wearily made my way back over to my desk and plopped down in my chair, when suddenly my door swung open and in walked Helen, smiling.

"Hello, Boris. You wanted to see me?"

"Helen. Yes. I have something for you," I said as I stood and opened my briefcase. I took out the divorce papers and handed them to her.

"Sorry it took me so long. I shouldn't have dragged it out like I did. It was unfair to you, and unfair to Walter. You were right, it's time to move on," I said with a heavy sigh.

Helen was stunned. This wasn't at all what she expected.

"Now you're free to marry Kyle," I said trying to sound happy for her.

Helen said flatly, "We broke up."

I shot her a look of surprise.

"Yes," she said. "To be honest, I think he was just a mid-life crisis. You know, like your Cinderella."

"My Cinderella?"

"I know all about her. Walter told me."

"H-he did?" I asked nervously.

"I'll admit, I was jealous when I saw you with such a pretty and *younger* girl. It made me realize we must have both been trying to recapture our youths."

"Oh, no. No. It's not like that at all," I said wanting to correct her.

"Please, Boris, I know I don't have to tell *you* about denial. Can't we just put all of this behind us and start again?"

"Y-you want to get back together?" I stammered. I couldn't believe what I was hearing.

Helen smiled. "More than anything."

My wish had come true. I couldn't believe it. I quickly went around my desk and hugged her. "Oh, Helen – I never stopped loving you,"

We kissed – a long, passionate kiss, and then we both giggled like teenagers when she pulled away.

"Kyle is out of my life forever. Now, you just have to end it with Cinderella."

"End it? No, I – I can't," I told her.

"But you just said you loved me. Obviously, she can't stay in the picture," Helen said, growing concerned.

"She's not in the picture. She's a patient," I clarified.

Helen stepped away, disgusted. "Dear God, Boris! You're dating a patient?"

"I'm not *dating* her," I said, insulted.

"Don't lie to me. I saw you two shopping, and found her blouse at the house."

I knew the look on my face was a guilty one. Yes, the blouse was at my house, but she had it all wrong. I began trying to explain the impossible. "Helen, I know you're not gonna believe this, but she really *is* Cinderella! She's here for therapy. She's going through an identity crisis and I'm helping her marriage with the Prince."

Helen looked at me, sad and worried. "Oh, no. This is tragic. It's genetic. Y-you're as unstable as your great grandfather.

"My great grandfather was *not* unstable. Everything he wrote and tried to tell the world was true. Cinderella and fairy tales *do* exist! I am no crazy, Helen."

"My God, Boris, do you really think I'm that stupid?"

"It's true," I said, my voice going a notch higher in octave. "The woman you saw me with *is* Cinderella!"

"Yeah, and I'm Sleeping Beauty," Helen said as shoved the papers in her purse and turned to leave.

I took a step toward her. "Wait! What about us?"

Helen glared at me. "Get rid of...whoever she is...then we'll talk," she said in a voice as cold as her eyes, and stormed out of the office.

I stood there, numb. How was I going to get Helen to understand that Cinderella was really Cinderella? It was impossible, but I didn't want to lose Helen. I also made a promise to Cinderella that I'd help her. Suddenly, my thoughts went to Walter. I couldn't put him through a divorce, and *I* sure as hell didn't want one. This was my chance to make this work for all of us. But Cinderella needed me.

Emotionally and professionally I was torn.

Forty-Two

⇝ DOWN THE SHORE ⇜

Once again, Cinderella left my office building and found Rodney parked out front waiting for her. He honked his car horn to catch her attention. She went over and peered in the open passenger side window.

"What do you want?" she asked, bothered to see him.

"I want to apologize for yesterday. I was only trying to help," he told her.

"I don't need your help," she said as she began to walk away.

"Wait!" shouted Rodney as he quickly got out of his car and followed her.

"I already have a doctor. I don't need another one," Cinderella told him as she kept walking.

"But I'm not trying to be your doctor. Just your friend."

"You're only using me to get to the prince," she said, coldly.

"What? Now, why would I do that?"

"Because he's a prince. He's rich and owns the entire kingdom."

"Whoa, whoa, whoa," said Rodney, grabbing her arm to stop her. "Are you really that blind?"

"No, I can see perfectly well, thank you," answered Cinderella, annoyed that he was holding her arm.

"No. *Blind* meaning you don't get it," he said.

"Get what?"

He let go of her arm. "In the kingdom, yeah, I'm sure the prince is "the man," but here? You're the one everybody knows, or wants to know. It's got nothing to do with money. You, you're magical, wonderful…fantastic!"

"I'm not," she said, sounding glum.

"Oh, but you *are*," Rodney corrected her, then, acting shy, said, "At least to me. I realized last night, as I was kicking myself for upsetting you, that since you've only been here a short time you haven't seen much of New Jersey. And I thought maybe if you weren't doing anything today, and forgave me for being such a horrible cad, I could give you a tour."

Cinderella began to soften. She loved his idea of getting away since she had been longing for something more fun to do than just going to therapy, but was still hesitant. "I don't know – "

"There are a lot of cool things to do," Rodney told her.

"Cool?" asked Cinderella.

"Uh, yeah. You know…" said Rodney.

"So, I will need a coat," said Cinderella, innocently.

Rodney laughed. "No, no, not that kind of cool. More like… stimulating, exciting."

Cinderella looked at him, confused.

"Look, you don't need a coat, just the need for a little freedom, to get away and have some fun."

Cinderella looked at him with distrustful eyes. He was sure he blew it, until she smiled and asked, "When do we leave?"

Rodney took Cinderella to Point Pleasant Beach, New Jersey, which is about an hour drive from Newark. Cinderella was amazed and delighted by the boardwalk that was filled with arcades, food, rides and gift shops. She laughed heartedly when he took her into a fun house that was filled with mirrors that contorted her image.

She especially loved going into the antique shops to look at the memorabilia and artifacts of times past. She wanted to bring something back for the Fairy Godmother, but couldn't decide what she would like, or didn't have, so she thought she'd simply tell her all about it upon her return.

Rodney then took Cinderella down to the water to watch the boats and described in detail of his time, as a young boy, when his father used to bring him there and they would go blue fishing. Cinderella loved hearing Rodney's stories of his youth since she understood the importance of childhood.

After some time on the boardwalk, they enjoyed a nice lunch at Red's Lobster Pot where Cinderella had a shrimp salad sandwich with fish and chips. This was where Rodney shared with her where he went to school to study to become a psychiatrist. He laid it on thick how important it was for him to "help" people, leaving out, of course, his destructive need for fame and power and willingness to do anything possible to achieve it. Cinderella listened intently, falling for every word hook, line and sinker. No pun, intended.

After lunch, they strolled again along the boardwalk, taking in the sea salt air, listening to the faint sound of Frank Sinatra singing a love song in the distance and picking at a large, pink head of cotton candy. Cinderella loved pulling out long strands of it, and shoving it into her mouth.

"We must have cotton candy in the kingdom. I will tell the King to make it so," said Cinderella as she licked the sugar off her fingertips.

As they continued on down the boardwalk, Rodney slipped his arm around Cinderella's waist and was relieved to find she didn't mind it at all. When something would catch Cinderella's eye and distract her, Rodney would glance over his shoulder as if looking for something. He found it with every glance. It was Billy who had been trailing them all day.

Billy made sure to keep a good, safe distance away so he would go unnoticed by Cinderella. This was something Billy didn't want to do, but he did it anyway only because he liked being liked by Rodney.

The day was growing long, and Cinderella was growing tired, although she enjoyed her time down the shore immensely. She was ready when Rodney suggested they return to Newark. He led her down an alley that was a "short cut" back to his car.

As they were cutting through, they passed a large dumpster where Billy jumped out from behind it to "mug" them. He nervously pointed at them what looked like a gun in his jacket pocket, and insisted that they give him all their money. Cinderella clung to Rodney in fear. Rodney pretended to be scared and nervous, but then went into a gallant hero act.

"Hurt me, but don't hurt her," he said fearlessly to Billy, as he pushed Cinderella behind him.

Billy thrust out his pocket that held the "gun," and, again demanded money. Rodney reached for his wallet, but instead took a swing at Billy. Billy ducked and took a swing in return at Rodney, all staged, of course for Cinderella's benefit. However, this backfired when, on instinct, Rodney ducked and Billy socked Cinderella hard in the face!

Cinderella nearly fell backward, but regained her balance and held her hand to her left cheek and eye. Billy, never having hit a girl before, began to freak out.

"Oh, my God...oh, my God...oh, my God," he repeated as he looked at Rodney in fear and remorse.

"I never meant to hit -" Billy began to say, but Rodney, in fear of him blowing their cover, quickly punched Billy square on the nose, causing him to fall backward and pass out.

Cinderella saw this, peering out with her good eye.

"Are you all right, Cinderella?" asked Rodney, coming to her "rescue."

"Y-yes," she answered, a bit dazed.

"Come on...let's get you out of here," he said taking her arm.

"But what about him?" Cinderella asked, pointing at Billy unconscious on the ground.

"Leave him. The police will pick him up," Rodney answered, as he carefully led Cinderella out of the alley to safety.

Rodney gently assisted Cinderella into the passenger seat of his car, then went around and got in himself. Cinderella held a small towel filled with Italian Ice to her now swollen eye and cheek that Rodney was able to get from a small stand that sold the frozen delight.

"Here," said Rodney, being gentle as he slowly pulled away the towel to look at Cinderella's eye. "You might have a shiner tomorrow, but at least you're safe."

"You were most brave to protect me like that," Cinderella told him, impressed.

"Oh, it was nothing," Rodney said with false modesty.

"Oh, but it wasn't! You might have gotten hurt...and badly," she insisted.

"I guess, but I'm more concerned about you right now."

He moved in closer to inspect the bruise on her cheek. Cinderella stared up at him as he did this. Rodney noticed. The urge to grab and kiss her was strong, but he didn't want to ruin his act that thus far was going perfectly.

"It's nice to be taken care of," she said, sweetly.

"It's my honor," Rodney said slowly getting pulled into her big, blue eyes, but he resisted. "You're Cinderella. It's not every day that a regular guy like me gets to save a princess."

"Then you *do* believe!" Cinderella exclaimed in glee.

"How can I not when you're the most beautiful woman I've ever seen," replied Rodney.

Cinderella blushed. Rodney smiled and sat back comfortable in his seat. "Let's get you home," he said, then started the car. As he drove out of the parking lot, he grinned. He has her now, he thought, and well on his way to super fame and fortune.

Forty-Three

odney pulled up in front of The Castle Condos and
parked.

"I had a lovely time, Rodney," Cinderella said,
pulling the now wet towel from the melted ice away from her
face.

Rodney reached over and gently touched her cheek. "So
did I," he said. "If you'd like, I can wait here while you go in
and change and we can have dinner."

Cinderella at first loved the idea, but then remembered her
obligations. "I can't. I have a date," she said, disappointed.

"A date?"

"Yes, with my husband," she said in a grumpy manner.

"Oh," said Rodney, as he uneasily shifted in his seat.
Damn. Just when the momentum was building, he thought.
Then, thinking fast, he said, "Well, maybe after? I'll be at the
Blue Mirror Lounge on Clinton Avenue. We can have a night-
cap."

"What's a nightcap?" asked Cinderella.

"A drink. An *after* date," Rodney explained with a smile.

Cinderella, liking the idea, smiled back. "All right."

As she turned to open the car door, Rodney took her other hand, brought it to his lips and kissed it.

"Thank you for a great afternoon," he said, pretending to be a gentleman.

Cinderella let out a soft giggle of appreciation, thanked him again and got out of the car. She stood on the sidewalk and waved as he drove off, then went into the building. She, again, did a little waltz as she headed for the stairs, still holding the wet towel to her face.

"A nightcap...a nightcap..." she sang softly to herself as she climbed the stairs and down the hall to the condo.

Once inside, she waltzed into her bedroom closet, closing the door behind her. She went straight to a small mirror that was on the wall and removed the towel away from her face. Seeing the swollen bruise on her once delicate cheek, she let out a loud gasp.

"Oh, dear," she said as she studied the strange contusion, something she'd never had before.

Cinderella went over to her things that were laid out on a small nightstand near the bed, in search for some make-up that might hide the bruise. She rummaged around and found a compact and her hairbrush. She then reached into her pockets, for maybe some lipstick, and slowly pulled out the letter from the Prince.

She made a disgusted face upon seeing it. The last thing she wanted to do that evening was to spend it with her husband.

Forty-Four

⇒ Do You Love Her? ⇐

Iarrived home earlier than usual since I wanted to help get the Prince ready for his date with Cinderella, though my mind was filled with worry about the ultimatum Helen gave me that afternoon. On the drive home I thought if perhaps this date went well, then maybe the Prince and Cinderella will want to return back to the kingdom together, and I could just easily tell Helen that "Cinderella" was out of my life for good.

I went up the stairs to my bedroom and found the Prince putting on one of my best suits. It was bluish/grey with a white shirt and a silver/blue tie, the kind that Cary Grant would wear, although he looked way more like Cary Grant than I ever could. It was a little snug for the Prince, but he still looked great in it.

"Wow. You look fantastic!" I said as I entered the room.

"Dr. Berger!" shouted the Prince. "I need to speak with you." He quickly reached for a book that was on the bed. It was a copy of the fairy tale, *Cinderella*. "I found this in Walter's bedroom and read it."

"Oh?" I asked, very interested in what he thought of it.

"This book...this story...this distorted tripe...it makes me out to be a mindless, pampered *nothing*!"

"I agree. There isn't much substance there," I said calmly.

"Substance? There is no *me* in it!" he said in dismay.

"Well, it is titled *Cinderella*, after all," I reminded him.

"Yes, but I am her husband. It tells nothing of who *I* am."

I sat on the edge of the bed and asked gently, "And, who are you?"

"I am the Prince!" he proclaimed.

"I know that, but who *are* you? What's inside?"

"Inside?"

"Yes, all anyone knows about you is that you're charming and perfect."

"Need there be more?" he asked.

I got his point, but he was missing mine. "Did you ever think that maybe being perfect is...oh, I don't know, a little...boring?"

"Boring?" he asked half insulted, half clueless.

I stood. "Have you ever done anything that was imperfect?" I asked.

"I don't know anything about that."

"Hmm," I muttered, and began to slowly pace the room, thinking. I stopped and said, "I have an idea. Come with me."

I led the Prince out of the bedroom and downstairs to my kitchen. I told him to take a seat at the table, which he did, and took a seat directly across from him.

"All right. Tonight you'll be having dinner with Cinderella. She expects you to be perfect. Why not surprise her and do something *not* perfect?"

He looked at me, puzzled.

Let's try it. Start with putting your elbows on the table."

The Prince chuckled, humored by such a simple task. "Dr. Berger, you *do* amuse me," he said, then leaned forward and bent his arms. As he began to lower them, with his elbows about ready to touch the table, he stopped. Pulling back, he let out a strained laugh, and then tried again with the same result. He shook his head, not ready for defeat and gave it another try. Again, as he came close to putting his elbows down, he stopped. Finally, he placed his hands on the table.

"Your elbows," I reminded him.

He gave me a disagreeing look then lifted his arms, bent his elbows and leaned forward, ready to put them once and for all on the table, but again put his hands on it.

"I can't. It's not right," he said, uneasy.

"You mean it's not *perfect*. It's really OK to put your elbows on the table. Granted, it's not proper etiquette, but it's not the end of the world. Give it another try."

And try he did. Again...and again...and again, growing frustrated with every attempt. He simply could not bring himself to do anything purposely imperfect. It was as if there was an invisible force stopping him. Finally, he placed his hands on the table and lowered his head in shame.

"It is of no use," he said. "I am too perfect. Disgustingly, unhappily perfect," he added as he slammed his fists down angrily."

"Whoa! It's OK. Really, it's OK," I assured him.

"It is *not* the letters O and K. It's perfection, and it's ruining my marriage!"

"Well, if you know that, then put your damn elbows on the table!" I shouted, using a bit of tough love.

He stared at me long and hard. A look that I thought meant he hated me, but I was wrong – he hated himself. He pushed his chair away from the table, stood and stormed out of the room, back toward the bedroom. I followed.

I found him standing in front of the mirror. His hands shook as he fumbled with his tie. I walked over and helped him.

"My hands, they're not working properly," he said with and uneasy chuckle.

"That's because you're nervous," I told him as I adjusted the tie. "All men get nervous when they are getting ready to spend time with the girl they love."

"But I have no reason to be," said the Prince, "She is my wife."

"She's also a lovely young woman, and maybe you're finally understanding that," I said.

The Prince looked at me, as if he got what I meant, then said, "I'm not used to being nervous. Does that count as imperfect?" he asked wanting desperately to be just that.

"No. It's only a feeling. And it's because you're in love. You do love her, don't you?"

The Prince looked at me with deep sincerity in his eyes. "Yes, very much so."

"Then let her know that," I suggested. "Sometimes that's all a woman needs to hear."

I stepped back after fixing his tie. He looked at himself for a long while in the mirror, then at me.

"Dr. Berger, I appreciate your help and will do my best to use these to win the affections of my beloved, Cinderella," he said lifting and pointing his elbows at me.

Oh, if only that's all it took, I thought to myself.

Forty-Five

✦ THE FIRST DATE ✦

When Cinderella arrived to the "date" that evening, the Prince was already there, waiting. He stood, alarmed to see the black and blue mark directly under her left eye and inquired about it.

"It's a bruise," said Cinderella, nonchalantly. "I was careless. There is no need to worry. I'm all right."

"B-but I've never seen such a thing, especially on a woman. My love, it's so...so..." he said as he began making his way around the table.

"Imperfect?" she asked as she took her seat, not waiting for him to help her with her chair.

"Yes, imperfect," the Prince said, bothered that she didn't wait and took his own seat. "But that's fine," he lied; trying to prove to Cinderella he'd changed.

Cinderella knew he was lying, and secretly liked that he had since she'd never known him to do such a thing. They ordered something safe and simple – chicken, and made small talk at first about the restaurant and me, as well as the strange custom of having a "date," but soon ran out of things to say. The Prince had the book on his mind. Cinderella had Rodney on hers.

"May I ask you a question?" asked the Prince.

Cinderella nodded.

"Do you think I have...substance?"

"You're a prince. That alone gives you substance, doesn't it?" Cinderella answered, bored.

"Yes, I suppose," said the Prince, unsatisfied.

He pretended to be interested in his meal, but wasn't hungry. They both sat in awkward silence.

"But what *does* give me substance besides royalty?" he asked.

Cinderella looked at him, suspicious of his question. "I've never known you to fish for compliments," she said.

"I'm not," said the Prince, mildly insulted. "I'm very serious. What gives me substance?"

"Why are you asking me this?"

The Prince looked down at his plate, not wanting to say, but knew he had to. "I read your book today."

"My book?"

"*Cinderella*...your story."

Cinderella glared at him. "That's *not* my story."

"Well, it's not *mine*, either. I come across as a one-dimensional dolt."

Cinderella was surprised that he was bothered, as well as being so honest. "Well, I come across as a two-dimensional fool who depends on wishes and the rescue of that one-dimensional dolt."

The Prince looked at her, unsure whether he should agree or be insulted. "We were never conferred on the writing of it," he said, incensed.

"I know!" Cinderella said in strong agreement.

The Prince was surprised and happy to be on the same "page" with his wife. "The part about me doing hardly a thing until you came along really got my goat," he said. "I'll have you know, I went on journeys before you entered my life. Protected damsels, fought battles, slayed dragons."

"And as for me, yes, I worked and slaved most of the time, but I also loved tending to my garden and flower beds. I also read a great deal. I'm quite knowledgeable, and cared for all animals, whom I adored."

They looked at each other, liking how they were, for the first time, organically learning about each other.

"The only part that was accurate was the description of my stepmother and stepsisters," said Cinderella. "Bitches," she muttered under her breath.

Hearing this made the Prince laughed. Cinderella laughed, too. Then they looked happily into each other's eyes. The Prince thought that right then would be the "perfect" moment to put his elbows on the table. He lifted his arms and leaned forward. As his elbows were about to touch down, he pulled away. He tried it again, but with the same results. After the third attempt, Cinderella asked what he was doing.

"I...well, I...nothing. Just stretching my arms," he answered, then placed his arms at his side, discouraged.

They both went back to their meal in silence, although neither was eating a thing. The Prince glanced over at Cinderella's plate.

"How is your dinner?"

"I'm not really hungry," she said looking glum.

The Prince put down his fork and said, "Nor am I. Shall we go for a walk?"

Cinderella nodded, happy to get out of the restaurant, and closer to ending this date.

Cinderella and the Prince walked along a path beside a large, serene lake in Branch Brook Park, one of the more beautiful parks in Newark. The moon was full.

"It's a lovely night," said the Prince in a soft voice. Then added, "For such a strange land."

"Yes," said Cinderella with a giggle.

The Prince smiled at her. "How I love your laugh. It's been some time since I've heard it."

Cinderella lowered her head and said, "I am sorry for that."

"No, it's my fault," said the Prince, as he lowered his head. "I've done little to amuse you lately."

Cinderella stopped. "I've never heard you say anything was your fault before," said Cinderella, stunned. "You're always so –"

"Perfect?" asked the Prince, looking back at her.

Cinderella nodded.

"Yes. Well, perhaps I am not," he humbly said.

Cinderella was taken aback. "And I've never heard you doubt yourself before."

The Prince lowered his head again. "You're seeing my weaknesses."

"You're vulnerable. I like it," Cinderella said sweetly.

"You do?" asked the Prince, liking her approval. Cinderella nodded.

The Prince then said, "And you were vulnerable the other day when you shared what happened to you as a child. I wanted to hold you so, and comfort you."

Cinderella looked surprised. "I thought you would be repulsed."

The Prince asked how she could think such a thing.

Cinderella sighed, "Because I'm not the perfection you thought you married."

The Prince looked downward. "Perhaps perfection is over-rated." He then looked at Cinderella. They both started to laugh.

"Some fairy tale heroes we are," she said between giggles.

"Indeed," said the Prince, chuckling. He looked at his wife, endearingly. "I love you, Cinderella."

Cinderella looked at him. "Do you?"

"Of course," he said, wondering why she would doubt him. She started to walk. He followed.

Cinderella then tried to explain her doubts. "But I come with so much...how did Dr. Berger put it? Baggage."

The Prince looked perplexed. "I did not see you pack before you left."

"I know!" exclaimed Cinderella, just as perplexed. "Their speech here is so strange. But I believe he means my past. It's unresolved. I-I don't know who I am."

"I do," said the Prince with confidence.

"No, you *don't*. It's not that easy," said Cinderella. "And I don't want you to love me because I fit some slipper. I need you to love me for me – the *real* me."

"But I do," swore the Prince as he went to put his arm around her.

She stopped him and said, "I need more time to think."

"And I need my princess," he said, getting a little annoyed.

"That might not be who I am," she said. "Let's be honest, I was just the last piece of furnishing you needed to complete the perfect picture in your castle, but you chose the wrong girl. I don't fit in there."

"Of course you do!"

"No…I don't," she said, finally expressing what she truly felt. "Everything in that castle is pristine and perfect whereas, I am flawed. Damaged goods. That morning you found me in the bathroom brushing my teeth I was really scrubbing the toilet to remove a stain. Why? Because I thought it made me feel like I was earning my keep, but the truth is *I* was that stain. And I was trying to remove what truly didn't belong."

"Oh, my darling – " said the Prince as he held out his arms again to embrace her.

"No! I don't want your sympathy or chivalry."

The Prince looked at her, confused. "But I want to help. I want to do whatever it is you need –"

"No! I don't want help. I don't want you to just magically make everything all right because, honestly, you can't."

The Prince was taken aback.

"That's right, you can't…at least not with me. I just want to be who I am, a common girl with a common life – who meets a man, not at a ball, but by bumping into him on the street. A man who takes me away and introduces me to things fun, such as cotton candy and Frank Sinatra."

"Who is this Frank Sinatra?" asked the Prince, jealous.

"A singer – from long ago. Don't get jealous, he's dead. He wasn't the one who took me out." Cinderella quickly regretted letting that slip.

"Someone else did?" asked the Prince growing more jealous.

"If you must know, yes. His name is Rodney, but that's not the point…"

"It most certainly is the point! My wife out with another man?"

"And what is wrong with that? Is it because I actually had fun, or because that doesn't fit the 'story'?"

"That book may have many inaccuracies, but it is true about us being *married*," barked the Prince.

"Well, maybe it's time we *change* the story," countered Cinderella.

The Prince stepped back, startled by the veiled threat in what she said. Cinderella had another quick moment of regret that soon passed. "I think I want to go home now," she said as she began to turn away.

"When you say "home," you mean *our* castle, don't you?"

"*Your* castle," said Cinderella corrected him.

The Prince began to ask, "What difference does it make where we live..."

But before he could finish his sentence, Cinderella bluntly shouted, "Don't you understand? I don't want to live *anywhere* with you anymore!"

The Prince stared at her, dumbfounded. Cinderella, too, was just as dumbfounded, then suddenly sad and remorseful because she knew she meant it. She quickly walked away...then ran. The Prince stood there unsure what to do. A long moment lapsed before he realized he was about to lose the most important thing in his life and went after her.

As he rushed out of the park, he saw Cinderella getting into the car I rented for her. It pulled away before he could get to it. Dejected, he watched its taillights disappear in the distance. He stood there, hurt until he remembered the slipper. The last time this happened, all he had to do was search for her slipper!

He began to search the ground, kicking leaves away in hopes it might be under them when suddenly, an old, white Camaro pulled up to the curb.

Nikki hung out of the passenger side and yelled, "Hey! Need a lift?"

The Prince looked up and was relieved to see Nikki and Angelina in the front seat.

"Hello! Yes," said the Prince as he made his way over to their car. "I've been stranded."

"Get in," Nikki said happily.

She swung opened the door and the Prince slid in next to her. They soon were all wedged together, tight and close, in the front seat. Before driving off, Nikki and Angelina gave each other happy, yet wicked, glances. They've just pulled off the ultimate "robbery."

Forty-Six

A car pulled up in front of my house and Cinderella jumped out. She ran to my door and, after several persistent knocks, I opened it. I was surprised to see her, but more shocked to see the horrible bruise on her face.

"Cinderella! What happened?"

"I don't know how I feel about the Prince any longer. I think it's over," she said exasperated.

"All right, all right," I said, trying to calm her, "But first, what happened to your face?"

Cinderella gently touched where the bruise was and, not wanting to tell me the truth, said, "Oh, I just had a little accident."

I looked at her suspiciously. "It wasn't the Prince…" I began to say, although I knew it would be impossible for him to ever harm her, but I needed to be sure.

"Oh, no. He would never do such a thing," she assured me.

I was relieved, and asked her to come inside. Thankfully, it was late and Walter was in bed asleep, so I knew we would have privacy. I led her into the living room where she took a seat in a chair. I sat on the couch and asked her to start from the beginning.

"We had our...*date*..." she began, "and it went fairly well, then we went for a walk. That's when everything just...fell apart. I am going to leave him," she said pointblank, and to my surprise.

"Hold on," I said, "let's talk this through. Are you sure this is something you really want to do?"

Cinderella thought for a moment, running her hands through her hair, then flopped back in her seat, confused. "Oh, I don't know! I do love him, but I can't be his princess...or anyone else's."

"You're tired of the label," I said, understanding.

"Yes! It's all too much. The weight of having to be this *thing* is smothering me. He grew up in it, so he knows nothing else, but I – "

"Won the lottery," I said, reminding her of what I told her on our first visit.

"No. I've won nothing. I've lost myself."

I was impressed by her insight, and nodded.

"It's always been about where, or how, I fit into the Prince's life, but now I don't know where he fits into mine."

"The first sign of real independence," I told her.

"I've always longed for independence, but why does it have to be at such a cost and so...frightening? I wish he hadn't followed me here. It's only complicated things."

"He followed you here because he loves you. I, personally, think it's a good thing that he did."

"Why?" she asked.

"Because if he hadn't, you would have gone back with all these new insights about yourself...changed, in other words...and he would still be the same, and this fall-out would happen over there. At least you're both here now to work this out."

"I don't want to work it out any longer. I've made up my mind," she said, determined.

I moved forward in my seat to get closer to her. "Have you really, Cinderella?"

"If you're trying to get me to stay with him because of that stupid story, and all those stupid people who believe in it -" she began.

"I don't care about the book, or the story...I care about *you*. This is about you and your happ –"

"My happiness?" she finished what I didn't. "My happily ever after?"

"Yes," I said. "With or without the prince, that's all I, and everyone else who knows you, or about you, truly wants."

She looked at me, wanting to believe me.

"What is it that you truly want that you *know* will make you happy?" I asked.

"Getting rid of that bloody book," she said.

"Well, that's a tall order, so how about...as a sugges-tion...rewriting it, and adding a new ending? One that works for you?"

Cinderella sat up. "Yes! I like that idea very much," she said smiling for the first time.

"Good!" I said, relieved. "Then tomorrow in our session, we will begin rewriting a better, happier ending for you. But I ask in the meantime not to make any haste decisions about the prince."

Cinderella frowned. It worried me to see how just the men-tion of his name changed her mood instantly.

I said gently, "Don't be so quick to toss away love, Cinder-ella. No matter what form it comes in."

Cinderella let out a heavy sigh. "I *do* love him. I'm just so tired."

"I understand," I said. I was also relieved to hear her say she still loved the prince. It was good to know there was some hope left there.

We both stood, and I led her to the door. I was glad to see the car I had hired was still waiting for her. After she stepped out onto the porch, she turned and managed a smile.

"Thank you, Dr. Berger."

I smiled back and said, "Ice -" pointing to the bruise on her face.

"Oh, yes. Italian Ice. I will get more," she said as she made her way off the porch and into the car.

I waved goodbye, then went back inside. When I turned off the living room light and headed up the stairs, I suddenly stopped and wondered, "Italian Ice?"

Forty-Seven

➤ PRINCE OF NEW JERSEY ◆

inderella was tired by the time she arrived back at the condo. She wearily headed for her bedroom closet when she heard peels of laughter coming from the living room. When she went to investigate, she stopped in the entrance with a horrified look on her face.

On the couch was Nikki and Angelina dressed in skimpy lingerie, drunk and falling over laughing. With them was the Prince wearing only boxers and another one of the girl's t-shirts. This one had the slogan, *"Yes, I drink Cawfee"* written on it. He, too, was drunk, with lipstick kisses on his face and neck. His back was to Cinderella as he told a story with slurred speech, trying to imitate their New Jersey accent.

"So, there I was in the freakin' ballroom, bored off my arse –"

Nikki and Angelina were laughing so hard they were crying. The Prince continued, "Then this ...*hot babe* appeared at the top of the stairs -"

The girls saw Cinderella standing in the doorway. They pointed at her, laughing. The Prince turned and saw her.

"Yo! Cinderella," he shouted.

Cinderella was shocked and appalled to see lipstick kisses all over his face. "W-what are you doing?"

"Telling the ladies a story," he said, followed by a loud burp.

Nikki and Angelina laughed. Cinderella, disgusted, turned to them and angrily asked, "What have you done to him?"

The Prince stepped in quickly, holding up his hands. "No, no. Don't attack them. They've done no harm. They are my...*wenches!*"

As the girls stood next to him, hanging suggestively on his arms and still laughing, Cinderella was trying to control her rage. She gritted her teeth at the Prince and said, "You need to leave now."

The Prince became irate. "No, I'm staying because they *want* me," implying that she didn't.

Cinderella looked hurt. "And what about me?"

The Prince gave her a hard look. "I don't know who...you...*are*. And you don't either."

Cinderella lowered her head, "You said you loved me."

The Prince snapped back, "And you said you loved *me*."

"Are you calling me a liar?" asked Cinderella, feeling betrayed.

The Prince snidely responded, "If the shoe fits."

Suddenly, he realized what he had said and repeated it to Nikki and Angelina. "If the shoe fits – get it?"

The girls started to laugh hysterically. So did the Prince. Cinderella was furious, but actually more heartbroken. Crushed, she ran to the front door and left the condo, slamming the door behind her.

Forty-Eight

❧ THE LAST WISH ❧

Rodney sat at the bar of the Blue Mirror Lounge eyeing and smiling at the attractive, and much younger, ladies as they stepped up to collect their drinks. A few smiled back, but most just rolled their eyes. I believe the term they use today for guys like him is "troll."

Rodney was bringing his drink to his lips when suddenly someone raced up behind him and shouted angrily, "I can't believe you left me on the pavement!"

Rodney turned and saw a very irate Billy. He was still dressed in his "mugger" clothes, which were now dirty from lying in an alley for several hours, and smelled like it, too.

"Shhh...keep it down," said Rodney, who looked around to make sure no one heard him, or was paying attention. He then turned on his sickening charm. "You were fantastic!" he said, grinning.

"I hit a girl!" said Billy, hating himself.

"If it's any consolation, she's not a girl, she's a...I'm not sure what she is...but don't worry about it."

"Whether she really is Cinderella or not, I hit her and that's just *wrong*," barked Billy.

"Hey, keep your voice down, and don't get all righteous on me. I have her right where I need her. Remember, this is going to be huge and you'll be with me every step of the way. You'll be famous, too," Rodney lied.

Billy liked that he was included, but still haunted by what he'd done. "But I never hit a woman, or anyone before. I feel so rotten."

"It's not a big deal," Rodney said with a wave of his hand.

Billy looked at him, disgusted.

"Sit down. I'll buy you a drink," offered Rodney, trying to appease his remorseful henchman.

Billy slowly sat on a stool. The bartender came over. "A ginger ale," said Billy, meekly.

Rodney let out a chuckle. "Ginger ale. You sure you don't want anything stronger?"

"No. I don't drink. I've never even been in a place…like this."

Rodney shook his head at the lack of experience the guy had, as Billy eyed a pretty girl who was at the other end of the bar. Rodney noticed.

"You like her?" he asked in his wolfish way.

Billy quickly diverted his eyes. "Well, she is pretty," he answered as he looked down at the bar, shy.

"Let me go and bring her over for you," Rodney said as he started to get off his stool.

"No! No!" Billy panicked, grabbing Rodney's arm.

Rodney let out a laugh. He enjoyed torturing this young innocent. He sat back down on his stool. "You gotta loosen up, kid," he said and took a swig from his glass.

Just then, the bartender came over with the ginger ale and

placed it in front of Billy with a napkin. Billy took a sip. Rodney watched, again shaking his head. Bored with his inexperienced partner, he turned around to check out more girls. Suddenly, he saw Cinderella enter the club. He quickly nudged Billy off his stool as he was taking another sip.

"You have to get out of here…now!" Rodney said, alarmed.

"W-what? Why?" asked Billy.

"She's here. Cinderella is here. She can't see you with me. Hide yourself. Go!" ordered Rodney.

Billy, without hesitation, quickly turned up the collar of his jacket and looked down at the floor. He started to move in one direction, then the other, not knowing which way to go.

"Go! That way!" said Rodney, pushing Billy away from him.

Billy hated being pushed, but did what he was told and swiftly moved to the other side of the club and into the shadows. Rodney watched, and was relieved once Billy was out of sight. He then gave a wave to Cinderella. She saw him and made her way over.

"So…you made it!" Rodney said, grinning.

"Yes. I made it," she said, disgruntled, as she sat on a stool.

"Can I get you a drink?" Rodney asked, taking the seat next to her.

"Yes. I'll have a Clarea of Water."

"A Clarea of…?" Rodney asked confused.

"I'm ready to prove anything you'd like," Cinderella said flatly, still hurt and angry with the prince.

Rodney looked at her surprised. "Y-you are?"

"Yes. It's time I rewrite my story. Just tell me what I need to do."

Rodney stared at her, dumbfounded, then grinned and shouted at the bartender, "Two Clarea's of Water"!

Forty-Nine

❧ The Promise ❧

The following afternoon, Rodney was in a meeting with several members from the board of the American Psychiatric Association. He was able to gather them together on short notice with the help of his publisher, the prestige of having a book on the New York Times bestseller's list and his excitement and promise that he had a "major discovery" to present to them.

Without going into specifics with them, he spoke enthusiastically about my great grandfather and the research he had been doing for his next book. He told them of this "mind-blowing" discovery he made, and asked for a special gathering of all the board members, as well as the top representatives from the New England Journal of Medicine.

To this, the several board members balked, but Rodney promised them it would be more than worth their time and consideration, and even went as far as to make the promise of stripping himself of his own license to practice as a doctor and therapist, along with his good standing with the APA, if what he had to show them was not one hundred percent to their satisfaction.

"You mean, you are willing to risk your entire career on this mystery of yours?" asked one of the skeptical board members.

"I am," said Rodney, looking brave and determined. "Gentlemen," he assured them, "I promise you, what you will witness is something that is going to change the world in a very, *very* big way."

The board members asked Rodney to leave the room momentarily as they conferred in private. After about fifteen minutes, they asked Rodney back into the room and agreed to bring the board together with a representative of the New England Journal of Medicine, but clearly warned him, "It better be good."

Fifty

❧ THE HANGOVER ❧

I was in my kitchen, having just sent Walter off to play with several of his friends, and pouring my second cup of coffee, when the Prince shuffled in looking like he had been swept through a hurricane. His hair was a floppy mess, his eyes bloodshot with dark circles under them and his skin pale. He took a seat at the table, put his face into his hands and let out a painful groan. When I offered him some coffee, he begged me not to yell.

"I'm not yelling," I said gently.

"I-I'm sorry. Everything seems exaggerated. I don't know what's happened to me. All I did last night was drink a little."

"I'd say a lot," I said as I poured him a cup of coffee, black, and put it in front of him. "Here, this will take the edge off a bit."

The Prince looked into the cup, and then slowly pushed it away.

"I take it the date didn't go very well?" I asked.

"It was terrible. I did everything you instructed. At first we laughed and were getting along splendidly, but then our talk

249

turned to that book and her mood changed. She hates the castle, and no longer wants to be married."

"I know. She stopped by last night and told me."

"She came here? Then is it true? Does she wish to leave me?" he asked, afraid of the answer.

"I don't think so, but it will take time for her to work things out. I'll speak with her."

"I am most grateful, especially after seeing me filled with spirits and cavorting with those two women," he said, ashamed.

"You were with two women?" I asked, surprised.

"Yes, the two women with whom she is staying with. Dreadful lasses, those two," said the Prince. "They filled me with endless ale."

"And Cinderella saw this?" I asked with a grimace.

"Yes. I was most decadent. I acted like such a fool."

"Well, at least you regret it. I'll be sure to let Cinderella know."

"Will you? I would be most indebted to you."

"I'll do the best I can. But why did you let it go so far?"

"Jealousy," replied the Prince.

"Jealousy? Of what?"

"She has been seeing someone else behind my back."

"Oh. Someone in the kingdom?" I asked interested to know who it was. Peter Pan, maybe?

"A man named Rodney."

"Rodney?!" I shouted, causing the Prince to wince in pain.

"Yes. He took her out yesterday – they spent the day together. She seemed most smitten with him. I want to wring his neck."

"So do I," I said, seething, as I quickly grabbed my briefcase.

"Do you know this scoundrel?" the Prince asked.

"All too well," I said through gritted teeth, as I began to leave the room. "That rotten, no good piece of – "

"Are you off to defend her honor for me?"

"I plan on doing much more than that," I assured him. "Take care of that hangover. I'll be back later."

I stormed out of the room and out of the house. Rodney had done a lot of despicable things in the past, but this one was the lowest – and most dangerous.

Fifty-One

✦ THE PUNCH ✦

It took me an hour with traffic to reach Rodney's office. He had just finished with a patient and had a few moments before his next. He said he was surprised to see me, but I knew it was an act. I wanted to punch that stupid grin right off his face.

"To what do I owe this visit?" he asked, closing his office door behind him.

"You know why I'm here," I said angrily.

"Let me guess – you've changed your mind, and you want to go in with me on the book about your great grandfather."

I glared at him. He chuckled as he took a seat and put his feet up on his desk, the cocky bastard.

"No," I said through gritted teeth.

"Then why the visit?" he asked.

I was stumped. I didn't want to mention Cinderella, admit that she was real, but I had to address what he was doing, otherwise there was no point in me being there. He waited for me to speak, then finally I said, "I found out you've been seeing one of my patients. It's unethical."

"Am I?" he asked, pretending to be shocked. "Which one?"

"You know which one," I said being careful.

"Let me think," he replied, enjoying this game. "Are you talking about…Cinderella?"

"That's not her real name, but yes," I said.

"Oh? And what's her real name? Gertrude?" he asked with a laugh.

Again, the urge to punch him was strong. It took everything in me to keep my cool. He kicked his feet off his desk and sat back. "She's an interesting girl, Boris. *Very* interesting."

"She's married and under my care. I think it would be in your best interest to leave her alone."

"My best interest? Are you sure you're not here to protect yours?"

I didn't respond.

"All right," he said, getting out of his chair. "Time to stop playing games. We both know who she is and what this is about. If you're going in with me on all of this, then let's talk terms."

"Terms? I'm not going in on anything with you. I want you to stop seeing my *married* patient."

"Oh, yeah, the Prince. Interesting magic he has, turning men into frogs."

I did my best to hide my surprise that he knew about the prince, but failed. Rodney was stupid, but not *that* stupid. He leaned excitedly forward, over his desk.

"I saw the whole thing in the parking lot. He's the real Prince Charming, and she really *is* Cinderella. And your great grandfather was telling the truth. It's all real, and *you* know it."

"What do you want, Rodney?" I asked, neither confirming, nor denying what he just said.

"To be the renowned doctor and psychiatrist that I'm meant to be."

"You're already well known. You have a best selling book out there," I reminded him.

"Oh, that," Rodney dismissed with the wave of his hand. "It isn't mine. I paid some lowly student to write it for me. I just came up with the title. Now this...*this* will be mine. The greatest discovery the world has ever known!"

"You're out of your mind. No one will believe you," I told him.

"They will if you go in on it with me, and it will validate your great grandfather. You won't have people laughing behind your back anymore. You'll have a bestseller, and you'll be more famous than Sigmund Freud!"

"You think I'm in it for the fame? I pity you, *and* your patients," I said still fighting the urge to slug him.

"We'll see how you feel once this is all out to the public," Rodney said, stepping around from his desk.

"You can't prove it," I told him.

"I can and I will. Just ask Cinderella. She's ready to "rewrite" the new ending of her story," he said. "And I'm going to be the one behind it."

"She won't listen to you," I insisted.

"She already has," he said, smiling. "We've made a deal. I'm going to give her what she wants...and she's going to give me what I want."

Not wanting to engage in this conversation any longer, I turned to leave. Rodney followed behind me.

"Oh, what you could have had, but you blew it just like your great grandfather."

That remark did it. I spun around and took a good swing at Rodney, but unfortunately, I missed. He ducked just in time and gave me a good, hard punch in the stomach. I doubled over in pain. Rodney laughed.

"You're so weak. When this is all over, you'll only be a footnote in *my* book...if I'm feeling generous."

He opened the door and, seeing his next patient in his waiting room, quickly turned on the sympathy act and told his secretary I was suffering from a stomach spasm and pawned me off to her as he escorted his next patient inside, closing the door behind him.

Fifty-Two

➤ A GRIMM BETRAYAL ❦

I paced my office waiting for Cinderella to arrive. I was doing my best to remain calm and professional, but after what happened with Rodney, it was tough. I couldn't believe she would do such a thing, and behind my back. Finally, Cinderella entered the room looking cheerful and refreshed. I stared at her suspiciously as she took her usual seat.

"Is there anything you want to tell me?" I asked her, trying not to sound like a scolding parent.

"No," she said as she gave me a look of concern. "But I do want to talk about how to put an end to that silly story, and get on with my life."

"I will work with you, Cinderella – in fact, I've *been* working with you, but there can't be any interferences."

"Interferences?"

"Yes. Other outside influences that might alter decisions you need to make."

"There are no outside influences," she said, looking down at her hands.

She had just lied to me. It was a blow that hurt me more than it should have. Perhaps I didn't make myself clear, I told myself, wanting to give her the benefit of the doubt.

"No others then the Prince and those you are staying with, correct?" I asked her.

She looked at me with suspicious eyes. All I wanted was the truth.

"No other doctors, or therapists?" I asked.

Her eyes widened. She was caught and she knew it. "There is another who is giving me counsel," she admitted.

I felt relieved. At least she was being honest. As long as the truth was still present between us, there was hope.

"Who?" I asked.

Cinderella hesitated. It was good to see that even she knew deep down what she was doing was wrong, or she wouldn't have stalled. Yet, she couldn't bring herself to tell me.

"I know about Rodney Klein," I said finally, and disappointed.

"Oh," said Cinderella, softly.

"Why?" I asked her.

"He's sweet to me...a friend," she said, fully convinced.

"He's not a friend, Cinderella, he is only using you."

"He is helping me. He has shown me only great kindness and respect," she argued.

"Respect?" I chuckled. "I don't even think he knows the meaning of the word."

"You are in competition with him," she said, as if she believed it. "I know all about that."

"Competition? Is that what he told you?" I responded, trying not to get angry.

"Yes, that you are jealous that he is a successful writer and you are not. And that you know very little about relationships since you have failed in yours."

That stung. Again, not because there was truth to the last part, but because Cinderella would give any credence to what Rodney told her, especially when my intentions were strictly to help her. Rodney *was* a master manipulator, and she was obviously under his spell. This was dangerous. I knew I had to be careful.

"It is true, Cinderella. I have failed in my relationship, but at least I've been in one. And as for Rodney's book..."

"A very popular book," she said, now sounding like him.

"Yes, popular, but I am not jealous."

"He told me you were ashamed of your great grandfather. Is this true?"

Now she was sounding like a scolding parent. If I was to have any hope in keeping her safe, and remaining on course, I had to stick with the truth.

"Yes," I said.

"Your own family? Even when I was with my stepmother and stepsisters, no matter how cruel and unjust they were to me, I never felt ashamed of them. They were family."

"My great grandfather," I began slowly and carefully, "experienced something that the world, our world, was not yet ready for. He took a great risk to his career and family when he published his book."

"But it was true!" she argued.

"Yes...I know that now, but – "

"But, you are not a risk taker like your great grandfather. What are you afraid of?"

That was a hard question, and one I really didn't know how to answer, but for her sake, I tried. "I'm afraid of..." I hesitated. "I'm afraid of..."

"Looking as bad as your great grandfather? Of being put away, or embarrassing your own family?"

"Well, yes. My son…"

"Believes in me," she said quickly.

"Yes, but when he gets older…when he enters adulthood…"

"Adulthood," she said with a frown. "A very sad thing, indeed."

"It's not sad," I protested.

"No, it's not sad…only filled with suspicion and gossip…internal strife, competition, lack of joy, wars…and fear. Lots of fear."

I stared at her, surprised. In such a short time she picked up on all of that? Then I quickly remembered what we were talking about.

"We're getting off subject here," I said abruptly. "Are you, or are you not, going to stop seeing Rodney Klein?"

"He is going to help me dispel all the lies that have been written about me, and finally tell the truth."

"How?" I asked.

"He is taking me to a special meeting with important people, so I can prove who I am with my final wish. Then he will write the most honest book about me, and it will make that special list."

"The New York Times list," I groaned.

"Yes," she said, proudly. "That is the one."

I sat down and rubbed my forehead anxiously. "Please don't tell me he's going in front of the APA," I asked, wearily.

"Yes, that's the one. And that is what he will be doing for me. What will *you* do instead?"

I looked at her. Was this a competition? Was she really asking me what I would do bigger, better or faster than Rodney to appease her? It was then I truly realized that Rodney had gotten his hooks very deep in her. I sat forward.

"Cinderella, you came to me for help at the recommendation of the Fairy Godmother –"

"She recommended your great grandfather...not you," she coldly reminded me.

That stung, too, but I didn't show it, and continued. "Cinderella, I am here to help you. Not exploit you for any personal gain. No good and honest therapist would do such a thing."

"I have only a short time here, and you told me therapy takes many sessions. I asked what happens when I am gone, and you said you would give me insights and exercises, as well as books, to take with me. But that's not enough. I need more."

"Then maybe we can ask the Fairy Godmother for more time," I suggested.

"How much more time?" she asked, impatiently.

"I...I don't know," I said. "But – "

"No. I am done with therapy, Dr. Berger, and I appreciate the help you have given me," she said as she began to get out of her chair.

"You can't leave! Cinderella, you're making a big mistake. Rodney is not your friend. He is only using you," I urged.

"And I am using *him*. I want only my story to be true – that will make me happy. And that is what I've come for."

"What about the Prince?"

She looked at me, hating that I mentioned his name. "That is over as well," she said, uncaringly, as she stood and headed for the door.

I leapt from my chair and reached the door before she did. "Rodney will destroy you, Cinderella. Allow me more time to work with you and help you find real happiness...not this dangerous quick fix. They don't exist in therapy. In fact, they don't exist at all!"

"As I didn't?" she asked. "You didn't even believe your own great grandfather. At least he was brave enough to *try* to enlighten others. You...you're *still* too afraid to even try. Goodbye."

Her words cut me to my core. All I could do was step aside when she reached for the door handle and walked out. I had never felt so beaten down and defeated as I had in that moment, for she was right about all of it.

Fifty-Three

After that unsuccessful session with Cinderella, I cancelled all of my afternoon appointments and went home. The conversation I had with her kept swimming around in my brain as I drove. My feelings were hurt, my ego crushed and my confidence shattered. Much of what she said was the truth and I felt at a complete loss of who I was, let alone what to do in regard to helping her with who she was.

I glumly entered my house, tossed my briefcase on a nearby chair and walked into the kitchen. It was there that I found the Prince still trying in vein to put his elbows on the table. How pathetic and useless he looked. It reminded me of how I felt. But I was wrong.

"Dr. Berger!" shouted the Prince. "I've been waiting for you...watch!"

I stood and watched as the Prince carefully lifted his bent arms and moved them over the kitchen table. As if about to skillfully make a chess move, he lowered them slowly onto the table and held them there.

"I did it! My elbows are on the table. I am officially imperfect!" He smiled that pearly white smile, so proud of himself.

"That's…that's great," I said weakly, then made my way over to the refrigerator, opened it and took out a beer. I leaned against the counter, tired.

The Prince stood. "I thought you would be more happy for me," he said.

"I am, but…it's too late," I said sadly.

"Too late? Did you not speak with Cinderella?" he asked growing concerned.

"Yes. She…she said she was going to go with Rodney and expose the truth. She also said she no longer wanted to be with you."

From the Prince's expression, you'd have thought I just told a child there was no Santa Claus. "But she is my wife…my beloved…" he said with staggered speech, then he looked at me and demanded, "You must do something!"

"I can't. I've tried."

"But are you not a doctor? You must help," he said desperately.

"I am a doctor, yes, but I can't make someone do something that they don't want to do."

"What are your powers?" he asked.

"I don't *have* powers," I said, angry that this was all falling on me. "I'm human. This world doesn't work that way."

The Prince stared at me with great disappointment and pity. It shamed me to the point where I had to divert my eyes to the floor. To look at him only made me feel more like a tremendous failure.

"I am going to lose my wife?" he asked, helplessly.

It was in that moment I knew exactly how he felt. I was where he was not too long ago when Helen walked out on me. It was soul crushing, and seeing him standing there in such anguish was nearly unbearable, but it raised in me that strange and sudden determination not to give up. I may have failed for myself, but I was not going to fail him...or Cinderella. I wracked my brain to figure out a way to help. Then suddenly, something came to me.

"Wait," I said, "How many wishes did the Fairy Godmother give you before you came here?"

"Three, of course," replied the Prince.

"You changed those two muggers into frogs, then back again, that was only two – you have one more, right?" I asked, hopeful.

"No. I was hungry when I first arrived here and wished for a mutton chop," he said, embarrassed and crestfallen.

"A mutton chop?" I asked, deflated.

"I had no currency and was hungry," he said defensively.

"It's OK...we'll figure out something else," I said as I put the still full beer bottle in the sink and began pacing the small space between the stove and the refrigerator.

"Perhaps I can find this Rodney and slay him with my sword," the Prince suggested.

As much as I personally loved the idea, I told him no. "That would be murder, and there are laws here against it," I added.

"What has this man done to her?" he asked bewildered.

"He poisoned her mind," I said, matter-of-fact.

"The evil scoundrel. Was it done with an apple or a thorny rose?" asked the Prince.

"No, he did it with manipulation...lies."

"Ah, he bewitched her. Then, what is his plan?"

"Plan?" I asked.

"Yes," said the Prince. "The wicked always have a plan."

"Oh. Well, he's taking her in front of the board of the American Psychiatric Association where he'll expose her to be real using her last wish."

The Prince looked at me as if I just told him a joke. "That's all?" he asked.

"That's *all*? He's going to expose her!"

"Then she is not in danger," he said, relieved.

"That includes *all* of you. You won't be safe anymore in your little fairy tale world. You don't understand, in this world they love to dissect and exploit, and ruin everything that's good and true. Just look at our landscapes, oceans and air."

"Yes, I've noticed. Why does that happen here?"

"Because of people like Rodney," I told him. "That's why you have to save her. She's in danger."

"But you've been telling me that she does not want to be saved."

"Then save yourself!" I urged him. "Rescue your kingdom."

"Will she want me back?"

"I don't know. I don't know what she wants anymore," I told him, throwing up my hands.

It was now the Prince who began to pace the small space in the kitchen. I'd never seen him in such deep thought before. His forehead creased, and his eyebrows aimed downward as he rubbed his chin. God only knows what was going on in that fairy tale mind of his. Suddenly, he stopped and looked at me with surprise.

"I know what she wants, *and* I will give it to her!" he exclaimed. "I will save her!"

"How?" I asked.

"No. I cannot tell you. This is for me alone to take care of. You must stay home, but tell me where this meeting will take place."

"I don't know, but I can find out," I said.

"Do," he demanded.

Although I was happy to see the Prince ready to take charge, I was also very worried. "Please don't do any-thing…well, stupid," I told him.

"My friend, you still have such little belief. All will be well, I give you my solemn promise."

With that, he put his hand on my shoulder and gave me the most confident smile I'd ever seen.

Fifty-Four

❧ A Very Real Fight ❧

staid home the next day, just as the Prince asked, and was happy to do so. I wouldn't have been able to bring myself to see what the Prince had planned to help Cinderella, nor did I want my presence to bring any further attraction to the circus Rodney had planned to create. I tried my damnedest to keep myself occupied with books, and even a little television, but my mind was solely on what was taking place at the meeting with Rodney Klein, Cinderella and the board of the American Psychiatric Association…

The board members, and two representatives from the New England Journal of Medicine, sat stoically behind a large table in a conference room located at Rutgers University. One of the members of the board was also a professor there and was able to secure the room for this. Rodney stood on the opposite side of the table doing his best to sound like a professional, but he sounded more like a two-bit hustler. He reminded them, again, after going into his spiel about making the "greatest discovery ever known to mankind," that he was ready to risk his entire career and reputation on it. The head of the board, already bored with his long-winded speech, told him to "just get on with it."

With that, Rodney opened the doors behind him and introduced the room to Cinderella, who entered with shy grace wearing a beautiful lavender dress.

The board looked at each other, perplexed. Rodney grinned after he pulled out a chair and helped Cinderella take a seat. He then went into yet another long-winded tale about my great grandfather's book (to which most of them, I'm sad to say, rolled their eyes), the research he had been working on, the story of the Fairy Godmother and how he came upon the one and only, Cinderella.

Thankfully, again, he left me completely out of it, making no mention of my name. Like the good, obedient girl she was, Cinderella remained silent and allowed Rodney to make his presentation.

The board members, tiring of what truly seemed like a huge waste of time, asked Rodney if this was some sort of joke.

"Gentlemen...and ladies...I assure you, this is no joke," he promised, and then asked Cinderella to stand. She did and, like a trained monkey, he moved her to the front of the table to speak.

"I am Cinderella," she began, "And I know you all need proof of that, so I'll need only a wish from one of you and I will make it come true."

The board members looked at each other. Some chuckled. Several found no humor in it at all. The two representatives from the New England Journal of Medicine began closing up their notebooks, preparing to leave. Seeing this, Rodney stepped forward.

"One wish from any of you, or all of you...and she'll make it come true. Trust me, this *is* real," he urged.

"Dr. Klein," began the Head of the Board, "We are all very busy people."

"I know that, and we can wrap this up in a matter of minutes if you'd only make one wish, a big one, and see what happens. I promise you, you will not regret it."

"Yes, please," Cinderella chimed in. "Let me prove to you that I really am Cinderella."

"Just one wish. Just one..." Rodney pleaded again, when suddenly the conference room doors swung open and in entered the Prince.

"Stop!" he shouted.

The board members looked baffled and surprised to see this stranger barge in wearing his royal uniform of dark blue with gold buttons and a sword at his side. At least he looked the part, most of them thought to themselves.

Cinderella spun around. "What are *you* doing here?" she hissed at the Prince.

Rodney grinned, happy to have the Prince there. In his mind, this was only more "proof" for the board. He stepped forward and announced, "Ladies and gentlemen...Prince Charming!"

Several of the board members laughed at the antics, but the others were not amused.

"Dr. Klein!" shouted the Head of the Board, his patience fast running out. "What is going on here?" he asked angrily.

"Please – just one wish. I guarantee it will be the most important wish you'll ever make," Rodney pleaded. "Cinderella, come here," he said, motioning her to stand next to him.

Cinderella was about to stand next to Rodney, but the Prince quickly stood between them.

"No, I can't let you do this," he said to Cinderella.

"This is none of your business," she growled.

"It is when my wife is about to ruin everything she's ever known."

"I don't care – this is for *me*," she snapped.

"Dr. Klein," said the Head of the Board, losing his patience. "You're wasting our time."

"But you *have* to believe," Rodney said to him, panicking.

"We've seen enough," said another annoyed board member, as he started to rise from his chair. Several others did the same.

"Sir," shouted the Prince to the board member, "I beg you to sit." He then turned to Rodney and said, "If this must be, then allow me to explain everything to them."

Cinderella, angrily, stepped forward, but the Prince pushed her back. "No, my love, if you are that tired of me and the kingdom, let it be me who puts an end to it all." He made a short bow to the board and began, "Your eminences, if I may..."

The board members looked at each other and sat back down. Rodney was momentarily relieved. The Prince looked at Cinderella hoping to get a smile, but she only glared at him.

"Good men and women," the Prince began, "I am the Prince, and I live in a kingdom...in a castle...with the King, my father, and the Queen, my mother. I am an only child."

"We all know the story...get to the point," Rodney whispered to the Prince.

"Yes, of course. Well..." said the Prince, clearing his throat. "It was on a day much like this one when..."

He glanced over at Cinderella again to make sure she was listening. She was – bitterly.

"When, once upon a time, I went on a long journey across the kingdom. I rode my best steed, Chase. We came upon a brook and I dismounted. As Chase drank from the brook…"

"Oh, geez," groaned Cinderella. She'd heard this before. She'd heard them *all* before.

"I watched a bird fly from a long branch on a tree to another, then back again," the Prince finished.

The board members looked at him, waiting to hear the rest of it, as did Rodney.

"And…?" asked the Head of the Board.

"And what?" asked the Prince.

"Then what happened?"

"I mounted Chase and returned home to the castle, of course," said the Prince, smiling.

Cinderella rolled her eyes. The board members looked at each other, confused.

"Dr. Klein…" the Head of the Board said, ready to give another warning.

"Good people, I will share with you another story," said the Prince. "Once upon a time, I went on a long journey across the kingdom. I rode my best steed, Chase. We came upon a meadow of…"

"Oh, for God's sake…shut up!" shouted Cinderella.

"But, my love…" the Prince began to say.

Unable to take this humiliation much longer, Cinderella tugged hare on the Prince's arm, then began to push him backwards, and continued to push until they both were out the door and in the hallway. She closed the doors behind them.

"My love…" said the Prince again, happy to be alone with her.

He reached out to put his arms around her, but she held up her hand fast.

"Don't! Don't you *dare* start that "my love" business. You've embarrassed me for the last time."

"No! It is *you* who has embarrassed *me!*" shouted the Prince.

Cinderella was taken aback.

"Yes. You have behaved abominably towards me and everyone else. And not just here, but back in the kingdom as well."

Cinderella's mouth dropped open in shock.

"Oh, you think I hadn't noticed? That I *am* just the one-dimensional dolt that appears in all the storybooks? I am much more than that, Cinderella, much more, but you've been too self-centered to notice."

"Self-centered? Me, self-centered?" she asked in angry surprise.

"Ha! You admit it," shouted the Prince.

Cinderella was beside herself with rage. "Why you arrogant, spoiled bastard," Cinderella growled. "How dare you!"

"How dare I? Easily, with such a wretched woman as my wife," snapped the Prince.

This infuriated Cinderella. "You're despicable," she hissed.

"And *you* are an adulteress," the Prince hissed back.

"I am no such thing! Rodney is a friend. I am not in love with him. How could you even *think* such a thing?" asked Cinderella as she turned her back to the Prince in a huff, with arms folded.

The Prince gave a look of relief knowing she didn't love Rodney, but quickly put on his angry face again once she turned back around.

"You were with those hideous sisters the other night in only your under garments. It should be *I* accusing you," Cinderella sneered.

"And it was the best time I've had in years," jeered the Prince, almost as if he was purposely egging her on. In fact, he was. Unbeknownst to Cinderella, he was giving her what she had asked for that morning in the castle at breakfast – an argument.

"Well, spending that day with Rodney was the best time I've had in my entire *life*," retorted Cinderella.

"Then maybe you should go and be with him. Stay here, for all I care. I'll go back to the kingdom where princesses like you come a dime a dozen," the Prince said, convincingly.

Cinderella was now fuming angry. " I don't know what I ever saw in you."

"My riches, of course," he chuckled.

"You think I...how *dare* you," she hissed again.

Then the Prince leaned against the wall in a cocky way, and said, "So, don't you think it's about time I got my money's worth?"

Cinderella let out a surprised and angry gasp, and then turned to leave. The Prince grabbed her roughly, pulled her to him and tried to kiss her. Cinderella wrestled to get away. When she did, she went for the conference room doors, turned and said, "Y-you cad! I wish you would just go away!" She then opened the door and ran inside as the door slowly closed behind her.

The Prince leaned his head sadly against it and whispered sincerely, "So be your wish. Goodbye, my love."

Back inside the conference room, Cinderella regained her composure. Rodney approached her and whispered, "I was able to talk them back into it...you do the rest."

Cinderella approached the table and said, "Forgive me for the disruption. We will not be disturbed any further."

"Young lady," began the Head of the Board, "We are all on very tight schedules. Though we are skeptical, to say the very least, we've decided on a 'wish.' Are you ready?"

"I am," said Cinderella, confidently.

"Even though it's against our better judgment, and a real question of our own sanity, the board and I discussed it and we "wish" to meet this Fairy Godmother of yours."

"You wish for me to make the Fairy Godmother appear here?" she asked.

"That's right," said the Head of the Board.

Rodney stood off to the side of the room, smiling. This was his big moment.

"I doubt she'll like this, but if that is what will convince you," Cinderella said, then took a step back and said softly, "I wish for the Fairy Godmother to appear."

The board and Rodney sat in anticipation. Nothing happened. Cinderella looked over at Rodney. He motioned for her to say it again. She did, louder.

"I wish for the Fairy Godmother to appear."

Again nothing. She looked at Rodney, confused. He looked just as confused and panicky. Just then, there was a knock at the door. Rodney let out a sigh of relief as he raced to the doors and announced, "Ladies and Gentlemen...the Fairy Godmother!"

He swung the doors open and in stepped Billy, carrying a satchel over his shoulder. Rodney, stunned, whispered, "What are *you* doing here?"

Billy walked angrily past him toward the table. He stood next to Cinderella. She gasped when she saw him.

"You! Y-you're the man who hit me!" she blurted out.

"I'm really sorry about that. Honest, I am...but *he* made me do it!" Billy shouted as he pointed at Rodney.

Rodney stepped forward, chuckling. "I've never seen this man before in my life."

"Oh, he knows me, all right," said Billy eyeing Rodney

with contempt. "And he's been pushing me around from day one. I never meant to hurt anyone…and I never meant to hit a girl. That's when I knew he really was no good and rotten."

"Dr. Klein?" the Head of the Board asked, now completely confused and tired of it all.

"I-I swear, I've never seen him before," stammered Rodney.

"Oh, no?" asked Billy. "Then maybe the board would like to see some proof…"

Billy opened his satchel, reached in and pulled out a large, handwritten manuscript. He placed it on the table and slid it toward the board members. One of them grabbed it and began to flip through it.

"That's the…rather, *my*…original manuscript of the book Rodney claimed he wrote, but he didn't. He paid me to write it."

"That's a lie!" Rodney declared nervously.

Billy reached again into his satchel, pulled out a letter and slid that across the table. "And that's my copyright infor-mation. I wrote it under a different title that Dr. Klein changed. *The Joy of Depression* – what a stupid title."

The board members looked at, then and passed around, the copyright letter, as well as Billy's manuscript. Rodney stood there, stunned and humiliated.

"I…I…" he stuttered.

"If this is true, Dr. Klein, you can be assured there will be an investigation, and you'll have to answer to all of it…as well as about all this Cinderella business," said the Head of the Board as he began to collect his things and stood.

The other members did as well, including the two repre-sentatives from the New England Journal of Medicine, who shook their heads as they filed out of the room.

"Make a wish," murmured one, feeling like a fool.

Rodney was sickened. He leaned against a chair with his head down.

"I'll see you in the morning about your resignation," said another member of the board as he passed Rodney.

Billy followed them out, giving Rodney a pathetic look as he did. Once they were all gone, Cinderella approached Rodney and asked, "Y-you lied to me. You promised you'd help me, and – " she began.

But before she could continue, Rodney looked at her with rage and yelled, "You've ruined me!" followed by a hard slap across her face.

Cinderella held her hand to her face, fighting tears and watched as Rodney stumbled out of the room leaving her alone where she sunk into a chair, hung her head and began to cry.

Fifty-Five

✦ THE REFUSAL ✦

I was home with Walter and Helen that evening. Earlier in the afternoon, to my great surprise, Helen phoned and asked if she could come over and make dinner for us. Of course I said yes. It had been so long since I've had one of her home cooked meals, and it was a way for the three of us to feel like a family again.

Plus, it took my mind off of Cinderella with the APA. As we were just about to sit down to eat, the doorbell rang. I excused myself to answer it. When I opened the door I was surprised to see Cinderella standing there, looking horribly lost and alone.

"Cinderella!"

"Oh, Dr. Berger…it was horrible. All of it. You were right, Rodney is evil and…and I was such a fool. Such a fool." She looked down at the ground, ashamed.

"The Prince…where is he?" I asked.

"I don't know," she said with little concern, which bothered me. "Everything is ruined."

"Did they believe you?" I asked.

"No. I failed. It all was just...so terrible," she said as she touched her face where Rodney slapped her and began to weep.

I wanted to put my arm around her, but I was still hurt and angry how we left it the last time we spoke. She got what she deserved, I thought, but my compassion was at battle with me. Also, I hated that I had to ask about the Prince, whom she gave little care about. It bothered me that she was more concerned about herself.

"May I come in?" she asked between sniffles.

I hesitated. I wasn't keen on giving her refuge, more importantly I couldn't let Helen see her, so I stammered as I lied, speaking in a low voice so no one would hear as I stepped out on the porch, closing the door behind me.

"Uh – it's kind of late, and Walter just went to bed, so –"

"Oh. Of course," she said. "I need your help, Dr. Berger. I've realized I made a big mess of things."

"Yes, you have," I said.

She shot me a look indicating that she knew I wasn't happy with her. She stepped forward and asked again as if testing me. "Please let me come inside so we can talk. I will be quiet as not to wake Walter."

I gently blocked her and said, "No, Cinderella."

She looked at me, stunned and confused. I saw this, and it only made it that much harder.

"My wife came to see me today and I have a real chance with her."

Cinderella's face brightened. "Oh, Dr. Berger, that's wonderful...but what does this have to do with –"

"She saw you when we were shopping, and you left one of your blouses here. She thinks we're –"

I looked at her hoping she'd catch on. Cinderella, getting it, exclaimed, "Oh, but we're not!"

"Right, but she doesn't believe me. The reason she left in the first place was because – well, she said I have too high of an ideal about love and relationships. I'm unrealistic."

"You're a dreamer," Cinderella said sweetly, as she sniffled.

I smiled, appreciating her observation. "You know," I began, "I'm able to sit with patients who are lost and unhappy because I believe in that better tomorrow, that silver lining. That –"

"Happily ever after," said Cinderella, softly.

"Yes," I said, "but I never saw the reality of my wife's unhappiness by being that way, which is one of the reasons why I can't see you anymore."

"You can't see me anymore? And that is only *one* reason? You have others?"

"Cinderella…our last conversation…"

"I deeply regret. Truly, I am sorry. I didn't believe –"

"In me," I said.

"No…I didn't," she said, looking down at the ground.

"You wounded me deeply, but more than that, the Prince. He was beside himself with worry. He loves you so much, but you gave little regard to his feelings."

"But he never should have come here…this therapy was for me," she tried to argue.

"Yes, but…he is your husband and you pushed him away."

"Dr. Berger, I am trying," she said. "Just give me another chance."

"Cinderella –" I said, shaking my head.

"But you said you would help me!" her voice rose in disappointment.

Now she was acting like a spoiled princess and I didn't like

279

it. "I can't," I told her. "You said so yourself, remember? You're forgetting this is real life here. And you – you're not real."

My words cut her deep, and I knew this, and saying it only made me grow more frustrated. "Look, you get to go back to Fairy Land, or wherever you came from, and live in your perfect world. I live in an imperfect one. Look around you, it's Newark, New Jersey, for God's sake!"

Cinderella looked at me with frightened eyes. She slowly stepped back, as if I had some contagious disease. "You are right, Dr. Berger. I cannot be helped by one who refuses to believe."

I took a step toward her, suddenly regretting everything I just said. "Cinderella, it's not that I don't believe – "

But it was too late. She turned and ran quickly away into the night. I called after her, but she was gone. Just then, Helen stepped out on the porch.

"I heard everything, Boris," she said as she looked with a cool stare in the direction where Cinderella took off. "Don't worry. She'll get over it."

Helen then gave me a smile, reminded me that our dinner was getting cold and went back inside the house. I stood there, confused about how everything turned out. A moment later, Walter stepped out. He saw the look on my face, the one that obviously read that I was feeling terrible and guilty for what I had just done. Still, when he asked me what was wrong, I shut out all my feelings by lying. "Nothing," I said, and we went back in the house and closed the door.

Some therapist I was, I think as I now write this. Not a proud moment for me, allowing my ego to get in the way of helping someone in need. In fact, I am ashamed to even put this to paper, but in telling the story, it's important that I be truthful.

Fifty-Six

✤ THE BOOK ✤

Cinderella ran down the sidewalk, fighting back tears. She kept running from one block to the next, never stopping. Soon one block turned into two, then three, then six…then several more. Feeling weak and overwhelmed, she gradually slowed down, passing a long concrete/brick wall and stopped. She came upon cement steps nearby and sat wearily to catch her breath and wipe her tears.

Eventually, she looked about to see where she was. It all looked oddly familiar to her. She then turned around, and that's when the building behind her came into focus. It *was* familiar and, yes, she had been there before. She was sitting on the steps of the Newark Public Library. Seeing the lights glowing inside, she stood, walked up the steps and entered.

The library was still and quiet with not as many people inside as the last time she was there. It was evening, so those who were there were mostly students studying and a few older people who preferred to bury themselves in a good book than watch TV.

Cinderella stared once again in awe of the massive marble structure and large marble staircases that led to special rooms. There was something very extraordinary about this place, so extraordinary that it made her forget how much she hated marble.

She slowly climbed the stairs, all the way to the third floor, clutching the iron banister for support, then wandered down a long, empty hallway. An elderly gentleman with white hair suddenly appeared from out of a room, and quietly came down the hall. He wore a white shirt with a brow sweater vest and corduroy pants. Wired framed glasses slid down his nose. He spotted Cinderella, smiled at her beauty, and then became curious as to what such a lovely young girl would be doing wandering the halls of a library so late at night.

When he approached her, his smile grew and he asked, "May I help you?"

Cinderella was startled at first, but upon seeing his warm expression, she smiled back and said, "I was only admiring the halls."

The elderly gentleman let out a chuckle. "Yes, the library is quite stunning, especially at this hour. Are you looking for anything in particular?"

"No," answered Cinderella. "I hope I am not being a bother. I have come a long way and just needed refuge."

"Well, we won't be closing for a couple more hours, so enjoy your...refuge," he said, still smiling. He continued down the hall, and then turned to notice Cinderella about to enter into a room. He walked back toward her. "Miss!" he whispered loudly, "You cannot go in there."

Cinderella stopped before entering. The elderly gentleman approached her. "That is the Special Collections room. It is off limits to the public. I'm sorry."

"Oh," said Cinderella, her curiosity piqued.

"What are the Special Collections?" she asked.

"Art work, memorabilia, rare books," answered the elderly gentleman.

"Sounds fascinating," said Cinderella. "But why is it not open for others to see?"

The elderly gentleman chuckled. "Because many of the materials are from a long time ago. They must be handled with great care."

"I see," said Cinderella.

"Why, some of the artifacts date back to Ancient Egypt. And some books are very old and fragile. Most date back over hundreds of years ago, and almost all are out of print."

"Out of print," repeated Cinderella softly. Those words sounded familiar. Then she remembered. She looked at the elderly gentleman and asked, "Would one of them be a book by a Dr. Boris Berger?"

The elderly gentleman's eyes widened. "Are you talking about *Fairy Tales Lost*?

"Yes," answered Cinderella. "Do you have it?"

"Why, yes. Are you a student of psychiatry?"

"No, just curious. May I see it?"

"You'll have to make an appointment."

"Can't I see it now?" asked Cinderella.

"No. I'm sorry," the elderly gentleman said with regret.

Cinderella looked down at the floor, dejected. The elderly gentleman watched, feeling the cause of her sadness. "I'll tell you what," he began. "If you have time now, and you absolutely promise to handle the book with utmost care, I'll let you have a look."

Cinderella looked up at him with surprised glee. "Oh, you are so very kind, sir."

"Call me William."

"Yes...William."

"Come with me," he said as he entered the room. Cinderella followed.

Inside, there were several reading tables with chairs. Long rows of bookcases filled most of the room, and were filled with thousands of old and rare books.

William went over to one of the tables, pulled out a chair for Cinderella and motioned for her to sit. She graciously did, appreciating his kindness.

"Stay right here," he said, and then disappeared down one of the rows of bookcases. Several moments passed before he reappeared holding the same looking thin volume that Cinderella saw the Fairy Godmother hand to me back at the cottage.

"Here it is," William said happily, and placed it carefully into Cinderella's hands.

Cinderella ran her delicate fingers gently across its cover.

"Be very careful with it. I will be right over there, so take your time. Enjoy," said William, and then he walked away.

As Cinderella slowly opened the book, it made a loud creaking sound due to its age and the tight binding. Cinderella turned to look at William, knowing he must have heard it. He did, and looked up from his desk. He gave Cinderella an understanding smile, and returned to his work.

Cinderella turned the first page and stared at the title: *Fairy Tales Lost – My Journey to the Other Realm* by Dr. Boris Berger.

Below that was the date: *1900*

Cinderella turned the page and looked at its table of contents. Then she opened to the first chapter and began to read. Much of it she already knew, so she found herself skimming paragraphs. She could not find anything out of the ordinary with what she was reading, and wondered why people would have such a difficult time accepting my great grandfather's findings.

She grew weary once she got to the fourth, then fifth chapter.

Not from boredom, but exhaustion due to all she had been through that day. She gently closed the book, leaned her forehead into the palm of her hand and closed her eyes.

Moments passed, when suddenly, she felt a presence of someone standing close by. She opened her eyes and looked up. It was William.

"I don't mean to disturb you," he said, "but I thought perhaps you'd be interested in this." He held out a short manuscript written on aged paper. "This is most rare. It was to be Dr. Berger's follow up book to that one. He never completed it. They put him in a sanatorium before he could. Only a few know of its existence. I thought you might like to take a look."

He held the pages out to Cinderella. She took them and William went back to his desk. Cinderella opened the manuscript and let out a silent gasp. She held her hand to her chest when she saw the title of the work: *Upon Study of Cinderella*.

Cinderella carefully turned the page and began to read. She was touched that my great grandfather, having never met her, took the time to give care and thought to her. She was also captivated by what he wrote. It was as if he knew and understood her. What moved her the most was a certain paragraph that addressed her most important issue…

Knowing the Fairy Godmother is limited in her powers, there is something that will more than likely surface for this dear girl that cannot be fixed with pixie dust or wishes. No, she will need to learn to love herself in another way, a human way. For she has experienced what no other of her kind has, and that is suffering. A daily suffering, not from a wicked queen bent on vanity, or an ogre angered by trespassers, but from the cruelty of her own family who, for no reason other than to satisfy their ego, greed and selfishness, inflict pain upon the good and kindhearted.

This suffering is the worst of its kind, and usually creates more of its own, which is what Cinderella must be wary of. For one day she may find herself in such misery and fall victim to becoming like one of those with whom she was raised. And it will take more than magic for Cinderella to learn self-acceptance, and more importantly, self-love. No riches will bring to her a cure. It will be through the example of true love, and the sacrifice of another, to which she allows herself to see, that she will understand that she has always had in her possession the infamous "key" to happiness. However, no key is ever necessary because where there is love, the door is never locked.

So, it is with that I leave Cinderella this simple lesson: Do not be so quick to toss love away. No matter what form it comes in.

"Dr. Berger..." Cinderella whispered, recalling the exact words I had said to her not too long ago, although I had not known of this manuscript and was unaware of what my great grandfather wrote.

Tears came to Cinderella's eyes as she closed the pages. "This is why I could not understand the Prince, nor endure all his possessions...he had never suffered as I had. It was never about perfection," she whispered again to herself.

She sat back, dazed in the realization. "He simply loves me. What would he know about suffer –" she began to say, when suddenly she remembered all that had happened earlier that day. "Oh, no! What have I done?" she shouted as she quickly stood, kicking back the chair, which caused a loud echo in the quiet room.

William looked up, startled. Cinderella gathered my great grandfather's book and manuscript and brought them over to him.

"Kind sir...'er, William...here...I must be off," she said, sounding in a panic.

William stood. "Is everything all right?" he asked, worried.

"No. I mean, yes...I mean..." Cinderella stammered. "Thank you, William. I shall never forget you, and will be sure to tell the Fairy Godmother and the Prince, should I find him, of your great kindness. Goodbye!"

Cinderella then turned and quickly left the room. William stood there holding my great grandfather's works, looking puzzled.

Fifty-Seven

✦ GONE ✦

When Cinderella got back to The Castle Condos, she made a mad dash up the stairs. As she approached the door, she took out her key and went to put it in the lock, but to her surprise, it was open. She rushed inside, but found no one was there.

She went first to the living room and found clothes and trash scattered all over, left of course, by Nikki and Angelina, but she wasn't concerned about that now, she needed to find out where the Prince was.

She then went into the kitchen where that room, too, was filled with dirty dishes and food left out on the counters. Cinderella went back out into the living room. As she stood there staring at the mess, trying to figure out where the girls might be, Mrs. Mortadella came out of her bedroom wearing her nightgown and looking half asleep.

"Oh, Mrs. Mortadella, where is everyone?" Cinderella asked in a desperate plea.

It was as if Mrs. Mortadella didn't hear her. She saw the

state of the living room and barked, "The place is a mess, Cinderella. Clean it up!"

"But –" Cinderella began to say, but Mrs. Mortadella turned her back and returned to her bedroom, slamming the door behind her.

Cinderella stood there, appalled at first by Mrs. Mortadella's indifference, but then moved over the couch, sat down in exhausted defeat and began to cry.

Fifty-Eight

❧ GREAT GRANDFATHER ❧

That same night, after a pleasant evening with Walter and Helen, though, it was a struggle keeping what happened between me and Cinderella out of my thoughts, Helen went home and I was in Walter's room putting him to bed.

"Is Mom coming back home?" he asked me.

"I don't know, maybe," I answered.

"I hope so. I miss having her here."

"Me, too," I replied, as I tucked him in, kissed his forehead and reached to turn out the light that was next to his bed.

Before I did, Walter asked, "Dad?"

I moved my hand away from the lamp. "Yeah?"

"How come you never talk about your great grandpa?"

I was taken aback by his question. "What made you ask that?"

"You never talk about him," Walter said, innocently.

I began to feel anger toward Helen. "Did your mother tell you about him?" I asked defensively.

"No, Cinderella did. She said he was a great man, and that he helped the Fairy Godmother, and if it wasn't for him, I might have never heard of her."

I was surprised that Cinderella did this, and a little touched, but at the same time I felt put on the spot, and seeming like a heel for never mentioning him myself to my son.

"Is it true?" he asked me. "Would I have never heard about Cinderella if not for great, great grandpa?"

Now I felt trapped. I had never lied to Walter, but worried about confirming that Cinderella was real in fear that he may start telling his friends. He would feel the shame and ridicule I felt when I told mine when I was his age. A part of me always hated my father for telling me at all. Should I finally break the "Berger Curse" and bury my great grandfather's memory once and for all, or should I embrace it? The time was forced upon me to decide, but I wasn't sure what to do.

Then I recalled Cinderella's words to me about how brave my great grandfather was with the risks he took to enlighten the world. It also reminded me of how brave I wasn't. I knew right then and there it was time I finally took a risk.

"Yes, Walter…it's true. All of it."

And with that, a funny thing happened. I felt an enormous sense of relief and pride having said those words to my son. For the first time, I felt a connection to my great grandfather and my heritage. The shame had disappeared.

"I figured as much, but I needed to hear it from you," said Walter. He then wiggled down further in the sheets and closed his eyes.

I smiled, reached for the light and turned it off. After I stood and walked toward the door, I heard Walter's voice come from across the darkened room.

"Hey, Dad?"

I turned toward him, but my eyes had not adjusted yet to the dark, so I couldn't see him. "Yeah?" I replied.

"You're lucky."

"Why is that?"

"Because you're named after him."

Those words could have knocked me over like a feather. I *was* lucky and I now knew it. I stepped out into the hall, leaned against the wall and thought about Walter...and my father...and his father...and his father...and how I was proud of all of them.

Fifty-Nine

❧ CASH FOR KINDNESS ❦

The next morning, Nikki and Angelina entered the condo looking sloppy and hung over. They both went in the kitchen and started knocking things around, attempting to make coffee.

Cinderella was curled up on the couch in the living room, asleep, still in her lavender dress from the day and night before. She awoke from the sounds being made in the kitchen. She groggily sat up then, realizing where she was, rushed into the kitchen.

"Where is the Prince?" she asked, frantic.

Nikki and Angelina winced from the sound of her voice, and ignored her.

"Please tell me where he is," she pleaded.

Nikki yawned and said, "What do you care?"

"He's my husband!" she declared in a stern, loud voice.

Nikki and Angelina stopped and looked at her, stunned at first, and then Angelina rolled her eyes and said, unconvinced, "Yeah, right."

"No, he is!" Cinderella insisted. "I came here because I was unhappy in the kingdom. He followed me here, and everything will be ruined if I don't find him!"

"Someone partied *way* too hard last night," Nikki said shooting a snide look at Angelina.

"Seriously," agreed Angelina.

"I *am* Cinderella!" shouted Cinderella.

Nikki and Angelina again winced as they looked at her, but were too exhausted to respond with one of their usual sarcastic retorts.

"I'll prove it to you," said Cinderella, desperate.

Nikki sighed. "OK, I'm game."

Angelina looked at her sister as if she was making a stupid move. "Really?"

"What? I want some coffee," she said to her, then looked at Cinderella. "Here...fill this cup with coffee with your *magical* powers."

"That will convince you?" asked Cinderella, thinking a simple cup of coffee wouldn't be enough.

"If you do it right now, yeah," said Nikki.

Cinderella closed her eyes and said aloud, "I wish for coffee to appear in Nikki's cup right now."

Nikki and Angelina looked in the cup. Nothing. Cinderella opened her eyes. She looked in the cup. There was nothing inside.

"I don't understand," Cinderella said, confused.

"I do. You're *whack*," said Nikki.

"No, my wishes must be...all gone," said Cinderella, confused.

"So are mine because you're still here," said Angelina giving her a tired look.

"My first wish was Snow White...then there was taking Dr.

Berger to the Fairy Godmother…" murmured Cinderella, trying to retrace her wishes.

"What is she saying?" asked Nikki in a whisper to Angelina.

"I don't know…maybe she's high on something," Angelina replied keeping a suspicious eye on Cinderella.

"I thought I had one more wish…I didn't use it for Rodney." Cinderella, too distraught to think, stopped trying to figure it out and tried to reason with the two sisters, "Well, whether you believe me or not –"

"We don't," Nikki said, cutting her off.

"You must tell me where he is," demanded Cinderella again.

The girls ignored her. Knowing she wasn't getting anywhere, Cinderella left the room. A moment later, Mrs. Mortadella entered, already dressed for the day. She shot a disgusted look at her hung-over daughters.

"Getting in at this hour?" she asked, displeased.

The girls ignored their mother, too, still trying to make coffee through their blurred and bloodshot eyes.

Cinderella rushed back in holding the burlap sack of money. "I'm leaving," she announced.

Nikki and Angelina spoke in union, "Good."

"But since you won't tell me where the Prince is out of simple, decent kindness, I will give you all of this if you do."

Cinderella opened the burlap sack and dumped all the cash on the floor. Dozens and dozens of crisp hundred dollar bills hit the tiled floor and scattered. Nikki, Angelina and Mrs. Mortadella's eyes widened with delicious greed.

Angelina snapped to and looked at Cinderella, answering quickly, "He stopped by last night, and we went to Guitar Bar."

"Where is that?" asked Cinderella.

"Railroad Ave.," she replied, and then looked at Nikki. "Was he still with us after that?"

"Yeah. Remember he was starting to kind of weird out at the XL?"

"What is XL?" asked Cinderella.

"A club," said Nikki. "In the Ironbound."

Cinderella nodded, making a mental note, then she asked, "What does 'weird out' mean?"

"Ya know," started Nikki, "he was saying stuff like, 'I must leave soon' and 'I'm being summoned back'. He didn't make any sense."

Cinderella looked at Nikki, Angelina and Mrs. Mortadella, and said in all sincerity, "I thank you. And I will not be seeing you ever again."

She turned and rushed out of the condo. Mrs. Mortadella looked at her daughters as if disappointed, but then broke into a devilish grin and shouted, "Girls -- we're RICH!!"

Then they all lunged to the floor like three starved vultures.

Sixty

⇢ THE SIMPLE TRUTH ⇠

I was at home that morning sifting through old papers on my desk. I had a couple of patients to see later in the afternoon, and one in the evening, so I thought I'd spend the day organizing my home office. As I was doing this, I came upon the note I had written during my first meeting with Cinderella. *"How does someone live happily ever after?"*

I stared at the note, discouraged, because I still didn't have the answer. But it made me think of the many sessions with Cinderella and my work in general. I also thought about Walter's easy acceptance of what others find so hard to believe, that fairy tales are real. I was proud of my son, and decided to find those papers belonging to my great grandfather that I had stashed away so many years ago, and share them with him.

Out in the garage, I began removing around dusty, old boxes to get to the one I knew contained my great grandfather's work. The more boxes I had to move, the more I realized how deeply I wanted his work "buried" away. I felt a twinge of shame seeing just how far I went to make sure they wouldn't be found. I was also surprised that I hadn't simply burned them. But I didn't, and I was relieved about that.

I finally came upon the box, which was deep inside a larger box that had the word "incidentals" marked on it in. Incidentals indeed. I shook my head at my stupidity. I pulled out the box and brought it into the house. I put it on the kitchen table and opened it. Inside, just as I remembered, were my great grandfather's letters and documents, now old and worn, some even brittle. I made sure to handle each with great care.

I skimmed over several until I found one that, upon reading it, made me pause for a long time. My great grandfather's words were wise and touched me deeply. He wrote:

"*Some things should be left to the imagination. In taking away our fairy tales, what is left to learn? They are our guides. The simple truth of what is right and wrong, good and evil. Without them, humanity suffers.*"

As I pondered this, it made me feel sick to my stomach recalling how I treated Cinderella. She had surely been a "guide" to me in so many ways, and how did I repay her? By sending her off. I felt even sicker that I allowed my ego and self-interests get in the way of truly helping her, no matter how stubborn or irresponsible she had been behaving. This was why she was in my care in the first place, and I failed her.

Just then, the doorbell rang. I went and answered it. Standing on my doorstep was Helen. She gave me a seductive smile, said, "Hello, Boris," and entered, breezing past me. I closed the door and began to follow her until she spun around, threw her arms around my neck and kissed me. I have to admit, I loved it.

When she pulled away she said, "I had fun last night."

"Me, too," I told her.

"It was like old times. The way it used to be. The way it should be. You, me and Walter," she said as she went into the kitchen.

She stopped when she saw the box on the kitchen table and the several papers next to it. Although she knew exactly what they were, she still asked, "What is this?"

"I was just going through some of my great grandfather's papers," I answered simply.

She gave me a suspicious and worried look. "What for?"

"To show Walter."

"Why on earth would you want to do that?" she asked, trying to control her displeasure.

"He wants to know more about him. Who he was...I think he should know."

"No, he shouldn't!" she said loud and angry. "You should burn them, burn the whole box. I don't want my son influenced by –"

"By what? A mad man?" I asked defensively.

"No, by fairy tales," she said.

I felt like a jerk being so defensive about my great grandfather, but her problem with fairy tales really bothered me. "There is nothing wrong with fairy tales," I told her.

"That Cinderella really got under your skin, hasn't she?" she asked in a jealous, accusatory way.

"She has nothing to do with this," I said.

"You got rid of her, didn't you?"

"Yes, I got "rid" of her," I answered. "Though I can't say I feel very good about it."

"Boris, who is more important to you? Me, or that girl?"

"I'm not so sure anymore," I muttered softly, which caused her to give me a worried look. "By the way, what about Kyle?" I asked.

"I told you he's out of my life," she said, diverting her eyes from mine.

"How did it end?" I asked.

Helen didn't answer.

"OK, then how did it begin?"

"What does it matter?" Helen asked, getting annoyed.

"It matters because I want to know."

She hesitated for a few moments, and then let out a heavy sigh, admitting, "OK, if you must know…he never existed."

My mouth dropped open, stunned. "Wait…Kyle isn't…*real*?"

"Yes. I only told you I had someone else to make you jealous. That was until you played me at my own game and found yourself a *real* girlfriend."

"You mean, you lied? This whole time?"

"I had to, Boris!" she shouted. "My words weren't getting through. You were always so deep in your work, then your book…always trying to out race this phantom madness of your great grandfather…I was desperate."

"But you were going to go through with a divorce," I said, still in shock.

"To be honest, that's when I began to get nervous. But then you wasted no time in replacing me with that girl!"

"There was never any *girl*!" I protested.

"So, then, we're even…there was never any Kyle!"

"Did you even think for a minute what this was doing to Walter?" I asked.

"I saw him every day, Boris, at school. You didn't know, but I made sure to be there every morning to greet him before he went inside. He knows I love him. I explained to him that I just needed a break."

A break. Like Cinderella needed one from the Prince, I thought to myself.

"I-I can't believe this," I said, running my hands through my hair.

"And I couldn't believe how fast you replaced me," she said, hurt.

"You were never replaced!" I shouted back.

"You really expect me to believe that girl really *is* Cinderella?" she asked as she reached into the box and lifted out several papers. "That all this stuff your great grandfather wrote was *true*?"

"Yes!" I said angrily.

"Oh, come on! Then you really *are* crazy," she said, tossing the papers back in the box and turning away.

There was that word. Crazy. I was tired of it, and so was she, but the only way we were going to get back on track, let alone have any sort of future, was if she was going to finally believe.

"Helen, listen to me. I am willing to forgive and forget about you lying about Kyle, if you will just say you believe in everything my great grandfather wrote, and that the girl you've been seeing me with really is Cinderella."

She turned and stared at me.

"It's the only way we can make it. You *must* believe," I pleaded.

She slowly shook her head. "No, Boris…I don't."

My heart sank. I looked at her, sad, and said, "You know what Cinderella called me last night when I was treating her like crap? A "dreamer." And she meant it as a compliment. But it made me sad because I'm not, but it's what I want to be. I am proud of my great grandfather. I want to be just like him – a dreamer. So, if there is any hope of us getting back together, you have to start dreaming with me."

Helen rolled her eyes, tired of this.

"Is it so bad to want to live happily ever after?" I asked her, softly.

"There's no such thing," she said, as if she was the authority on the subject.

"Then leave," I told her, my tone flat and serious.

Helen looked at me, shocked. "What?" she asked, though she heard me clearly.

"Get out," I said in a more direct manner as I started to lead her toward the door.

Although she tried to protest, I opened the door and said, "Go back to harsh, cold reality, Helen, because that's what you get when you stop dreaming. Now go!"

Helen, stunned, stepped outside as I slammed the door hard behind her. On my side of the door, I was crushed and heartbroken. I hung my head for a moment, fighting tears even, but didn't let them fall and walked stoically back into the kitchen.

Outside, Helen stood there, numb. She looked around realizing for the first time she was alone. Tears welled up in her eyes. She grabbed a tissue from her purse and started dabbing her eyes. Just then, Walter came up the sidewalk carrying his backpack. He saw his mother and happily ran to her.

"Hi, Mom!" he shouted excitedly.

Helen wiped her tears. Walter stopped when he saw she was crying. "What's wrong?" he asked, becoming sad, too.

She spoke to Walter straight forward, as it had always been her way. "I-I'm afraid your father wants Cinderella more than me."

Walter smiled. "No, he doesn't. Cinderella is married to the Prince."

Helen smiled through her sadness, appreciating his attempt to make her feel better. "That's very sweet of you, Walter," she said patting him on the head.

"It's true! Cinderella loves the Prince – I could tell. They're just having problems right now, but they'll work it out. Just like you and dad will."

Helen looked at her son and sighed. "You're so optimistic, just like your father, but the reality is –"

"Cinderella told me. And the Prince did, too," Walter said, wanting his mother to understand.

"The Prince told you?" asked Helen, unsure.

"Yeah. He said that Cinderella was his princess and no matter what, he wasn't ever gonna let her go. That's why he came here – to bring her back home."

"You've met the Prince?" asked Helen, perplexed.

"Yeah. And dad's been helping them. And if he can help them, he's gotta be able to get you back home, too. You just gotta believe."

Helen looked at her son with tears in her eyes. She leaned down, hugged him tight and whispered, "I'm trying."

Sixty-One

⇾ DISBELIEF ⇽

Cinderella stepped out of the Guitar Bar looking frantic and overwhelmed. She obviously had no luck finding the Prince there, but quickly headed down the street to continue her search. She was prepared to search every club in Newark to find him. And that's just what she did. Hours later, she walked out of the XL Club looking weary and defeated.

She stood on a sidewalk and wondered aloud, "Where could he have gone? Why would he just go away like this?" Suddenly, it dawned on her. "Go away. Oh, no. I wished him to go away! *That* was my last wish. Oh, no!" she wailed, then hung her head and began to cry.

The reception area of my office was empty. By now it was evening and Rachel had gone home for the night. I opened my office door and walked out with a patient. I sometimes see patients during late hours to accommodate their schedules. This was one of those times. He quietly thanked me and, as he left, I loosened my tie, ready to go home when I saw Cinderella slowly come off the elevator. I was so surprised and happy to see her, since there was so much I needed to clear up.

"Cinderella!" I called out to her.

Looking beaten down, Cinderella approached me and said resignedly, "Dr. Berger, I wanted to apologize for saying you were not a good doctor – that was wrong of me."

I was happy to hear her say this, but shook my head. "No, no. You were right. I should never have shut you out like that. In my profession, that's the worst thing a doctor can do. And I'm sorry for saying you're not real. You're very, *very* real, Cinderella."

Cinderella sighed. "I came here looking for happiness, but did not realize I've had it all along. I just didn't allow myself to see it."

"I guess we all do that," I said with a wistful smiled. "You know, I've been thinking a lot about how to live happily ever after, and I don't think it's possible –"

Cinderella looked at me, sad.

Then I quickly said, "*All* of the time. But it is *most* of the time, when we allow it...and remember we deserve it."

Cinderella smiled briefly, but then tears came to her eyes. "Oh, Dr. Berger, I did it. I didn't mean to, but I did the most horrible thing."

"What did you do?"

"I killed my husband. I had fantasized about it for so long, and now it finally happened. I'm a terrible, terrible person!"

"Y-you killed the Prince?" I asked, shocked and dismayed.

She slowly nodded her head yes. "I wished it and it happened."

I didn't know what to say. This was a horrible turn of events. "Oh, Cinderella," I said as I took her in my arms and held her.

At that moment, the elevator's doors opened and Helen stepped out with Walter. She saw me hugging Cinderella causing her eyes to narrow with jealousy.

When Walter saw Cinderella, he shouted out her name, ran to her and hugged her tight. Cinderella wiped her tears away, not wanting him to see her cry. Helen shot me a dirty look as she approached me.

"What are you doing here?" I asked her.

"Walter kept begging me to bring him here to see...*her*," Helen said, not liking any of this.

"Where's the Prince?" Walter asked Cinderella, excited.

Cinderella looked down at Walter, pained to have to tell him the truth. "I accidentally wished him gone, and now he is...gone forever."

"What do you mean he's gone forever?" Walter asked.

"Yeah – what does that *mean*, Boris?" Helen asked, annoyed.

I gently pushed Cinderella aside and squatted down to be at eye level with Walter. "Son, sometimes things happen. Sometimes just by accident, or mistake," I told him gently as I looked up at Cinderella, hoping she would understand that it *was* a mistake. "What Cinderella is trying to say is..."

"I've killed him!" Cinderella blurted out, then burst into tears.

I hung my head, sad for Cinderella...sad for Walter, and sad for myself.

"No you didn't," said Walter.

"Son," I said, still holding Walters arms, "the Prince is –"

"Going back home on the carriage," Walter said, excited.

"What?" I asked.

"Yeah. He came by last night after you went to bed. He came to my window to say goodbye. He said he had to go away."

"But – that's impossible," whispered Cinderella.

I stood and took hold of Cinderella's arms. "When you made your wish about the Prince, what exactly did you wish for? Your *exact* words?"

"I said, 'I wish you would just go away'," she said.

"So, you didn't wish him to be dead?"

"No. Just to go away, but it means the same -"

"It means he's still alive!" I said.

"But that was last night. The spell happened last night. He's gone," said Cinderella.

"Wait," I said, and turned to Walter. "Walter, when did the Prince come by your window?"

"After you went to bed. He was looking for you, too."

"I didn't go to bed until…it was way after 12:30 – which means he's still alive. He must be leaving tonight."

"But how can he? The Fairy Godmother said if one of our kind wishes harm or malice against another, they'd perish by stroke of midnight."

"In the *kingdom*, not in Newark! As long as he's still here, he's alive," I explained. I then turned to my son. "Walter, where is the Prince? Did he say where he was going?"

"That's what I've been trying to tell you. I asked him how he was getting back to the kingdom, and he told me the carriage was picking him up at midnight at 75th and Central Park."

I muttered under my breath, "New York City."

Cinderella heard this. "Yes! New York! That's where he'll be. We must get there before the carriage arrives…before stroke of midnight. I must save him! Will you take me there?"

307

I looked at my watch. "We've got time. Hopefully traffic won't be too bad. Let's go!"

Cinderella, Walter and I made a mad dash for the elevator. Helen stood there looking at us as if we'd all lost our minds.

"Wait! You can't be serious," she said, taking a sarcastic tone.

"Please, we must make haste," said Cinderella.

"Look, sister -" Helen said, getting defensive. I went back over to Helen with a look of determination.

"Helen, if there was ever a time when you needed to believe, it's now. So – are you coming, or aren't you?"

"To save a Prince Charming from getting into a carriage at midnight, so he won't "perish" when he returns to the kingdom?" she asked, sarcastically.

I stared at her. My eyes letting her know that this was hers, and ours, last chance. Helen looked back at me. Seeing I was serious, she glanced over at Cinderella, then at Walter then back at me again.

Against her better judgment, she said, "Oh, hell…let's go."

Traffic was jammed in the Holland Tunnel that crossed into New York City, and smack in the middle of it was my car. I was at the wheel and Walter sat next to me. Cinderella and Helen were in the backseat. Helen kept shooting jealous, perplexed glances at Cinderella. To start conversation, she asked, "So, you left the prince because you were bored?"

"No, not bored," answered Cinderella, "Dissatisfied…but with myself. The prince had been nothing but perfect, only I could not appreciate it due to my own unhappiness."

Helen looked at her, still unsure. "Was there, you know, another man? Or dwarf…or whatever you're into?"

"Oh, no," insisted Cinderella. "My heart has always been for the prince alone. I just hope we find him so I can save him and tell him my true feelings."

"Before this magical carriage made from a pumpkin whisks him back to fairy tale land," said Helen, in snide disbelief.

"That's right," said Cinderella, innocently.

Helen squinted her eyes, not buying any of it. Just then, traffic started to move.

Cinderella leaned forward in her seat and tapped on my shoulder. "Oh, please, Dr. Berger – we must hurry!"

"Yeah, step on it, Boris, this I gotta see," said Helen, rolling her eyes.

I shot her a disapproving glance in my rearview mirror. Helen shot one back at me. Suddenly, the traffic opened up and I was able to maneuver my car through, and out of, the tunnel. When I saw an opening in another lane, I quickly swerved into it then stepped on the gas and headed as legally possible to 75th and Central Park.

Sixty-Two

❧ CENTRAL PARK ❦

O f course, I hit traffic in downtown Manhattan. People were either just heading out, or heading home, so we sat for long stretches. When we did move, we would sail pretty easily toward the next traffic light, getting our hopes up, only to come to a halt and sit for another long stretch again. It went on like this for well over an hour.

Finally, and miraculously, I found a spot to park in front of 75th and Central Park. We all got out, relieved to be free from such a tiresome drive, and looked around. I stepped up to Cinderella and asked, "Is the carriage going to pick him up out here in the open?"

Cinderella looked at me worried, "I don't know."

I looked down at my watch. "We have about thirty minutes. Maybe he's in the park?"

Cinderella, looking hopeful, said, "Let's search!"

We all headed into the park, spacing out without losing sight of one another and began to shout for the Prince. Helen looked at us as if we had all gone mad. Perhaps we had. Central Park at

310

midnight was not the safest place on earth. Since it was quite dark, I made sure that Walter remained close to me. Helen looked down at her shoes and saw they were getting dirty. This pissed her off, naturally.

After what seemed like a long time searching through thick and dark trails, and nervously dismissing the scurrying sounds of rats in the shrubbery, we all came to a small clearing where the Prince, looking weary and forlorn, was sitting on what looked like a rock, near a large bronze statue. Walter spotted him immediately.

"There he is! Prince!" he shouted.

The Prince saw Walter and quickly stood. Then he saw Cinderella. She stopped when she saw him. I'd never seen two people stare at each other with such love and longing before. It's the look, I'm sure, that they must have first given each other at the ball so long ago.

The Prince let out a happy and relieved sigh, and said softly, "My darling."

Cinderella rushed to him. "Oh, thank God you're still alive!" she exclaimed, and then embraced him. "I was so worried it would be too late."

"Perhaps it is," said the Prince, sadly.

Cinderella looked up at him, and pulled away. "No. No, it's not. You're still here. *We're* still here."

"But your wish –"

"Only works in the kingdom. As long as you're here, you're safe."

The Prince looked at her and smiled. "And you came to *rescue* me?"

Cinderella happily sighed, "Yes," and then held him again.

The Prince said gallantly, "And now you have the new ending to your story."

With tact, I stepped forward. "Uh…I hate to intrude on this truly beautiful moment, but we still have one little problem. If you don't get on that carriage tonight, does that mean you're…staying here?"

Cinderella and the Prince looked at each other.

"Oh, dear," Cinderella said.

"He's right," said the Prince. "If I return, I will surely perish."

Cinderella, realizing the magnitude of her wish, began berating herself. "Oh, I should never have come here. This is *all* my fault."

"No, no, my love. It is mine," said the Prince. "If I had been more understanding of what you needed –"

Overcome with regret, Cinderella lowered her head and began to weep. The Prince gently lifted her chin.

"You had to come here to find yourself, and we both had to come here to find each other. And we did. You, my beloved, *fit the slipper*. When I said that in Dr. Berger's office, it was not intended as it sounded. "You fit the slipper," means only that you fit my heart. No one else ever will. I will always love you, and no matter where you are, where *we* are, you will always be my princess."

Cinderella looked up at him lovingly, then they locked into another passionate embrace.

As Helen was watching this, she came over to me and whispered, "Wow. She really *does* love the guy."

The Prince then gently pulled away and said to Cinderella, "I cannot live in Newark, my love. Alive or dead, the kingdom is where I belong. You know this to be so."

Cinderella stared up at him, stunned, even though, yes, she did know and understand this. "But…I cannot live without you."

"You must, to carry on the tale of our love, and the story of how you *saved* our love forever."

"Oh, my darling," cried Cinderella, as she held him tighter.

Suddenly, a burst of stardust came out of nowhere, and sparkles appeared. They swirled around Cinderella and the Prince, becoming bigger and brighter.

Helen gasped and stood closer to me, afraid. "W-what's happening? What is that?!"

"I'm not sure," I said as I stared in wonderment.

Walter stood next to me, staring at the spectacular site in complete awe. The stardust and sparkles blended, and turned the Prince and Cinderella's clothes into their usual regal stunning gown and uniform. Then, finally, from the sparkles, a magnificent carriage with horses appeared, with two coachmen at its reins.

I grinned when I saw this and said to Helen without taking my eyes off the carriage, "Helen, now do you believe –"

When I turned to look at her, she wasn't there. I nervously looked around and saw that she had fainted on the grass near my feet. I quickly tried to revive her, but she was out cold.

As I tended to Helen, I looked over and saw the door of the carriage swing open. Squeezing herself out of it was the Fairy Godmother. She swung one leg over, then the other and stumbled out. A bit dazed and frazzled, she pushed back her hair and took a look around.

"Hey...this isn't Jersey," she said, disgruntled.

I stepped forward and said, "No, it's New York...Central Park."

"Oh, hi, Boris," she said, half interested to see me, and then looked around. "Now I'm all confused. I was told you all were in Newark."

"We were, but...well, it's a long story," I sighed.

313

"Don't tell it. In fairy tales, we like to keep our stories short."

"What are you doing here?" I asked.

"I came to make sure these clowns got it right this time," she said motioning to the coachmen.

"Hey! We're not the one with the wand, you know," snapped one of the coachmen, overhearing her remark.

"Yeah, yeah," said the Fairy Godmother, waving him off.

She then began moving her shoulders in a clockwork manner and winced. She caught me watching her.

"The damn carriage...kind of cramped," she explained. "So, are we about ready to get going here? I haven't got all night."

"Well, not really. We...they...are in a bit of a problem," I said.

"How little is a 'bit'?" asked the Fairy Godmother.

"OK, a big problem. You see, Cinderella -"

"I wished against the prince," Cinderella said, stepping forward. "I wished him to go away."

"Oh, geez. Really Cinderella? You *know* you're not supposed to wish against your own kind."

Cinderella lowered her head, embarrassed and hurt.

"If he gets in that carriage, he'll never step foot in the kingdom. He'll perish before he does," she reminded us.

"We know," I said.

The Fairy Godmother looked at me, then at Cinderella and the Prince...then at Walter.

"Hey, kid," she said to him.

Walter smiled, happy to be addressed by her.

"Well," she said to me, shrugging her shoulders, "I guess they're yours now," then turned back toward the carriage.

"Hey...wait a minute. You're just gonna leave them here?"

"Ya got any better ideas?" she asked.

"Yes! I mean, no. I mean you just can't leave them to live in Newark! Don't you have any spells, or something to reverse Cinderella's wish?"

"What do you think I'm made out of? Pixie dust? No, the wish was spoken. What's done is done," she said, and then looked up at the coachmen. "Come on, let's get out of here."

"Wait!" shouted the Prince. "I am going with you."

"No!" wailed Cinderella, as she grabbed his arm.

The Prince gently moved her hand away, but held it. "My love, as I told you, I must live...and die, in my kingdom. Remember me always." He brought her hand to his lips and kissed it.

Cinderella wept as he let go of her hand, and quickly made his way to the carriage, not looking back. Just as he began to step inside, Walter screamed, "No!"

With tears streaming down his face, he rushed over to the Prince and grabbed hold of his arm. "No! You can't go! You can't die! I won't let you. I don't want you to die! Please!" he sobbed.

Cinderella hung her head and turned away, crying herself, unable to watch such a desperate scene.

Between tearful gasps, Walter moaned, "If you leave, who am I going to believe in?"

Tears now filled my eyes. In Walter I saw myself, and every other little boy, even the ones that still live in every man, crying for their lost heroes. Oh, how important it was to believe.

The Prince stepped down from the carriage, grabbed Walter and hugged him. "Be brave, my little friend. We both must be brave." Then he let Walter go and turned away, unable to look at him any longer.

Walter tried to be brave, but it was impossible. He so loved the Prince, and looked utterly shattered as he stood there, with his head down, crying uncontrollably. I started to make my way over to my son, but the Fairy Godmother stopped me. She went over to him instead, and gently took his tear-stained face into her hands. She gave him a warm smile, then took her finger and carefully caught one of his tears.

Holding it up for everyone to see, she said, "The tear of a child. It's all that was needed to break the spell of the wish." Then she looked at Walter, and smiled. "You have saved the Prince from perishing, and the dreams and beliefs of every child living, as well as those to come."

Cinderella turned around, holding her hand to her lips in stunned happiness. I stood there, surprised and, oh, so very proud of my son. The Prince turned around and graciously stood before him.

"You have saved my life, Walter. I am forever indebted to you," then he bowed, a very slow and regal bow, to my son.

Walter wiped the tears from his face and jumped into the Prince's arms. The Prince grabbed Walter and held him tight as he spun him around. As he did this, he saw Cinderella, stopped and gently put Walter down.

Cinderella rushed over to him. They locked into a passionate embrace, and kissed. The Prince then pulled away and asked his princess, "Will you return with me now to *our* kingdom?"

"Yes. Oh, yes," she exclaimed and they embraced again.

The Prince happily whirled her around, and when he stopped, Cinderella peered over his shoulder. Something caught her eye. She pulled away from him and stared intently at the large statue behind them. It was of Alice, from *Alice In Wonderland*, with the Mad Hatter and the March Hare at her side.

"Are you kidding me? I can't believe this. Alice gets a statue?" Cinderella exclaimed bitterly. "*She* gets a big statue in a park? I mean, really! What do I get?"

The Prince stood behind her and said gently, "Eternal happiness…with me."

Cinderella turned to the prince and smiled, quickly forgetting all about Alice. They embraced once again, kissed, and then headed for the carriage.

The Fairy Godmother glanced over at me, and then noticed Helen lying on the ground. She did a double take and asked, "Who's that?"

"It's 'er…it's my wife," I said, embarrassed.

The Fairy Godmother looked like she was going to make some sort of snarky comment, but instead she just shook her head and walked over to the carriage.

"Did Boris fix you?" she asked Cinderella, concerned.

"Yes, Fairy Godmother. He fixed me," she answered as she looked over at me and smiled.

"And are you happy now?" she asked, just to make sure.

"Oh, yes. I am very happy now," she replied.

The Fairy Godmother turned and gave me a "thumb's up." "Ya done good, Boris. Just like your great grandfather."

I gave her an appreciative "thumbs up" in return.

Well, I'll be seeing ya 'round!" And with that, the Fairy Godmother climbed back into the carriage. The Prince stepped up and held out his hand to Cinderella. "Come, my love –"

Cinderella was about to take it, but turned and saw Walter. She held up her finger to the Prince and said, "One moment," then went over to my son.

"You've been so very kind, and oh, so brave, Walter."

"And you're the coolest girl…*ever*," Walter said without any hint of shyness.

317

LeeAnna Neumeyer

Cinderella giggled as she gave him a hug. Then she came over to me and saw Helen on the ground. "Oh, my! Is she all right?"

I smiled. "Yeah. She's just never seen a real princess before," I said looking at Cinderella sincerely. "A very *real* princess."

"I cannot thank you enough, Dr. Berger."

"Call me Boris. Please."

Cinderella nodded. "Yes – Boris. I shall never forget all you've taught me."

"I think I've learned much more from you. Thank you," I said as I reached out and hugged her. Then something occurred to me, and I pulled away. "Hey, what about all the clothes you bought, and your sack of money?"

"I won't be needing them any longer. And once the spell is broken, the money turns back to cabbage," Cinderella said with a sly grin…

At that very moment, in a department store, somewhere in Newark, Mrs. Mortadella, Nikki and Angelina were standing in front of a giant mountain of clothes and jewelry that was placed on a counter. A young female sales clerk had just finished totaling up the cost.

"OK, it all comes to fourteen thousand, six hundred and fifteen dollars," she said.

Mrs. Mortadella, Nikki and Angelina all greedily opened the burlap sack and reached in to grab the cash. Looks of surprise, horror and embarrassment spread across their faces as they pulled out fists of cabbage leaves. Realizing what had happened, they all began to cry.

Cinderella walked back to the carriage, and then turned one last time to Walter and me. "Fair well, my friends. My good, *good* friends," she called out.

She waved, took the Prince's hand and stepped into the carriage. Before the Prince got in he, too, waved to us. We waved back.

The coachman pulled on the reins and the carriage started to move. It bounced down a small path, picked up speed then lifted into the sky. We watched as it disappeared into the night.

Walter leaned his head back as far as it would go, staring up at the sky. "Wow! That was so cool!"

I put my arm around my son's shoulder and said, "Yes. Yes, it was."

Suddenly, we heard the sound of Helen groaning on the ground. Walter and I quickly squatted down, and I lifted her head. She spoke in a groggy voice, "W-what happened?"

"You've fainted," I said, gently, then helped her to sit up.

Helen looked around, trying to focus. "W-where's Cinderella?"

"She's gone. The carriage took her back to her castle."

Helen looked at me, bewildered. "W-was that *real*, Boris?"

"If you believe…yes," I answered.

She looked at me, surprised. Then she smiled. I leaned in and kissed her.

Sixty-Three

✤ Never Ending ✦

The large crowd stood patiently in line at the Barnes & Noble bookstore in Clifton, New Jersey. Each had a copy of their newly purchased book, waiting to get it signed. There was a huge display at the front of the store that read: The New York Times #1 Bestseller *How To Live Happily Ever After – What I've Learned From Cinderella in Therapy* by Dr. Boris Berger.

And there I was, sitting at a table, happily signing copies of my book for my readers.

Several hours later, after I finished signing the last book for the evening, I smiled and, feeling content, stood to stretch my legs and rub my tired hand. It had been a long, eventful and *very* satisfying day.

As I turned to put on my jacket, an older gentleman with a large moustache meekly approached the table. He was wearing a rumpled looking suit, held a red cap in his hand and spoke with an Italian accent. "Pardon me...Dr. Berger?"

I turned and smiled at him. Although my hand felt strained, I knew I could sign at least one more book.

"I hear you are a very good doctor. You might help me with a problem I have?" he asked me as he nervously twisted his hat in his hands. "My son. He is very active. He gets in a lot of trouble. I don't know how to take care of him."

I smiled broadly. "I understand. I have a seven year old myself."

The older gentleman grinned. "Ah, yes! Yes! Well, my son, he used to be made of wood – a puppet. Now he is a real boy."

I stared at the older gentleman, and then fear and recognition set in. "Wait...y-you're not –"

"Geppetto. Yes," he nodded, excited.

I looked at him nervously. "Y-your son is –"

"Pinocchio. You've heard of him!" exclaimed Geppetto, looking happy and relieved as he pulled a business card from his vest pocket. "Cinderella – she gave me your card. She's been recommending you to everyone."

I froze. "E-everyone?" I muttered uneasily.

Geppetto nodded again, and extended his arm as he turned. Behind him I saw a small group of fairy tale characters standing in a line looking at me with hopeful expressions. There was Goldilocks, Captain Hook, Hansel and Gretel, Rapunzel, the Seven Dwarfs, Aladdin, etc. To the average person, it looked like a costume party, but to me...

I let out an overwhelming sigh and muttered under my breath, "Oh, Cinderella. What have you done?"

❯ Epilogue ❮

I t was a dark night in the kingdom. As usual – an enchanted evening. The sky was a dark, velvety blue. Stars twinkled. Inside the castle all was quiet, as Cinderella and the Prince slept peacefully in their bed.

The clock on the mantle struck midnight, the soft chime signifying the hour. Cinderella stirred in bed several times. Suddenly, her eyes opened wide and she sat up, looking restless and confused. The Prince, too, awoke. He sat up and pushed his sleeping mask up on his head.

"Cinderella, my darling – what is it?"

Cinderella looked at him, frustrated. "Why *don't* we have any children?" she asked.

The Prince looked at her, perplexed. Slowly a devilish grin came across his face. Cinderella smiled coyly back at him as they both deliberately slid under the covers.

And they lived happily ever after...*Most Of The Time.*

The End

✤ ABOUT THE AUTHOR ✤

LeeAnna Neumeyer is the author of *Lonely Heart Of The Little Prince*, as well as this one...even though she'd like you to believe Boris wrote it. She is currently working on the next one.

www.ingramcontent.com/pod-product-compliance
Lightning Source LLC
Chambersburg PA
CBHW020400260626
47156CB00007B/2188